MAGGIE: A GIRL OF THE STREETS
& other stories

MAGGIE
A Girl of the Streets
& other stories

Stephen Crane

WORDSWORTH AMERICAN CLASSICS

The paper in this book is produced from pure wood
pulp, without the use of chlorine or any other substance
harmful to the environment. The energy used in its
production consists almost entirely of hydroelectricity
and heat generated from waste material, thereby
conserving fossil fuels and contributing little to the
greenhouse effect.

This edition published 1995 by
Wordsworth Editions Limited
Cumberland House, Crib Street
Ware, Hertfordshire SG12 9ET

ISBN 1 85326 559 4

© Wordsworth Editions Limited 1995

Typeset in the UK by Antony Gray
Printed and bound in Denmark by Nørhaven

INTRODUCTION

Stephen Crane (1871–1900) was part of the realist movement among American writers who examined the life of ordinary people. His first novel (published in 1893), *Maggie: A Girl of the Streets*, is considered to be the first piece of fiction to give a truthful rendering of urban slum life, through the struggles of a well-meaning girl reared in an environment of drunkenness and grime.

The Bowery district of New York City in the 1890s, where *Maggie* is set, was a world that Crane knew well. As an aspiring young journalist in his early twenties, he had gone to the city to work as a newspaper reporter and thereby experience 'all the sensations of life'. While working and living in the seedy apartments of artistic friends, he was developing his powers as an observer of human behaviour and social reality.

Already, Crane thought of the novel as a succession of sharply outlined pictures that 'pass before the reader like a panorama, leaving each its definite impression'. Thus *Maggie* consists of a succession of impressionistic vignettes and scenes, with mood defining the relationship between the episodes. At his own expense Crane published the first edition of *Maggie*, with its vivid depiction of the street language of the time and descriptions of the Bowery:

> a dark region where, from a careening building, a dozen gruesome doorways gave up loads of babies to the street and the gutter. A wind of early autumn raised yellow dust from cobbles and swirled it against a hundred windows. Long streamers of garments fluttered from fire-escapes. In all unhandy places there were buckets, brooms, rags and bottles. In the street infants played or fought with other infants or sat stupidly in the way of vehicles. Formidable women, with uncombed hair and disordered dress, gossiped while leaning on railings, or screamed in frantic quarrels. Withered persons, in curious postures of submission to something, sat

smoking pipes in obscure corners. A thousand odours of cooking food came forth to the street. The building quivered and creaked from the weight of humanity stamping about in its bowels.

Born into this tenement world, Maggie, as a young girl neglected by her violent father and drunken mother, has an inner goodness which somehow remains intact. She is a collarworker in a sweatshop, appalled by the prospect of the other grizzled women working alongside her who seem 'mechanical contrivances sewing seams and grinding out, with heads bent over their work, tales of imagined or real girlhood happiness, or of past drunks, or the baby at home, and unpaid wages'.

Like most girls doing a grinding job in a world of hardship and insults, Maggie wonders how long her youth and looks will last. When her brother introduces her to his tough friend Pete, it's not surprising that she quickly falls for him. Here is a man who shrugs off all adversity and seems part of a world of elegance that Maggie envies. She is also seduced by Sunday afternoons spent at the Central Park Menagerie and the Museum of Art and by evenings at the theatre, also provided by Pete. For a brief time she leaves home to live with him.

However, as Crane constantly suggests in the novel, it is a world without mercy or justice for Maggie, who is forced into prostitution and must again contend with her drunken mother and hard-hearted brother. The reader when finishing the story of her tragic life has caught a glimpse of an overwhelming city and its furtive inhabitants, a world of faces and façades, gravel heaps and mud puddles, boys and girls of the street.

With the publication of his first novel, Stephen Crane voiced his belief in human beings as helpless creatures whose fate was determined by their environment. Along with many of his contemporaries, he saw that the demands that the industrial age placed on individuals threatened the traditional American values of family, practicality and moral restraint.

In the same year as *Maggie* was published Crane had begun work on his best-known work, *The Red Badge of Courage: An Episode of the American Civil War*. With its publication the following year, he became internationally known as an exponent of modern realism.

He also began to get newspaper assignments as a roving reporter in the West and Mexico, a period that would provide the background for his Western stories 'Moonlight on the Snow', 'Twelve O'Clock' and 'The Blue Hotel', which were to be published five years later in the collection known as *The Monster and Other Stories*.

In the intervening years Crane continued to demonstrate his interest in conflict by reporting on the Graeco-Turkish War and the Spanish American War for American newspapers. During this period he had settled in England where he was greatly admired and made friends with the American writer Henry James and various English writers, including Joseph Conrad, H.G. Wells and Ford Maddox Ford.

Published in 1899, *The Monster and Other Stories* represents several strands of Crane's style. Three of the stories – 'The Monster', 'His New Mittens' and 'An Illusion in Red and White' – have as their setting the various towns of his boyhood in New Jersey and Port Jervis, New York. 'His New Mittens' is best described as a boy's story and could be analysed in terms of Crane's relationship with his mother, who had been absorbed in piety before her death when Crane was eighteen. The centre of interest in 'The Monster' is the negro Henry Johnson, who also represents the first instance in a novel by a white American author of a negro performing an heroic act. His subsequent ostracism is symbolic of the unceasing state of civil war in America.

Of the three Western stories collected together in *The Monster and Other Stories*, 'The Blue Hotel' is the best known, with Crane juxtaposing the two cultures of East and West in America, debunking the tough Wild West and the Easterner's fixed ideas about it. The murders in these Western stories show his obsession with death at that time and perhaps in 'Twelve O'Clock' with the meaninglessness of the extravagant life he himself was leading with his fellow writers in England. As with most of Crane's writing, these are stories of social ostracism with the protagonist pitted against convention; and, particularly in 'The Blue Hotel', he expresses his mature vision of human beings as so many lice clinging 'to a whirling, fire-smote, ice-locked, disease-stricken, space-lost bulb'.

The publication of *Maggie* and the short stories in this one volume provides a revealing summary of the work of Stephen Crane, a writer in the forefront of two major directions in modern American fiction, realism and symbolism.

LEE BENNETT

FURTHER READING

Edwin H. Cady, *Stephen Crane*, 1980
Eric Solomon, *Stephen Crane: From Parody to Realism*, 1966
Chester L. Wolford, *The Anger of Stephen Crane: Fiction and the Epic Tradition*, 1983
James P. Colvert, *Stephen Crane*, 1984
Bettina L. Knapp, *Stephen Crane*, 1987

CONTENTS

Maggie: A Girl of the Streets

❦ I ❦

A very little boy stood upon a heap of gravel for the honour of Rum Alley. He was throwing stones at howling urchins from Devil's Row, who were circling madly about the heap and pelting him.

His infantile countenance was livid with the fury of battle. His small body was writhing in the delivery of oaths.

'Run, Jimmie, run! Dey'll git yehs!' screamed a retreating Rum Alley child.

'Naw,' responded Jimmie with a valiant roar, 'dese mugs can't make me run.'

Howls of renewed wrath went up from Devil's Row throats. Tattered gamins on the right made a furious assault on the gravel heap. On their small convulsed faces shone the grins of true assassins. As they charged, they threw stones and cursed in shrill chorus.

The little champion of Rum Alley stumbled precipitately down the other side. His coat had been torn to shreds in a scuffle and his hat was gone. He had bruises on twenty parts of his body, and blood was dripping from a cut in his head. His wan features looked like those of a tiny insane demon.

On the ground, children from Devil's Row closed in on their antagonist. He crooked his left arm defensively about his head and fought with madness. The little boys ran to and fro, dodging, hurling stones, and swearing in barbaric trebles.

From a window of an apartment house that uprose from amid squat ignorant stables there leaned a curious woman. Some labourers, unloading a scow at a dock at the river, paused for a moment and regarded the fight. The engineer of a passive tugboat hung lazily over a railing and watched. Over on the island a worm of yellow convicts came from the shadow of a grey ominous building and crawled slowly along the river's bank.

A stone had smashed in Jimmie's mouth. Blood was bubbling over his chin and down upon his ragged shirt. Tears made furrows on his dirt-stained cheeks. His thin legs had begun to tremble and turn weak, causing his small body to reel. His roaring curses of the first part of the fight had changed to a blasphemous chatter.

In the yells of the whirling mob of Devil's Row children there were notes of joy like songs of triumphant savagery. The little boys seemed to leer gloatingly at the blood upon the other child's face.

Down the avenue came boastfully sauntering a lad of sixteen years, although the chronic sneer of an ideal manhood already sat upon his lips. His hat was tipped over his eye with an air of challenge. Between his teeth a cigar stump was tilted at the angle of defiance. He walked with a certain swing of the shoulders which appalled the timid. He glanced over into the vacant lot in which the little raving boys from Devil's Row seethed about the shrieking and tearful child from Rum Alley.

'Gee!' he murmured with interest, 'a scrap. Gee!'

He strode over to the cursing circle, swinging his shoulders in a manner which denoted that he held victory in his fists. He approached at the back of one of the most deeply engaged of the Devil's Row children.

'Ah, what d' hell,' he said, and smote the deeply engaged one on the back of the head. The little boy fell to the ground and gave a tremendous howl. He scrambled to his feet, and perceiving, evidently, the size of his assailant, ran quickly off, shouting alarms. The entire Devil's Row party followed him. They came to a stand a short distance away and yelled taunting oaths at the boy with the chronic sneer. The latter, momentarily, paid no attention to them.

'What's wrong wi'che, Jimmie?' he asked of the small champion.

Jimmie wiped his blood-wet features with his sleeve.

'Well, it was dis way, Pete, see! I was goin' teh lick dat Riley kid and dey all pitched on me.'

Some Rum Alley children now came forward. The party stood for a moment exchanging vainglorious remarks with Devil's Row. A few stones were thrown at long distances, and words of challenge passed between small warriors. Then the Rum Alley contingent turned slowly in the direction of their home street. They began to give, each to each, distorted versions of the fight. Causes of retreat in particular cases were magnified. Blows dealt in the fight were enlarged to catapultian power, and stones thrown were alleged to have hurtled with infinite accuracy. Valour grew strong again, and the little boys began to brag with great spirit.

'Ah, we blokies kin lick d' hull damn Row,' said a child, swaggering.

Little Jimmie was striving to stanch the flow of blood from his cut lips. Scowling, he turned upon the speaker.

'Ah, where was yehs when I was doin' all deh fightin'?' he demanded. 'Youse kids makes me tired.'

'Ah, go ahn!' replied the other argumentatively.

Jimmie replied with heavy contempt. 'Ah, youse can't fight, Blue Billie! I kin lick yeh wid one han'.'

'Ah, go ahn!' replied Billie again.

'Ah!' said Jimmie threateningly.

'Ah!' said the other in the same tone.

They struck at each other, clinched, and rolled over on the cobble-stones.

'Smash 'im, Jimmie, kick d' face off 'im!' yelled Pete, the lad with the chronic sneer, in tones of delight.

The small combatants pounded and kicked, scratched and tore. They began to weep and their curses struggled in their throats with sobs. The other little boys clasped their hands and wriggled their legs in excitement. They formed a bobbing circle about the pair.

A tiny spectator was suddenly agitated.

'Cheese it, Jimmie, cheese it! Here comes yer fader,' he yelled.

The circle of little boys instantly parted. They drew away and waited in ecstatic awe for that which was about to happen. The two little boys, fighting in the modes of four thousand years ago, did not hear the warning.

Up the avenue there plodded slowly a man with sullen eyes. He was carrying a dinner pail and smoking an apple-wood pipe.

As he neared the spot where the little boys strove, he regarded them listlessly. But suddenly he roared an oath and advanced upon the rolling fighters.

'Here, you Jim, git up, now, while I belt yer life out, yeh disorderly brat.'

He began to kick into the chaotic mass on the ground. The boy Billie felt a heavy boot strike his head. He made a furious effort and disentangled himself from Jimmie. He tottered away.

Jimmie arose painfully from the ground and confronting his father began to curse him. His parent kicked him. 'Come home, now,' he cried, 'an' stop yer jawin', er I'll lam the everlasting head off yehs.'

They departed. The man paced placidly along with the apple-wood emblem of serenity between his teeth. The boy followed a dozen feet in the rear. He swore luridly, for he felt that it was degradation for one who aimed to be some vague kind of a soldier, or a man of blood with a sort of sublime licence, to be taken home by a father.

Eventually they entered a dark region where, from a careening building, a dozen gruesome doorways gave up loads of babies to the street and the gutter. A wind of early autumn raised yellow dust from cobbles and swirled it against a hundred windows. Long streamers of garments fluttered from fire-escapes. In all unhandy places there were buckets, brooms, rags and bottles. In the street infants played or fought with other infants or sat stupidly in the way of vehicles. Formidable women, with uncombed hair and disordered dress, gossiped while leaning on railings, or screamed in frantic quarrels. Withered persons, in curious postures of submission to something, sat smoking pipes in obscure corners. A thousand odours of cooking food came forth to the street. The building quivered and creaked from the weight of humanity stamping about in its bowels.

A small ragged girl dragged a red, bawling infant along the crowded ways. He was hanging back, baby-like, bracing his wrinkled, bare legs.

The little girl cried out: 'Ah, Tommie, come ahn. Dere's Jimmie and fader. Don't be a-pullin' me back.'

She jerked the baby's arm impatiently. He fell on his face, roaring. With a second jerk she pulled him to his feet, and they went on. With the obstinacy of his order, he protested against being dragged in a chosen direction. He made heroic endeavours to keep on his legs, denounced his sister, and consumed a bit of orange peeling which he chewed between the times of his infantile orations.

As the sullen-eyed man, followed by the blood-covered boy, drew near, the little girl burst into reproachful cries. 'Ah, Jimmie, youse bin fightin' agin.'

The urchin swelled disdainfuliy.

'Ah, what d' hell, Mag. See?'

The little girl upbraided him. 'You'se allus fightin', Jimmie, an' yeh knows it puts mudder out when yehs come home half dead, an' it's like we'll all get a poundin'.'

She began to weep. The babe threw back his head and roared at his prospects.

'Ah,' cried Jimmie, 'shut up er I'll smack yer mout'. See?'

As his sister continued her lamentations, he suddenly struck her. The little girl reeled, and, recovering herself, burst into tears and quaveringly cursed him. As she slowly retreated, her brother advanced, dealing her cuffs. The father heard, and turned about.

'Stop that, Jim, d'yeh hear? Leave yer sister alone on the street. It's like I can never beat any sense into yer wooden head.'

The urchin raised his voice in defiance to his parent, and continued his attacks. The babe bawled tremendously, protesting with great violence. During his sister's hasty manœuvres he was dragged by the arm.

Finally the procession plunged into one of the gruesome doorways. They crawled up dark stairways and along cold, gloomy halls. At last the father pushed open a door, and they entered a lighted room in which a large woman was rampant.

She stopped in a career from a seething stove to a pan-covered table. As the father and children filed in she peered at them.

'Eh, what? Been fightin' agin!' She threw herself upon Jimmie. The urchin tried to dart behind the others, and in the scuffle the babe, Tommie, was knocked down. He protested with his usual vehemence because they had bruised his tender shins against a table leg.

The mother's massive shoulders heaved with anger. Grasping the urchin by the neck and shoulder she shook him until he rattled. She dragged him to an unholy sink, and, soaking a rag in water, began to scrub his lacerated face with it. Jimmie screamed in pain, and tried to twist his shoulders out of the clasp of the huge arms.

The babe sat on the floor watching the scene, his face in contortions like that of a woman at a tragedy. The father, with a newly ladened pipe in his mouth, sat in a backless chair near the stove. Jimmie's cries annoyed him. He turned about and bellowed at his wife:

'Let the kid alone for a minute, will yeh, Mary? Yer allus poundin' 'im. When I come nights I can't get no rest 'cause yer allus poundin' a kid. Let up, d'yeh hear? Don't be allus poundin' a kid.'

The woman's operations on the urchin instantly increased in violence. At last she tossed him to a corner, where he limply lay weeping.

The wife put her immense hands on her hips, and with a chieftain-like stride approached her husband.

'Ho!' she said, with a great grunt of contempt. 'An' what in the devil are you stickin' your nose for?'

The babe crawled under the table, and, turning, peered out cautiously. The ragged girl retreated, and the urchin in the corner drew his legs carefully beneath him.

The man puffed his pipe calmly and put his great muddied boots on the back part of the stove.

'Go t' hell,' he said tranquilly.

The woman screamed, and shook her fists before her husband's eyes. The rough yellow of her face and neck flared suddenly crimson. She began to howl.

He puffed imperturbably at his pipe for a time, but finally arose and went to look out of the window into the darkening chaos of backyards.

'You've been drinkin', Mary,' he said. 'You'd better let up on the bot', ol' woman, or you'll git done.'

'You're a liar. I ain't had a drop,' she roared in reply. They had a lurid altercation.

The babe was staring out from under the table, his small face working in his excitement. The ragged girl went stealthily over to the corner where the urchin lay.

'Are yehs hurted much, Jimmie?' she whispered timidly.

'Not a little bit. See?' growled the little boy.

'Will I wash d' blood?'

'Naw!'

'Will I – '

'When I catch dat Riley kid I'll break 'is face! Dat's right! See?'

He turned his face to the wall as if resolved grimly to bide his time.

In the quarrel between husband and wife the woman was victor. The man seized his hat and rushed from the room, apparently determined upon a vengeful drunk. She followed to the door and thundered at him as he made his way downstairs.

She returned and stirred up the room until her children were bobbing about like bubbles.

'Git outa d' way,' she bawled persistently, waving feet with their dishevelled shoes near the heads of her children. She shrouded herself, puffing and snorting, in a cloud of steam at the stove, and eventually extracted a frying-pan full of potatoes that hissed.

She flourished it. 'Come t' yer suppers, now,' she cried with sudden exasperation. 'Hurry up, now, er I'll help yeh!'

The children scrambled hastily. With prodigious clatter they arranged themselves at table. The babe sat with his feet dangling high from a precarious infant's chair and gorged his small stomach. Jimmie forced, with feverish rapidity, the grease-enveloped pieces between his wounded lips. Maggie, with side glances of fear of interruption, ate like a small pursued tigress.

The mother sat blinking at them. She delivered reproaches, swallowed potatoes, and drank from a yellow-brown bottle. After a time her mood changed, and she wept as she carried little Tommie into another room and laid him to sleep, with his fists doubled, in an old quilt of faded red and green grandeur. Then she came and moaned by the stove. She rocked to and fro upon a chair, shedding tears and crooning miserably to the two children about their 'poor mother 'and 'yer fader, damn 'is soul.'

The little girl plodded between the table and the chair with a dish pan on it. She tottered on her small legs beneath burdens of dishes.

Jimmie sat nursing his various wounds. He cast furtive glances at his mother. His practised eye perceived her gradually emerge from a mist of muddled sentiment until her brain burned in drunken heat. He sat breathless.

Maggie broke a plate.

The mother started to her feet as if propelled.

'Good Gawd!' she howled. Her glittering eyes fastened on her child with sudden hatred. The fervent red of her face turned almost to purple. The little boy ran to the halls, shrieking like a monk in an earthquake.

He floundered about in darkness until he found the stairs. He stumbled, panic-stricken, to the next floor. An old woman opened a door. A light behind her threw a flare on the urchin's face.

'Eh, child, what is it dis time? Is yer fader beatin' yer mudder, or yer mudder beatin' yer fader?'

❧ 3 ❧

Jimmie and the old woman listened long in the hall. Above the muffled roar of conversation, the dismal wailings of babies at night, the thumping of feet in unseen corridors and rooms, and the sound of varied hoarse shoutings in the street and the rattling of wheels over cobbles, they heard the screams of the child and the roars of the mother die away to a feeble moaning and a subdued bass muttering.

The old woman was a gnarled and leathery personage who could don at will an expression of great virtue. She possessed a small music-box capable of one tune, and a collection of 'God bless yehs' pitched in assorted keys of fervency. Each day she took a position upon the stones of Fifth Avenue, where she crooked her legs under her and crouched, immovable and hideous, like an idol. She received daily a small sum in pennies. It was contributed, for the most part, by persons who did not make their homes in that vicinity.

Once, when a lady had dropped her purse on the sidewalk, the gnarled woman had grabbed it and smuggled it with great dexterity beneath her cloak. When she was arrested she had cursed the lady into a partial swoon, and with her aged limbs, twisted from rheumatism, had kicked the breath out of a huge policeman whose conduct upon that occasion she referred to when she said, 'The police, damn em!'

'Eh, Jimmie, it's a shame,' she said. 'Go, now, like a dear, an' buy me a can, an' if yer mudder raises 'ell all night yehs can sleep here.'

Jimmie took a tendered tin pail and seven pennies and departed. He passed into the side door of a saloon and went to the bar. Straining up on his toes he raised the pail and pennies as high as his arms would let him. He saw two hands thrust down to take them. Directly the same hands let down the filled pail, and he left.

In front of the gruesome doorway he met a lurching figure. It was his father, swaying about on uncertain legs.

'Give me deh can. See?' said the man.

'Ah, come off! I got dis can fer dat ol' woman, an' it 'ud be dirt teh swipe it. See?' cried Jimmie.

The father wrenched the pail from the urchin. He grasped it in both hands and lifted it to his mouth. He glued his lips to the under edge and tilted his head. His throat swelled until it seemed to grow near his chin. There was a tremendous gulping movement and the beer was gone.

The man caught his breath and laughed. He hit his son on the head with the empty pail. As it rolled clanging into the street, Jimmie began to scream, and kicked repeatedly at his father's shins.

'Look at deh dirt what yeh done me,' he yelled. 'Deh ol' woman 'ill be trowin' fits.'

He retreated to the middle of the street, but the old man did not pursue. He staggered towards the door.

'I'll paste yeh when I ketch yeh!' he shouted, and disappeared.

During the evening he had been standing against a bar drinking whiskies, and declaring to all comers confidentially: 'My home reg'lar livin' hell! Why do I come an' drin' whisk' here thish way? 'Cause home reg'lar livin' hell!'

Jimmie waited a long time in the street and then crept warily up through the building. He passed with great caution the door of the gnarled woman, and finally stopped outside his home and listened.

He could hear his mother moving heavily about among the furniture of the room. She was chanting in a mournful voice, occasionally interjecting bursts of volcanic wrath at the father, who, Jimmie judged, had sunk down on the floor or in a corner.

'Why deh blazes don' chere try teh keep Jim from fightin'? I'll break yer jaw!' she suddenly bellowed.

The man mumbled with drunken indifference. 'Ah, w'ats bitin' yeh? W'a's odds? Wha' makes kick?'

'Because he tears 'is clothes, yeh fool!' cried the woman in supreme wrath.

The husband seemed to become aroused. 'Go chase yerself!' he thundered fiercely in reply. There was a crash against the door and something broke into clattering fragments. Jimmie partially suppressed a yell and darted down the stairway. Below he paused and listened. He heard howls and curses, groans and shrieks – a confused chorus as if a battle were raging. With it all there was the crash of splintering furniture. The eyes of the urchin glared in his fear that one of them would discover him.

Curious faces appeared in doorways, and whispered comments passed to and fro. 'Ol' Johnson's playin' horse agin.'

Jimmie stood until the noises ceased and the other inhabitants of the tenement had all yawned and shut their doors. Then he crawled upstairs with the caution of an invader of a panther's den. Sounds of laboured breathing came through the broken door panels. He pushed the door open and entered, quaking.

A glow from the fire threw red hues over the bare floor, the cracked and soiled plastering, and the overturned and broken furniture.

In the middle of the floor lay his mother asleep. In one corner of the room his father's limp body hung across the seat of a chair.

The urchin stole forward. He began to shiver in dread of awakening his parents. His mother's great chest was heaving painfully. Jimmie paused and looked down at her. Her face was inflamed and swollen from drinking. Her yellow brows shaded eyelids that had grown blue. Her tangled hair tossed in waves over her forehead. Her mouth was set in the same lines of vindictive hatred that it had, perhaps, borne during the fight. Her bare, red arms were thrown out above her head in an attitude of exhaustion, something, mayhap, like that of a sated villain.

The urchin bent over his mother. He was fearful lest she should open her eyes, and the dread within him was so strong that he could not forbear to stare, but hung as if fascinated over the woman's grim face. Suddenly her eyes opened. The urchin found himself looking straight into an expression, which, it would seem, had the power to change his blood to salt. He howled piercingly and fell backward.

The woman floundered for a moment, tossed her arms about her head as if in combat, and again began to snore.

Jimmie crawled back into the shadows and waited. A noise in the next room had followed his cry at the discovery that his mother was awake. He grovelled in the gloom, his eyes riveted upon the intervening door.

He heard it creak, and then the sound of a small voice came to him. 'Jimmie! Jimmie! Are yehs dere?' it whispered. The urchin started. The thin, white face of his sister looked at him from the doorway of the other room. She crept to him across the floor.

The father had not moved, but lay in the same deathlike sleep. The mother writhed in an uneasy slumber, her chest wheezing as if she were in the agonies of strangulation. Out at the window a florid moon was peering over dark roofs, and in the distance the waters of a river glimmered pallidly.

The small frame of the ragged girl was quivering. Her features were haggard from weeping, and her eyes gleamed with fear. She grasped the urchin's arm in her little trembling hands and they huddled in a corner. The eyes of both were drawn, by some force, to stare at the woman's face, for they thought she need only to awake and all the fiends would come from below.

They crouched until the ghost mists of dawn appeared at the window, drawing close to the panes, and looking in at the prostrate, heaving body of the mother.

❦ 4 ❦

The babe, Tommie, died. He went away in an insignificant coffin, his small waxen hand clutching a flower that the girl, Maggie, had stolen from an Italian.

She and Jimmie lived.

The inexperienced fibres of the boy's eyes were hardened at an early age. He became a young man of leather. He lived some red years without labouring. During that time his sneer became chronic. He studied human nature in the gutter, and found it no worse than he thought he had reason to believe it. He never conceived a respect from the world, because he had begun with no idols that it had smashed.

He clad his soul in armour by means of happening hilariously in at a mission church where a man composed his sermons of 'yous'. Once a philosopher asked this man why he did not say 'we' instead of 'you'. The man replied, 'What?'

While they got warm at the stove he told his hearers just where he calculated they stood with the Lord. Many of the sinners were impatient over the pictured depths of their degradation. They were waiting for soup tickets.

A reader of the words of wind demons might have been able to see the portions of a dialogue pass to and fro between the exhorter and his hearers.

'You are damned,' said the preacher. And the reader of sounds might have seen the reply go forth from the ragged people: 'Where's our soup?'

Jimmie and a companion sat in a rear seat and commented upon the things that didn't concern them, with all the freedom of English tourists. When they grew thirsty and went out, their minds confused the speaker with Christ.

Momentarily, Jimmie was sullen with thoughts of a hopeless altitude where grew fruit. His companion said that if he should ever go to heaven he would ask for a million dollars and a bottle of beer.

Jimmie's occupation for a long time was to stand at street corners and watch the world go by, dreaming blood-red dreams at the passing of pretty women. He menaced mankind at the intersections of streets.

At the corners he was in life and of life. The world was going on and he was there to perceive it.

He maintained a belligerent attitude towards all well-dressed men. To him fine raiment was allied to weakness, and all good coats covered faint hearts. He and his orders were kings, to a certain extent, over the men of untarnished clothes, because these latter dreaded, perhaps, to be either killed or laughed at.

Above all things he despised obvious Christians and ciphers with the chrysanthemums of aristocracy in their buttonholes. He considered himself above both of these classes. He was afraid of nothing.

When he had a dollar in his pocket his satisfaction with existence was the greatest thing in the world. So, eventually, he felt obliged to work. His father died and his mother's years were divided up into periods of thirty days.

He became a truck driver. There was given to him the charge of a painstaking pair of horses and a large rattling truck. He invaded the

turmoil and tumble of the down-town streets, and learned to breathe
maledictory defiance at the police, who occasionally used to climb up,
drag him from his perch, and punch him.

In the lower part of the city he daily involved himself in hideous
tangles. If he and his team chanced to be in the rear he preserved a
demeanour of serenity, crossing his legs and bursting forth into yells
when foot passengers took dangerous dives beneath the noses of his
champing horses. He smoked his pipe calmly, for he knew that his pay
was marching on.

If his charge was in the front, and if it became the key-truck of chaos,
he entered terrifically into the quarrel that was raging to and fro among
the drivers on their high seats, and sometimes roared oaths and
violently got himself arrested.

After a time his sneer grew so that it turned its glare upon all things.
He became so sharp that he believed in nothing. To him the police
were always actuated by malignant impulses, and the rest of the world
was composed, for the most part, of despicable creatures who were all
trying to take advantage of him, and with whom, in defence, he was
obliged to quarrel on all possible occasions. He himself occupied a
down-trodden position, which had a private but distinct element of
grandeur in its isolation.

The greatest cases of aggravated idiocy were, to his mind, rampant
upon the front platforms of all of the street cars. At first his tongue
strove with these beings, but he eventually became superior. In him
grew a majestic contempt for those strings of street cars that followed
him like intent bugs.

He fell into the habit, when starting on a long journey, of fixing his
eye on a high and distant object, commanding his horses to start and
then going into a trance of observation. Multitudes of drivers might
howl in his rear, and passengers might load him with opprobrium, but
he would not awaken until some blue policemen turned red and began
frenziedly to seize bridles and beat the soft noses of the responsible
horses.

When he paused to contemplate the attitude of the police towards
himself and his fellows, he believed that they were the only men in the
city who had no rights. When driving about, he felt that he was held
liable by the police for anything that might occur in the streets, and
that he was the common prey of all energetic officials. In revenge, he
resolved never to move out of the way of anything, until formidable
circumstances or a much larger man than himself forced him to it.

Foot passengers were mere pestering flies with an insane disregard for their legs and his convenience. He could not comprehend their desire to cross the streets. Their madness smote him with eternal amazement. He was continually storming at them from his throne.

He sat aloft and denounced their frantic leaps, plunges, dives, and straddles.

When they would thrust at, or parry, the noses of his champing horses, making them swing their heads and move their feet, and thus disturbing a stolid, dreamy repose, he swore at the men as fools, for he himself could perceive that Providence had caused it clearly to be written that he and his team had the unalienable right to stand in the proper path of the sun chariot, and if they so minded, to obstruct its mission or take a wheel off.

And if the god driver had had a desire to step down, put up his flame-coloured fists, and manfully dispute the right of way, he would have probably been immediately opposed by a scowling mortal with two sets of hard knuckles.

It is possible, perhaps, that this young man would have derided, in an axle-wide alley, the approach of a flying ferry boat. Yet he achieved a respect for a fire-engine. As one charged towards his truck, he would drive fearfully upon a side-walk, threatening untold people with annihilation. When an engine struck a mass of blocked trucks, splitting it into fragments, as a blow annihilates a cake of ice, Jimmie's team could usually be observed high and safe, with whole wheels, on the side-walk. The fearful coming of the engine could break up the most intricate muddle of heavy vehicles at which the police had been storming for half an hour.

A fire-engine was enshrined in his heart as an appalling thing that he loved with a distant, doglike devotion. It had been known to overturn a street car. Those leaping horses, striking sparks from the cobbles in their forward lunge, were creatures to be ineffably admired. The clang of the gong pierced his breast like a noise of remembered war.

When Jimmie was a little boy he began to be arrested. Before he reached a great age, he had a fair record.

He developed too great a tendency to climb down from his truck and fight with other drivers. He had been in quite a number of miscellaneous fights, and in some general bar-room rows that had become known to the police. Once he had been arrested for assaulting a Chinaman. Two women in different parts of the city, and entirely unknown to each other, caused him considerable annoyance by breaking forth, simultaneously, at fateful intervals, into wailings about marriage and support and infants.

Nevertheless, he had, on a certain star-lit evening, said wonderingly and quite reverently, 'Deh moon looks like hell, don't it?'

❦ 5 ❧

The girl, Maggie, blossomed in a mud puddle. She grew to be a most rare and wonderful production of a tenement district, a pretty girl.

None of the dirt of Rum Alley seemed to be in her veins. The philosophers, upstairs, downstairs, and on the same floor, puzzled over it.

When a child, playing and fighting with gamins in the street, dirt disgusted her. Attired in tatters and grime, she went unseen.

There came a time, however, when the young men of the vicinity said, 'Dat Johnson goil is a puty good looker.' About this period her brother remarked to her: 'Mag, I'll tell yeh dis! See? Yeh've edder got t' go on d' toif er go t' work!' Whereupon she went to work, having the feminine aversion to the alternative.

By a chance, she got a position in an establishment where they made collars and cuffs. She received a stool and a machine in a room where sat twenty girls of various shades of yellow discontent. She perched on the stool and treadled at her machine all day, turning out collars with a name which might have been noted for its irrelevancy to anything connected with collars. At night she returned home to her mother.

Jimmie grew large enough to take the vague position of head of the family. As incumbent of that office, he stumbled upstairs late at night, as his father had done before him. He reeled about the room, swearing at his relations, or went to sleep on the floor.

The mother had gradually arisen to such a degree of fame that she could bandy words with her acquaintances among the police justices. Court officials called her by her first name. When she appeared they pursued a course which had been theirs for months. They invariably grinned, and cried out, 'Hello, Mary, you here again?' Her grey head wagged in many courts. She always besieged the bench with voluble excuses, explanations, apologies, and prayers. Her flaming face and rolling eyes were a familiar sight on the island. She measured time by means of sprees, and was eternally swollen and dishevelled.

One day the young man Pete, who as a lad had smitten the Devil's

Row urchin in the back of the head and put to flight the antagonists of his friend Jimmie, strutted upon the scene. He met Jimmie one day on the street, promised to take him to a boxing match in Williamsburg, and called for him in the evening.

Maggie observed Pete.

He sat on a table in the Johnson home, and dangled his checked legs with an enticing nonchalance His hair was curled down over his forehead in an oiled bang. His pugged nose seemed to revolt from contact with a bristling moustache of short, wire-like hairs. His blue, double-breasted coat, edged with black braid, was buttoned close to a red puff tie, and his patent leather shoes looked like weapons.

His mannerisms stamped him as a man who had a correct sense of his personal superiority. There were valour and contempt for circumstances in the glance of his eye. He waved his hands like a man of the world who dismisses religion and philosophy, and says 'Rats!' He had certainly seen everything, and with each curl of his lip he declared that it amounted to nothing. Maggie thought he must be a very 'elegant' bartender.

He was telling tales to Jimmie.

Maggie watched him furtively, with half-closed eyes, lit with a vague interest.

'Hully gee! Dey makes me tired,' he said. 'Mos' e'ry day some farmer comes in an' tries t' run d' shop. See? But d' gits t'rowed right out. I jolt dem right out in d' street before dey knows where dey is. See?'

'Sure,' said Jimmie.

'Dere was a mug come in d' place d' odder day wid an idear he wus goin' t' own d' place. Hully gee! he wus goin' t' own d' place. I see he had a still on, an' I didn' wanna giv 'im no stuff, so I says, "Git outa here an' don' make no trouble," I says like dat. See? "Git outa here an' don' make no trouble"; like dat. "Git outa here," I says. See?'

Jimmie nodded understandingly. Over his features played an eager desire to state the amount of his valour in a similar crisis, but the narrator proceeded.

'Well, deh blokie he says: "T' blazes wid it! I ain' lookin' for no scrap," he says – see? "but," he says, "I'm 'spectable cit'zen an' I wanna drink, an' quick, too." See? "Aw, goahn!" I says, like dat. "Aw, goahn," I says. See? "Don' make no trouble," I says, like dat. "Don' make no trouble." See? Den d' mug he squared off an' said he was fine as silk wid his dukes – see? an' he wanned a drink – quick. Dat's what he said. See?'

'Sure,' repeated Jimmie.

Pete continued. 'Say, I jes' jumped d' bar, an' d' way I plunked dat blokie was outa sight. See? Dat's right! In d' jaw! See? Hully gee! he t'rowed a spittoon true d' front windee. Say, I taut I'd drop dead. But d' boss, he comes in after, an' he says: "Pete, yehs done jes' right! Yeh've gota keep order, an' it's all right." See? "It's all right," he says. Dat's what he said.'

The two held a technical discussion.

'Dat bloke was a dandy,' said Pete, in conclusion, 'but he hadn' oughta made no trouble. Dat's what I says t' dem: "Don' come in here an' make no trouble," I says, like dat. "Don' make no trouble." See?'

As Jimmie and his friend exchanged tales descriptive of their prowess, Maggie leaned back in the shadow. Her eyes dwelt wonderingly and rather wistfully upon Pete's face. The broken furniture, grimy walls, and general disorder and dirt of her home of a sudden appeared before her and began to take a potential aspect. Pete's aristocratic person looked as if it might soil. She looked keenly at him, occasionally wondering if he was feeling contempt. But Pete seemed to be enveloped in reminiscence.

'Hully gee!' said he, 'dose mugs can't phase me. Dey knows I kin wipe up d' street wid any tree of dem.'

When he said, 'Ah, what d' hell!' his voice was burdened with disdain for the inevitable and contempt for anything that fate might compel him to endure.

Maggie perceived that here was the ideal man. Her dim thoughts were often searching for faraway lands where the little hills sing together in the morning. Under the trees of her dream gardens there had always walked a lover.

❧ 6 ❧

Pete took note of Maggie.

'Say, Mag, I'm stuck on yer shape. It's outa sight,' he said, parenthetically, with an affable grin.

As he became aware that she was listening closely, he grew still more eloquent in his descriptions of various happenings in his career. It appeared that he was invincible in fights.

'Why,' he said, referring to a man with whom he had had a misunderstanding, 'dat mug scrapped like a dago. Dat's right. He was dead easy. See? He tau't he was a scrapper. But he foun' out diff'ent. Hully gee!'

He walked to and fro in the small room, which seemed then to grow even smaller and unfit to hold his dignity, the attribute of a supreme warrior. That swing of the shoulders which had frozen the timid when he was but a lad had increased with his growth and education in the ratio of ten to one. It, combined with the sneer upon his mouth, told mankind that there was nothing in space which could appal him. Maggie marvelled at him and surrounded him with greatness. She vaguely tried to calculate the altitude of the pinnacle from which he must have looked down upon her.

'I met a chump deh odder day way up in deh city,' he said. 'I was goin' teh see a frien' of mine. When I was a-crossin' deh street deh chump runned plump inteh me, an' den he turns aroun' an' says, "Yer insolen' ruffin!" he says, like dat. "Oh, gee!" I says, "oh, gee! git off d' eart'!" I says, like dat. See? "Git off d' eart'!" like dat. Den deh blokie he got wild. He says I was a contempt'ble scoun'el, er somethin' like dat, an' he says I was doom' teh everlastin' pe'dition, er somethin' like dat. "Gee!" I says, "gee! Yer joshin' me," I says. "Yer joshin' me." All' den I slugged 'im. See?'

With Jimmie in his company, Pete departed in a sort of a blaze of glory from the Johnson home. Maggie, leaning from the window, watched him as he walked down the street.

Here was a formidable man who disdained the strength of a world full of fists. Here was one who had contempt for brass-clothed power; one whose knuckles could ring defiantly against the granite of law. He was a knight.

The two men went from under the glimmering street lamp and passed into shadows.

Turning, Maggie contemplated the dark, dust-stained walls, and the scant and crude furniture of her home. A clock, in a splintered and battered oblong box of varnished wood, she suddenly regarded as an abomination. She noted that it ticked raspingly. The almost vanished flowers in the carpet pattern, she conceived to be newly hideous. Some faint attempts which she had made with blue ribbon to freshen the appearance of a dingy curtain, she now saw to be piteous.

She wondered what Pete dined on.

She reflected upon the collar-and-cuff factory. It began to appear to her mind as a dreary place of endless grinding. Pete's elegant occupation brought him, no doubt, into contact with people who had money and manners. It was probable that he had a large acquaintance with pretty girls. He must have great sums of money to spend.

To her the earth was composed of hardships and insults. She felt instant admiration for a man who openly defied it. She thought that if the grim angel of death should clutch his heart, Pete would shrug his shoulders and say, 'Oh, ev'ryt'ing goes.'

She anticipated that he would come again shortly. She spent some of her week's pay in the purchase of flowered cretonne for a lambrequin. She made it with infinite care, and hung it to the slightly careening mantel over the stove in the kitchen. She studied it with painful anxiety from different points in the room. She wanted it to look well on Sunday night when, perhaps, Jimmie's friend would come. On Sunday night, however, Pete did not appear.

Afterwards the girl looked at it with a sense of humiliation. She was now convinced that Pete was superior to admiration for lambrequins.

A few evenings later Pete entered with fascinating innovations in his apparel. As she had seen him twice and he wore a different suit each time, Maggie had a dim impression that his wardrobe was prodigious.

'Say, Mag,' he said, 'put on yer bes' duds Friday night an' I'll take yehs t' d' show. See?'

He spent a few moments in flourishing his clothes, and then vanished without having glanced at the lambrequin.

Over the eternal collars and cuffs in the factory Maggie spent the most of three days in making imaginary sketches of Pete and his daily environment. She imagined some half-dozen women in love with him, and thought he must lean dangerously towards an indefinite one, whom she pictured as endowed with great charms of person, but with an altogether contemptible disposition.

She thought he must live in a blare of pleasure. He had friends and people who were afraid of him.

She saw the golden glitter of the place where Pete was to take her. It would be an entertainment of many hues and many melodies, where she was afraid she might appear small and mouse coloured.

Her mother drank whisky all Friday morning. With lurid face and tossing hair she cursed and destroyed furniture all Friday afternoon. When Maggie came home at half-past six her mother lay asleep amid the wreck of chairs and a table. Fragments of various household utensils were scattered about the floor. She had vented some phase of drunken fury upon the lambrequin. It lay in a bedraggled heap in the corner.

'Hah!' she snorted, sitting up suddenly, 'where yeh been? Why don' yeh come home earlier? Been loafin' 'round d' streets. Yer gettin' t' be a reg'lar devil.'

When Pete arrived, Maggie, in a worn black dress, was waiting for him in the midst of a floor strewn with wreckage. The curtain at the window had been pulled by a heavy hand and hung by one tack, dangling to and fro in the draught through the cracks at the sash. The knots of blue ribbons appeared like violated flowers. The fire in the stove had gone out. The displaced lids and open doors showed heaps of sullen grey ashes. The remnants of a meal, ghastly, lay in a corner. Maggie's mother, stretched on the floor, blasphemed, and gave her daughter a bad name.

❧ 7 ☙

An orchestra of yellow silk women and bald-headed men, on an elevated stage near the centre of a great green-hued ball, played a popular waltz. The place was crowded with people grouped about little tables. A battalion of waiters slid among the throng, carrying trays of beer glasses, and making change from the inexhaustible vaults of their trousers pockets. Little boys, in the costumes of French chefs, paraded up and down the irregular aisles vending fancy cakes. There was a low rumble of conversation and a subdued clinking of glasses. Clouds of tobacco smoke rolled and wavered high in air about the dull gilt of the chandeliers.

The vast crowd had an air throughout of having just quitted labour. Men with calloused hands, and attired in garments that showed the wear of an endless drudging for a living, smoked their pipes contentedly and spent five, ten, or perhaps fifteen cents for beer. There was a mere sprinkling of men who smoked cigars purchased elsewhere. The great body of the crowd was composed of people who showed that all day they strove with their hands. Quiet Germans, with maybe their wives and two or three children, sat listening to the music, with the expressions of happy cows. An occasional party of sailors from a warship, their faces pictures of sturdy health, spent the earlier hours of the evening at the small round tables. Very infrequent tipsy men, swollen with the value of their opinions, engaged their companions in earnest and confidential conversation. In the balcony, and here and there below, shone the impassive faces of women. The nationalities of the Bowery beamed upon the stage from all directions.

Pete walked aggressively up a side aisle and took seats with Maggie at a table beneath the balcony.

'Two beehs!'

Leaning back, he regarded with eyes of superiority the scene before them. This attitude affected Maggie strongly. A man who could regard such a sight with indifference must be accustomed to very great things.

It was obvious that Pete had visited this place many times before, and was very familiar with it. A knowledge of this fact made Maggie feel little and new.

He was extremely gracious and attentive. He displayed the consideration of a cultured gentleman who knew what was due.

'Say, what's eatin' yeh? Bring d' lady a big glass! What use is dat pony?'

'Don't be fresh, now,' said the waiter, with some warmth, as he departed.

'Ah, git off d' eart'!' said Pete, after the other's retreating form.

Maggie perceived that Pete brought forth all his elegance and all his knowledge of high-class customs for her benefit. Her heart warmed as she reflected upon his condescension.

The orchestra of yellow silk women and bald-headed men gave vent to a few bars of anticipatory music, and a girl, in a pink dress with short skirts, galloped upon the stage. She smiled upon the throng as if in acknowledgment of a warm welcome, and began to walk to and fro, making profuse gesticulations, and singing, in brazen soprano tones, a song the words of which were inaudible. When she broke into the swift rattling measures of a chorus some half-tipsy men near the stage joined in the rollicking refrain, and glasses were pounded rhythmically upon the tables. People leaned forward to watch her and to try to catch the words of the song. When she vanished there were long rollings of applause.

Obedient to more anticipatory bars, she reappeared among the half-suppressed cheering of the tipsy men. The orchestra plunged into dance music, and the laces of the dancer fluttered and flew in the glare of gas jets. She divulged the fact that she was attired in some half dozen skirts. It was patent that any one of them would have proved adequate for the purpose for which skirts are intended. An occasional man bent forward, intent upon the pink stockings. Maggie wondered at the splendour of the costume and lost herself in calculations of the cost of the silks and laces.

The dancer's smile of enthusiasm was turned for ten minutes upon the faces of her audience. In the finale she fell into some of those grotesque attitudes which were at the time popular among the dancers in the theatres uptown, giving to the Bowery public the diversions of the aristocratic theatre-going public at reduced rates.

'Say, Pete,' said Maggie, leaning forward, 'dis is great.'

'Sure!' said Pete, with proper complacence.

A ventriloquist followed the dancer. He held two fantastic dolls on his knees. He made them sing mournful ditties and say funny things about geography and Ireland.

'Do dose little men talk?' asked Maggie.

'Naw,' said Pete, 'it's some big jolly. See?'

Two girls, set down on the bills as sisters, came forth and sang a duet which is heard occasionally at concerts given under church auspices. They supplemented it with a dance, which, of course, can never be seen at concerts given under church auspices.

After they had retired, a woman of debatable age sang a negro melody. The chorus necessitated some grotesque waddlings supposed to be an imitation of a plantation darky, under the influence, probably, of music and the moon. The audience was just enthusiastic enough over it to make her return and sing a sorrowful lay, whose lines told of a mother's love, and a sweetheart who waited, and a young man who was lost at sea under harrowing circumstances. From the faces of a score or so in the crowd the self-contained look faded. Many heads were bent forward with eagerness and sympathy. As the last distressing sentiment of the piece was brought forth, it was greeted by the kind of applause which rings as sincere.

As a final effort, the singer rendered some verses which described a vision of Britain annihilated by America, and Ireland bursting her bonds. A carefully prepared climax was reached in the last line of the last verse, when the singer threw out her arms and cried, 'The star-spangled banner.' Instantly a great cheer swelled from the throats of this assemblage of the masses, most of them of foreign birth. There was a heavy rumble of booted feet thumping the floor. Eyes gleamed with sudden fire, and calloused hands waved frantically in the air.

After a few moments' rest, the orchestra played noisily, and a small fat man burst out upon the stage. He began to roar a song and to stamp back and forth before the footlights, wildly waving a silk hat and throwing leers broadcast. He made his face into fantastic grimaces until he looked like a devil on a Japanese kite. The crowd laughed gleefully. His short, fat legs were never still a moment. He shouted and roared and bobbed his shock of red wig until the audience broke out in excited applause.

Pete did not pay much attention to the progress of events upon the stage. He was drinking beer and watching Maggie.

Her cheeks were blushing with excitement and her eyes were glistening. She drew deep breaths of pleasure. No thoughts of the atmosphere of the collar-and-cuff factory came to her.

With the final crash of the orchestra they jostled their way to the sidewalk in the crowd. Pete took Maggie's arm and pushed a way for her, offering to fight with a man or two. They reached Maggie's home at a late hour and stood for a moment in front of the gruesome doorway.

'Say, Mag,' said Pete, 'give us a kiss for takin' yeh t' d' show, will yer?'

Maggie laughed, as if startled, and drew away from him.

'Naw, Pete,' she said, 'dat wasn't in it.'

'Ah, why wasn't it?' urged Pete.

The girl retreated nervously.

'Ah, go ahn!' repeated he.

Maggie darted into the hall, and up the stairs. She turned and smiled at him, then disappeared.

Pete walked slowly down the street. He had something of an astonished expression upon his features. He paused under a lamp-post and breathed a low breath of surprise.

'Gee!' he said, 'I wonner if I've been played fer a duffer.'

❦ 8 ❧

As thoughts of Pete came to Maggie's mind, she began to have an intense dislike for all of her dresses.

'What ails yeh? What makes ye be allus fixin' and fussin'?' her mother would frequently roar at her.

She began to note with more interest the well-dressed women she met on the avenues. She envied elegance and soft palms. She craved those adornments of person which she saw every day on the street, conceiving them to be allies of vast importance to women.

Studying faces, she thought many of the women and girls she chanced to meet smiled with serenity as though for ever cherished and watched over by those they loved.

The air in the collar-and-cuff establishment strangled her. She knew she was gradually and surely shrivelling in the hot, stuffy room. The begrimed windows rattled incessantly from the passing of elevated trains. The place was filled with a whirl of noises and odours.

She became lost in thought as she looked at some of the grizzled women in the room, mere mechanical contrivances sewing seams and grinding out, with heads bent over their work, tales of imagined or real girlhood happiness, or of past drunks, or the baby at home, and unpaid wages. She wondered how long her youth would endure. She began to see the bloom upon her cheeks as something of value.

She imagined herself, in an exasperating future, as a scrawny woman with an eternal grievance. She thought Pete to be a very fastidious person concerning the appearance of women.

She felt that she should love to see somebody entangle their fingers in the oily beard of the fat foreigner who owned the establishment. He was a destestable creature. He wore white socks with low shoes. He sat all day delivering orations in the depths of a cushioned chair. His pocket-book deprived them of the power of retort.

'What do you sink I pie fife dolla a week for? Play? No, py damn!'

Maggie was anxious for a friend to whom she could talk about Pete. She would have liked to discuss his admirable mannerisms with a reliable mutual friend. At home, she found her mother often drunk and always raving. It seemed that the world had treated this woman very badly, and she took a deep revenge upon such portions of it as came within her reach. She broke furniture as if she were at last getting her rights. She swelled with virtuous indignation as she carried the lighter articles of household use, one by one, under the shadows of the three gilt balls, where Hebrews chained them with chains of interest.

Jimmie came when he was obliged to by circumstances over which he had no control. His well-trained legs brought him staggering home, and put him to bed some nights when he would rather have gone elsewhere.

Swaggering Pete loomed like a golden sun to Maggie. He took her to a dime museum, where rows of meek freaks astonished her. She contemplated their deformities with awe, and thought them a sort of chosen tribe.

Pete, racking his brains for amusement, discovered the Central Park Menagerie and the Museum of Arts. Sunday afternoons would some-times find them at these places. Pete did not appear to be particularly interested in what he saw. He stood around looking heavy, while Maggie giggled in glee.

Once at the menagerie he went into a trance of admiration before the spectacle of a very small monkey threatening to thrash a cageful because one of them had pulled his tail and he had not wheeled about quickly enough to discover who did it. Ever after Pete knew that monkey by sight, and winked at him, trying to induce him to fight with other and larger monkeys.

At the museum, Maggie said, 'Dis is outa sight!'

'Aw, rats!' said Pete; 'wait till next summer an' I'll take yehs to a picnic.'

While the girl wandered in the vaulted rooms, Pete occupied himself in returning stony stare for stony stare, the appalling scrutiny of the watch-dogs of the treasures. Occasionally he would remark in loud tones, 'Dat jay has got glass eyes,' and sentences of the sort. When he tired of this amusement he would go to the mummies and moralise over them.

Usually he submitted with silent dignity to all that he had to go through, but at times he was goaded into comment.

'Aw!' he demanded once. 'Look at all dese little jugs! Hundred jugs in a row! Ten rows in a case, an' 'bout a t'ousand cases! What d' blazes use is dem?'

In the evenings of weekdays he often took her to see plays in which the dazzling heroine was rescued from the palatial home of her treacherous guardian by the hero with the beautiful sentiments. The latter spent most of his time out at soak in pale-green snow-storms, busy with a nickel-plated revolver rescuing aged strangers from villains.

Maggie lost herself in sympathy with the wanderers swooning in snow-storms beneath happy-hued church windows, while a choir within sang 'Joy to the World'. To Maggie and the rest of the audience this was transcendental realism. Joy always within, and they, like the actor, inevitably without. Viewing it, they hugged themselves in ecstatic pity of their imagined or real condition.

The girl thought the arrogance and granite-heartedness of the magnate of the play were very accurately drawn. She echoed the maledictions that the occupants of the gallery showered on this individual when his lines compelled him to expose his extreme selfishness.

Shady persons in the audience revolted from the pictured villainy of the drama. With untiring zeal they hissed vice and applauded virtue. Unmistakably bad men evinced an apparently sincere admiration for virtue. The loud gallery was overwhelmingly with the unfortunate and the oppressed. They encouraged the struggling hero with cries, and jeered the villain, hooting and calling attention to his whiskers. When anybody died in the pale-green snow-storms, the gallery mourned. They sought out the painted misery and hugged it as akin.

In the hero's erratic march from poverty in the first act, to wealth and triumph in the final one, in which he forgives all the enemies that he has left, he was assisted by the gallery, which applauded his generous and noble sentiments and confounded the speeches of his opponents by making irrelevant but very sharp remarks. Those actors who were cursed with the parts of villains were confronted at every turn by the gallery. If one of them rendered lines containing the most subtle distinctions between right and wrong, the gallery was immediately aware that the actor meant wickedness, and denounced him accordingly.

The last act was a triumph for the hero, poor and of the masses, the representative of the audience, over the villain and the rich man, his pockets stuffed with bonds, his heart packed with tyrannical purposes, imperturbable amid suffering.

Maggie always departed with raised spirits from these melodramas. She rejoiced at the way in which the poor and virtuous eventually overcame the wealthy and wicked. The theatre made her think. She wondered if the culture and refinement she had seen imitated, perhaps grotesquely, by the heroine on the stage, could be acquired by a girl who lived in a tenement house and worked in a shirt factory.

❧ 9 ❧

A group of urchins were intent upon the side door of a saloon. Expectancy gleamed from their eyes. They were twisting their fingers in excitement.

'Here she comes!' yelled one of then suddenly.

The group of urchins burst instantly asunder and its individual fragments were spread in a wide, respectable half circle about the point of interest. The saloon door opened with a crash, and the figure of a woman appeared upon the threshold. Her grey hair fell in knotted masses about her shoulders. Her face was crimsoned and wet with perspiration. Her eyes had a rolling glare.

'Not a cent more of me money will yehs ever get – not a red! I spent me money here for t'ree years, an' now yehs tells me yeh'll sell me no more stuff! Go fall on yerself, Johnnie Murckre! "Disturbance?" Disturbance be blowed! Go fall on yerself, Johnnie –'

The door received a kick of exasperation from within, and the woman lurched heavily out on the sidewalk.

The gamins in the half circle became violently agitated. They began to dance about and hoot and yell and jeer. A wide dirty grin spread over each face.

The woman made a furious dash at a particularly outrageous cluster of little boys. They laughed delightedly, and scampered off a short distance, calling out to her over their shoulders. She stood tottering on the curb-stone and thundered at them.

'Yeh devil's kids!' she howled, shaking her fists. The little boys whooped in glee. As she started up the street they fell in behind and marched uproariously. Occasionally she wheeled about and made charges on them. They ran nimbly out of reach and taunted her.

In the frame of a gruesome doorway she stood for a moment cursing them. Her hair straggled, giving her red features a look of insanity. Her great fists quivered as she shook them madly in the air.

The urchins made terrific noises until she turned and disappeared. Then they filed off quietly in the way they had come.

The woman floundered about in the lower hall of the tenement house, and finally stumbled up the stairs. On an upper hall a door was opened and a collection of heads peered curiously out, watching her. With a wrathful snort the woman confronted the door, but it was slammed hastily in her face and the key was turned.

She stood for a few minutes, delivering a frenzied challenge at the panels.

'Come out in deh hal', Mary Murphy, if yehs want a scrap! Come ahn! yeh overgrown terrier, come ahn!'

She began to kick the door. She shrilly defied the universe to appear and do battle. Her cursing trebles brought heads from all doors save the one she threatened. Her eyes glared in every direction. The air was full of her tossing fists.

'Come ahn! deh hull gang of yehs, come ahn!' she roared at the spectators. An oath or two, catcalls, jeers, and bits of facetious advice were given in reply. Missiles clattered about her feet.

'What's wrong wi' che?' said a voice in the gathered gloom, and Jimmie came forward. He carried a tin dinner pail in his hand and under his arm a truckman's brown apron done in a bundle. 'What's wrong?' he demanded.

'Come out! all of yehs, come out,' his mother was howling. 'Come ahn an' I'll stamp yer faces tru d' floor.'

'Shet yer face, an' come home, yeh old fool!' roared Jimmie at her.

She strode up to him and twirled her fingers in his face. Her eyes were darting flames of unreasoning rage and her frame trembled with eagerness for a fight.

'An' who are youse? I ain't givin' a snap of me fingers fer youse!' she bawled at him. She turned her huge back in tremendous disdain and climbed the stairs to the next floor.

Jimmie followed, and at the top of the flight he seized his mother's arm and started to drag her towards the door of their room.

'Come home!' he gritted between his teeth.

'Take yer hands off me! Take yer hands off me!' shrieked his mother.

She raised her arm and whirled her great fist at her son's face. Jimmie dodged his head and the blow struck him in the back of the neck. 'Come home!' he gritted again. He threw out his left hand and writhed his fingers about her middle arm. The mother and the son began to sway and struggle like gladiators.

'Whoop!' said the Rum Alley tenement house. The hall filled with interested spectators.

'Hi, ol' lady, dat was a dandy!'

'Tree t' one on d' red!'

'Ah, quit yer scrappin'!'

The door of the Johnson home opened and Maggie looked out. Jimmie made a supreme cursing effort and hurled his mother into the room. He quickly followed and closed the door. The Rum Alley tenement swore disappointedly and retired.

The mother slowly gathered herself up from the floor. Her eyes glittered menacingly upon her children.

'Here now,' said Jimmie, 'we've had enough of dis. Sit down, an' don' make no trouble.'

He grasped her arm, and twisting it, forced her into a creaking chair.

'Keep yer hands off me!' roared his mother again.

'Say, yeh ol' bat! Quit dat!' yelled Jimmie, madly. Maggie shrieked and ran into the other room. To her there came the sound of a storm of crashes and curses. There was a great final thump and Jimmie's voice cried: 'Dere, now! Stay still.' Maggie opened the door now, and went warily out. 'Oh, Jimmie!'

He was leaning against the wall and swearing. Blood stood upon bruises on his knotty forearms where they had scraped against the floor or the walls in the scuffle. The mother lay screeching on the floor, the tears running down her furrowed face.

Maggie, standing in the middle of the room, gazed about her. The usual upheaval of the tables and chairs had taken place. Crockery was strewn broadcast in fragments. The stove had been disturbed on its legs, and now leaned idiotically to one side. A pail had been upset and water spread in all directions.

The door opened and Pete appeared. He shrugged his shoulders. 'Oh, gee!' he observed.

He walked over to Maggie and whispered in her ear: 'Ah, what d' hell, Mag? Come ahn and we'll have a out-a-sight time.'

The mother in the corner upreared her head and shook her tangled locks.

'Aw, yer bote no good, needer of yehs,' she said, glowering at her daughter in the gloom. Her eyes seemed to burn balefully. 'Yeh've gone t' d' devil, Mag Johnson, yehs knows yehs have gone t' d' devil. Yer a disgrace t' yer people. An' now, git out an' go ahn dat doe-faced jude of yours. Go wid him, curse yeh, an' a good riddance. Go, an' see how yeh likes it.'

Maggie gazed long at her mother.

'Go now, an' see how yeh likes it. Git out. I won't have sech as youse in me house! Git out, d'yeh hear! Damn yeh, git out!'

The girl began to tremble.

At this instant Pete came forward. 'Oh, what d' hell, Mag, see,' whispered he softly in her ear. 'Dis all blows over. See? D' ol' woman 'ill be all right in d' mornin'. Come ahn out wid me! We'll have a out-a-sight time.'

The woman on the floor cursed. Jimmie was intent upon his bruised forearms. The girl cast a glance about the room filled with a chaotic mass of *débris*, and at the writhing body of her mother.

'Git th' devil outa here.'

Maggie went.

❦ 10 ❦

Jimmie had an idea it wasn't common courtesy for a friend to come to one's home and ruin one's sister. But he was not sure how much Pete knew about the rules of politeness.

The following night he returned home from work at a rather late hour in the evening. In passing through the halls he came upon the gnarled and leathery old woman who possessed the music box. She was grinning in the dim light that drifted through dust-stained panes. She beckoned to him with a smudged forefinger.

'Ah, Jimmie, what do yehs t'ink I tumbled to, las' night! It was deh funnies' t'ing I ever saw,' she cried, coming close to him and leering. She was trembling with eagerness to tell her tale. 'I was by me door las' night when yer sister and her jude feller came in late, oh, very late. An' she, the dear, she was a-cryin' as if her heart would break, she was. It was deh funnies' t'ing I ever saw. An' right out here by me door she asked him did he love her, did he. An' she was a-crying as if her heart would break, poor t'ing. An' him, I could see be deh way what he said it dat she had been askin' orften, he says, "Oh, gee, yes," he says, says he, "Oh, gee, yes."'

Storm clouds swept over Jimmie's face, but he turned from the leathery old woman and plodded on upstairs.

'Oh, gee, yes,' she called after him. She laughed a laugh that was like a prophetic croak.

There was no one in at home. The rooms showed that attempts had been made at tidying them. Parts of the wreckage of the day before had been repaired by an unskilled hand. A chair or two and the table stood uncertainly upon legs. The floor had been newly swept. The blue ribbons had been restored to the curtains, and the lambrequin, with its immense sheaves of yellow wheat and red roses of equal size, had been returned, in a worn and sorry state, to its place at the mantel. Maggie's jacket and hat were gone from the nail behind the door.

Jimmie walked to the window and began to look through the blurred glass. It occurred to him to wonder vaguely, for an instant, if some of the women of his acquaintance had brothers.

Suddenly, however, he began to swear.

'But he was me frien'! I brought 'im here! Dat's d' devil of it!'

He fumed about the room, his anger gradually rising to the furious pitch.

'I'll kill deh jay! Dat's what I'll do! I'll kill deh jay!'

He clutched his hat and sprang towards the door. But it opened and his mother's great form blocked the passage.

'What's d' matter wid yeh?' exclaimed she, coming into the rooms.

Jimmie gave vent to a sardonic curse and then laughed heavily.

'Well, Maggie's gone teh d' devil! Dat's what! See?'

'Eh?' said his mother.

'Maggie's gone teh d' devil! Are yehs deaf?' roared Jimmie, impatiently.

'Aw, git out?' murmured the mother, astounded.

Jimmie grunted, and then began to stare out of the window. His mother sat down in a chair, but a moment later sprang erect and delivered a maddened whirl of oaths. Her son turned to look at her as she reeled and swayed in the middle of the room, her fierce face convulsed with passion, her blotched arms raised high in imprecation.

'May she be cursed for ever!' she shrieked. 'May she eat nothin' but stones and deh dirt in deh street. May she sleep in deh gutter an' never see deh sun shine again. D' bloomin' – '

'Here now,' said her son. 'Go fall on yerself, an' quit dat.'

The mother raised lamenting eyes to the ceiling.

She's d' devil's own chil', Jimmie,' she whispered. 'Ah, who would tink such a bad girl could grow up in our fambly, Jimmie, me son. Many d' hour I've spent in talk wid dat girl an' tol' her if she ever went on d' streets I'd see her damned. An' after all her bringin' up an' what I tol' her and talked wid her, she goes teh d' bad, like a duck teh water.'

The tears rolled down her furrowed face. Her hands trembled.

'An' den when dat Sadie MacMallister next door to us was sent teh d' devil by dat feller what worked in d' soap factory, didn't I tell our Mag dat if she – '

'Ah, dat's anudder story,' interrupted the brother. 'Of course, dat Sadie was nice an' all dat – but – see – it ain't dessame as if – well, Maggie was diff'ent – see – she was diff'ent.'

He was trying to formulate a theory that he had always unconsciously held, that all sisters, excepting his own, could, advisedly, be ruined.

He suddenly broke out again. 'I'll go t'ump d' mug what done her d' harm. I'll kill 'im! He tinks he kin scrap, but when he gits me a-chasin' 'im he'll fin' out where he's wrong, d' big stuff! I'll wipe up d' street wid 'im.'

In a fury he plunged out of the doorway. As he vanished the mother raised her head and lifted both hands, entreating.

'May she be cursed for ever!' she cried.

In the darkness of the hallway Jimmie discerned a knot of women talking volubly. When he strode by they paid no attention to him.

'She allus was a bold thing,' he heard one of them cry in an eager voice. 'Dere wasn't a feller come teh deh house but she'd try teh mash 'im. My Annie says deh shameless t'ing tried teh ketch her feller, her own feller, what we useter know his fader.'

'I could a' tol' yehs dis two years ago,' said a woman, in a key of triumph. 'Yes, sir, it was over two years ago dat I says teh my ol' man, I says, "Dat Johnson girl ain't straight," I says. "Oh, rats!" he says. "Oh, hell!" "Dat's all right," I says, "but I know what I knows," I says, an' it'll come out later. You wait an' see," I says, "you see." '

'Anybody what had eyes could see dat dere was somethin' wrong wid dat girl. I didn't like her actions.'

On the street Jimmie met a friend. 'What's wrong?' asked the latter.

Jimmie explained. 'An' I'll tump 'im till he can't stand.'

'Oh, go ahn!' said the friend. 'What's deh use! Yeh'll git pulled in! Everybody ill be on to it! An' ten plunks! Gee!'

Jimmie was determined. 'He t'inks he kin scrap, but he'll fin' out diff'ent.'

'Gee!' remonstrated the friend, 'what's d' use?'

❧ I I ❧

On a corner a glass-fronted building shed a yellow glare upon the pavements. The open mouth of a saloon called seductively to passengers to enter and annihilate sorrow or create rage.

The interior of the place was papered in olive and bronze tints of imitation leather. A shining bar of counterfeit massiveness extended down the side of the room. Behind it a great mahogany-imitation sideboard reached the ceiling. Upon its shelves rested pyramids of shimmering glasses that were never disturbed. Mirrors set in the face of the sideboard multiplied them. Lemons, oranges, and paper napkins, arranged with mathematical precision, sat among the glasses. Many-hued decanters of liquor perched at regular intervals on the lower shelves. A nickel-plated cash register occupied a place in the exact centre of the general effect. The elementary senses of it all seemed to be opulence and geometrical accuracy.

Across from the bar a smaller counter held a collection of plates upon which swarmed frayed fragments of crackers, slices of boiled ham, dishevelled bits of cheese, and pickles swimming in vinegar. An odour of grasping, begrimed hands and munching mouths pervaded all.

Pete, in a white jacket, was behind the bar bending expectantly toward a quiet stranger. 'A beeh,' said the man. Pete drew a foam-topped glassful, and set it dripping upon the bar.

At this moment the light bamboo doors at the entrance swung open and crashed against the wall. Jimmie and a companion entered. They swaggered unsteadily but belligerently toward the bar, and looked at Pete with bleared and blinking eyes.

'Gin,' said Jimmie.

'Gin,' said the companion.

Pete slid a bottle and two glasses along the bar. He bent his head sideways as he assiduously polished away with a napkin at the gleaming wood. He wore a look of watchfulness.

Jimmie and his companion kept their eyes upon the bartender and conversed loudly in tones of contempt.

'He's a dandy masher, ain't he?' laughed Jimmie.

'Well, ain't he!' said the companion, sneering. 'He's great, he is. Git on to deh mug on deh blokie. Dat's enough to make a feller turn handsprings in 'is sleep.'

The quiet stranger moved himself and his glass a trifle further away and maintained an attitude of obliviousness.

'Gee! ain't he hot stuff?'

'Git on to his shape!'

'Hey!' cried Jimmie, in tones of command. Pete came along slowly, with a sullen dropping of the under lip.

'Well,' he growled, 'what's eatin' yehs?'

'Gin,' said Jimmie.

'Gin,' said the companion.

As Pete confronted them with the bottle and the glasses they laughed in his face. Jimmie's companion, evidently overcome with merriment, pointed a grimy forefinger in Pete's direction.

'Say, Jimmie,' demanded he, 'what's dat behind d' bar?'

'Looks like some chump,' replied Jimmie. They laughed loudly. Pete put down a bottle with a bang and turned a formidable face toward them. He disclosed his teeth and his shoulders heaved restlessly.

'You fellers can't guy me,' he said. 'Drink yer stuff an' git out an' don' make no trouble.'

Instantly the laughter faded from the faces of the two men, and expressions of offended dignity immediately came.

'Aw, who has said anyt'ing t' you?' cried they in the same breath.

The quiet stranger looked at the door calculatingly.

'Ah, come off,' said Pete to the two men 'Don't pick me up for no jay. Drink yer rum an' git out an' don' make no trouble.'

'Aw, go ahn!' airily cried Jimmie.

'Aw, go ahn!' airily repeated his companion.

'We goes when we git ready! See?' continued Jimmie.

'Well,' said Pete in a threatening voice, 'don' make no trouble.'

Jimmie suddenly leaned forward with his head on one side. He snarled like a wild animal.

'Well, what if we does? See?' said he.

Hot blood flushed into Pete's face, and he shot a lurid glance at Jimmie.

'Well, den we'll see who's d' bes' man, you or me,' he said.

The quiet stranger moved modestly toward the door.

Jimmie began to swell with valour.

'Don' pick me up fer no tenderfoot. When yeh tackles me yeh tackles one of d' bes' men in d' city. See? I'm a scrapper, I am. Ain't dat right, Billie?'

'Sure, Mike,' responded his companion in tones of conviction.

'Aw!' said Pete, easily. 'Go fall on yerself.'

The two men again began to laugh.

'What is dat talking?' cried the companion.

'Don' ast me,' replied Jimmie with exaggerated contempt.

Pete made a furious gesture. 'Git outa here now, an' don' make no trouble. See? Youse fellers er lookin' fer a scrap an' it's like yeh'll fin' one if yeh keeps on shootin' off yer mout's. I know yehs! See? I kin lick better men dan yehs ever saw in yer lifes. Dat's right! See? Don' pick me up fer no stuff er yeh might be jolted out in d' street before yeh knows where yeh is. When I comes from behind dis bar, I t'rows yehs boat inteh d' street. See?'

'Aw, go ahn!' cried the two men in chorus.

The glare of a panther came into Pete's eyes. 'Dat's what I said! Unnerstan'?'

He came through a passage at the end of the bar and swelled down upon the two men. They stepped promptly forward and crowded close to him.

They bristled like three roosters. They moved their heads pugnaciously and kept their shoulders braced. The nervous muscles about each mouth twitched with a forced smile of mockery.

'Well, what yer goin' t' do?' gritted Jimmie.

Pete stepped warily back, waving his hands before him to keep the men from coming too near.

'Well, what yer goin' t' do?' repeated Jimmie's ally. They kept close to him, taunting and leering. They strove to make him attempt the initial blow.

'Keep back now! Don' crowd me,' said Pete ominously.

Again they chorused in contempt. 'Aw, go ahn!'

In a small, tossing group, the three men edged for positions like frigates contemplating battle.

'Well, why don' yeh try t' t'row us out?' cried Jimmy and his ally with copious sneers.

The bravery of bulldogs sat upon the faces of the men. Their clinched fists moved like eager weapons.

The allied two jostled the bartender's elbows, glaring at him with feverish eyes and forcing him toward the wall.

Suddenly Pete swore furiously. The flash of action gleamed from his eyes. He threw back his arm and aimed a tremendous, lightning-like blow at Jimmie's face. His foot swung a step forward and the weight of his body was behind his fist. Jimmie ducked his head, Bowery-like, with the quickness of a cat. The fierce, answering blows of Jimmie and his ally crushed on Pete's bowed head.

The quiet stranger vanished.

The arms of the combatants whirled in the air like flails. The faces of the men, at first flushed to flame-coloured anger, now began to fade to the pallor of warriors in the blood and heat of a battle. Their lips curled back and stretched tightly over the gums in ghoul-like grins. Through their white, gripped teeth struggled hoarse whisperings of oaths. Their eyes glittered with murderous fire.

Each head was huddled between its owner's shoulders and arms were swinging with marvellous rapidity. Feet scraped to and fro with a loud scratching sound upon the sanded floor. Blows left crimson blotches upon the pale skin. The curses of the first quarter-minute of the fight died away. The breaths of the fighters came wheezingly from their lips and the three chests were straining and heaving. Pete at intervals gave vent to low, laboured hisses, that sounded like a desire to kill. Jimmie's ally gibbered at times like a wounded maniac. Jimmie was silent, fighting with the face of a sacrificial priest. The rage of fear shone in all their eyes and their blood-coloured fists whirled.

At a critical moment a blow from Pete's hand struck the ally and he crashed to the floor. He wriggled instantly to his feet, and grasping the quiet stranger's beer glass from the bar, hurled it at Pete's head.

High on the wall it burst like a bomb, shivering fragments flying in all directions. Then missiles came to every man's hand. The place had heretofore appeared free of things to throw, but suddenly glasses and bottles went singing through the air. They were thrown point-blank at bobbing heads. The pyramids of shimmering glasses, that had never been disturbed, changed to cascades as heavy bottles were flung into them. Mirrors splintered to nothing.

The three frothing creatures on the floor buried themselves in a frenzy for blood. There followed in the wake of missiles and fists some unknown prayers, perhaps for death.

The quiet stranger had sprawled very pyrotechnically out on the sidewalk. A laugh ran up and down the avenue for the half of a block.

'Dey've trowed a bloke inteh deh street.'

People heard the sound of breaking glass and shuffling feet within the saloon and came running. A small group, bending down to look under the bamboo doors, and watching the fall of glass and three pairs of violent legs, changed in a moment to a crowd.

A policeman came charging down the sidewalk and bounced through the doors into the saloon. The crowd bent and surged in absorbing anxiety to see.

Jimmie caught the first sight of the oncoming interruption. On his feet he had the same regard for a policeman that, when on his truck, he had for a fire-engine. He howled and ran for the side door.

The officer made a terrific advance, club in hand. One comprehensive sweep of the long night stick threw the ally to the floor and forced Pete to a corner. With his disengaged hand he made a furious effort at Jimmie's coat-tails. Then he regained his balance and paused.

'Well, well, you are a pair of pictures. What have yeh been up to?'

Jimmie, with his face drenched in blood, escaped by a side street, pursued a short distance by some of the more law-loving or excited individuals of the crowd.

Later, from a safe dark corner, he saw the policeman, the ally, and the bartender emerge from the saloon. Pete locked the doors and then followed up the avenue in the rear of the crowd-encompassed policeman and his charge.

At first Jimmie, with his heart throbbing at battle heat, started to go desperately to the rescue of his friend, but he halted.

'Ah, what's d' use?' he demanded of himself.

❧ 12 ❧

In a hall of irregular shape sat Pete and Maggie drinking beer. A submissive orchestra dictated to by a spectacled man with frowsy hair and in soiled evening dress, industriously followed the bobs of his head and the waves of his baton. A ballad singer, in a gown of flaming scarlet sang in the inevitable voice of brass. When she vanished, men seated at the tables near the front applauded loudly, pounding the polished wood with their beer-glasses. She returned attired in less gown, and sang again. She received another enthusiastic encore. She reappeared in still less gown and danced. The deafening rumble of glasses and clapping of hands that followed her exit indicated an overwhelming desire to have her come on for the fourth time, but the curiosity of the audience was not gratified.

Maggie was pale. From her eyes had been plucked all look of self-reliance. She leaned with a dependent air toward her companion. She was timid, as if fearing his anger or displeasure. She seemed to beseech tenderness of him.

Pete's air of distinguished valour had grown upon him until it threatened to reach stupendous dimensions. He was infinitely gracious to the girl. It was apparent to her that his condescension was a marvel.

He could appear to strut even while sitting still, and he showed that he was a lion of lordly characteristics by the air with which he spat.

With Maggie gazing at him wonderingly, he took pride in commanding the waiters, who were, however, indifferent or deaf.

'Hi, you, git a russle on yehs! What yehs lookin' at? Two more beehs, d'yeh hear?'

He leaned back and critically regarded the person of a girl with a straw-coloured wig who was flinging her heels about upon the stage in somewhat awkward imitation of a well-known *danseuse*.

At times Maggie told Pete long confidential tales of her former home life, dwelling upon the escapades of the other members of the family and the difficulties she had had to combat in order to obtain a degree of comfort. He responded in the accents of philanthropy. He pressed her arm with an air of reassuring proprietorship.

'Dey was cursed jays,' he said, denouncing the mother and brother.

The sound of the music which, through the efforts of the frowsy-headed leader, drifted to her ears in the smoke-filled atmosphere, made the girl dream. She thought of her former Rum Alley environment and turned to regard Pete's strong protecting fists. She thought of a collar-and-cuff manufactory and the eternal moan of the proprietor: 'What een hale do you sink I pie fife dolla a week for? Play? No, py tamn!' She contemplated Pete's man-subduing eyes and noted that wealth and prosperity were indicated by his clothes. She imagined a future, rose-tinted, because of its distance from all that she had experienced before.

As to the present she perceived only vague reasons to be miserable. Her life was Pete's, and she considered him worthy of the charge. She would be disturbed by no particular apprehensions so long as Pete adored her as he now said he did. She did not feel like a bad woman. To her knowledge she had never seen any better.

At times men at other tables regarded the girl furtively. Pete, aware of it, nodded at her and grinned. He felt proud.

'Mag, yer a bloomin' good-looker,' he remarked, studying her face through the haze. The men made Maggie fear, but she blushed at Pete's words as it became apparent to her that she was the apple of his eye.

Grey-headed men, wonderfully pathetic in their dissipation, stared at her through clouds. Smooth-cheeked boys, some of them with faces of stone and mouths of sin, not nearly so pathetic as the grey heads, tried to find the girl's eyes in the smoke wreaths. Maggie considered she was not what they thought her. She confined her glances to Pete and the stage.

The orchestra played negro melodies, and a versatile drummer pounded, whacked, clattered, and scratched on a dozen machines to make noise.

Those glances of the men shot at Maggie from under half-closed lids made her tremble. She thought them all to be worse men than Pete.

'Come, let's go,' she said.

As they went out Maggie perceived two women seated at a table with some men. They were painted, and their cheeks had lost their roundness. As she passed them the girl, with a shrinking movement, drew back her skirts.

❧ 13 ❧

Jimmie did not return home for a number of days after the fight with Pete in the saloon. When he did, he approached with extreme caution.

He found his mother raving. Maggie had not returned home. The parent continually wondered how her daughter could come to such a pass. She had never considered Maggie as a pearl dropped unstained into Rum Alley from Heaven, but she could not conceive how it was possible for her daughter to fall so low as to bring disgrace upon her family. She was terrific in denunciation of the girl's wickedness.

The fact that the neighbours talked of it maddened her. When women came in, and in the course of their conversation casually asked 'Where's Maggie dese days?' the mother shook her fuzzy head at them and appalled them with curses. Cunning hints inviting confidence she rebuffed with violence.

'All' wid all d' bringin' up she had, how could she?' moaningly she asked of her son. 'Wid all d' talkin' wid her I did an' d' t'ings I tol' her to remember. When a girl is bringed up d' way I bringed up Maggie, how kin she go teh d'devil?'

Jimmie was transfixed by these questions. He could not conceive how, under the circumstances, his mother's daughter and his sister could have been so wicked.

His mother took a drink from a bottle that sat on the table. She continued her lament.

'She had a bad heart dat girl did, Jimmie. She was wicked t' d' heart an' we never knowed it.'

Jimmie nodded, admitting the fact.

'We lived in d' same house wid her an' I brought her up, an' we never knowed how bad she was.'

Jimmie nodded again.

'Wid a home like dis an' a mudder like me, she went teh d' bad,' cried the mother, raising her eyes.

One day Jimmie came home, sat down in a chair, and began to wriggle about with a new and strange nervousness. At last he spoke shamefacedly.

'Well, look-a-here, dis t'ing queers us! See? We're queered! An' maybe it 'ud be better if I – well, I t'ink I kin look 'er up an' – maybe it 'ud be better if I fetched her home an –'

The mother started from her chair and broke forth into a storm of passionate anger.

'What! Let 'er come an' sleep under deh same roof wid her mudder agin! Oh, yes, I will, won't I? Sure? Shame on yehs, Jimmie Johnson, fer sayin' such a t'ing teh yer own mudder! Little did I tink when yehs was a babby playin' about me feet dat ye'd grow up teh say sech a t'ing teh yer mudder – yer own mudder. I never taut – '

Sobs choked her and interrupted her reproaches.

'Dere ain't nottin' teh make sech trouble about,' said Jimmie. 'I on'y says it 'ud be better if we keep dis t'ing dark, see? It queers us! See?'

His mother laughed a laugh that seemed to ring through the city and be echoed and re-echoed by countless other laughs. 'Oh, yes, I will, won't I! Sure!'

'Well, yeh must take me fer a damn fool,' said Jimmie, indignant at his mother for mocking him. 'I didn't say we'd make 'er inteh a little tin angel, ner nottin', but deh way it is now she can queer us! Don' che see?'

'Aye, she'll git tired of deh life atter a while an' den she'll wanna be a-comin' home, won' she, deh beast! I'll let 'er in den, won' I?'

'Well, I didn't mean none of dis prod'gal bus'ness anyway,' explained Jimmie.

'It wa'n't no prod'gal dauter, yeh fool,' said the mother. 'It was prod'gal son, anyhow.'

'I know dat,' said Jimmie.

For a time they sat in silence. The mother's eyes gloated on the scene which her imagination called before her. Her lips were set in a vindictive smile.

'Aye, she'll cry, won' she, an' carry on, an' tell how Pete, or some odder feller, beats 'er an' she'll say she's sorry an' all dat an' she ain't happy, she ain't, and she wants to come home agin, she does.'

With grim humour the mother imitated the possible wailing notes of the daughter's voice.

'Den I'll take 'er in, won't I? She kin cry 'er two eyes out on deh stones of deh street before I'll dirty d' place wid her. She abused an' ill-treated her own mudder – her own mudder what loved her, an' she'll never git anodder chance.'

Jimmie thought he had a great idea of women's frailty, but he could not understand why any of his kin should be victims.

'Curse her!' he said fervidly.

Again he wondered vaguely if some of the women of his acquaintance had brothers. Nevertheless, his mind did not for an instant confuse himself with those brothers nor his sister with theirs. After the mother had, with great difficulty, suppressed the neighbours, she went among them and proclaimed her grief. 'May Heaven forgive dat girl,' was her continual cry. To attentive ears she recited the whole length and breadth of her woes.

'I bringed 'er up deh way a dauter oughta be bringed up, an' dis is how she served me! She went teh deh devil deh first chance she got! May Heaven forgive her.'

When arrested for drunkenness she used the story of her daughter's downfall with telling effect upon the police justices. Finally one of them said to her, peering down over his spectacles: 'Mary, the records of this and other courts show that you are the mother of forty-two daughters who have been ruined. The case is unparalleled in the annals of this court, and this court thinks – '

The mother went through life shedding large tears of sorrow. Her red face was a picture of agony.

Of course Jimmie publicly damned his sister that he might appear on a higher social plane. But, arguing with himself, stumbling about in ways that he knew not, he, once, almost came to a conclusion that his sister would have been more firmly good had she better known why. However, he felt that he could not hold such a view. He threw it hastily aside.

❧ 14 ☙

In a hilarious hall there were twenty-eight tables and twenty-eight women and a crowd of smoking men. Valiant noise was made on a stage at the end of the hall by an orchestra composed of men who looked as if they had just happened in. Soiled waiters ran to and fro, swooping down like hawks on the unwary in the throng; clattering along the aisles with trays covered with glasses; stumbling over women's skirts and charging two prices for everything but beer, all with a swiftness that blurred the view of the cocoanut palms and dusty monstrosities painted upon the walls of the room. A 'bouncer', with an immense load of business upon his hands, plunged about in the crowd, dragging bashful strangers to prominent chairs, ordering waiters here and there, and quarrelling furiously with men who wanted to sing with the orchestra.

The usual smoke cloud was present, but so dense that heads and arms seemed entangled in it. The rumble of conversation was replaced by a roar. Plenteous oaths heaved through the air. The room rang with the shrill voices of women bubbling over with drink laughter. The chief element in the music of the orchestra was speed. The musicians played in intent fury. A woman was singing and smiling upon the stage, but no one took notice of her. The rate at which the piano, cornet, and violins were going, seemed to impart wildness to the half-drunken crowd. Beer glasses were emptied at a gulp and conversation became a rapid chatter. The smoke eddied and swirled like a shadowy river hurrying toward some unseen falls. Pete and Maggie entered the hall and took chairs at a table near the door. The woman who was seated there made an attempt to occupy Pete's attention and, failing, went away.

Three weeks had passed since the girl had left home. The air of spaniel-like dependence had been magnified and showed its direct effect in the peculiar off-handedness and ease of Pete's ways toward her.

She followed Pete's eyes with hers, anticipating with smiles gracious looks from him.

A woman of brilliance and audacity, accompanied by a mere boy, came into the place and took a seat near them.

At once Pete sprang to his feet, his face beaming with glad surprise. 'Hully gee, dere's Nellie!' he cried.

He went over to the table and held out an eager hand to the woman. 'Why, hello, Pete, me boy, how are you?' said she, giving him her fingers.

Maggie took instant note of the woman. She perceived that her black dress fitted her to perfection. Her linen collar and cuffs were spotless. Tan gloves were stretched over her well-shaped hands. A hat of a prevailing fashion perched jauntily upon her dark hair. She wore no jewellery and was painted with no apparent paint. She looked clear eyed through the stares of the men.

'Sit down, and call your lady friend over,' she said to Pete. At his beckoning Maggie came and sat between Pete and the mere boy.

'I thought yeh were gone away fer good,' began Pete, at once. 'When did yeh git back? How did dat Buff'lo bus'ness turn out?'

The woman shrugged her shoulders. 'Well, he didn't have as many stamps as he tried to make out, so I shook him, that's all.'

'Well, I'm glad teh see yehs back in deh city,' said Pete, with gallantry.

He and the woman entered into a long conversation, exchanging reminiscences of days together. Maggie sat still, unable to formulate an intelligent sentence as her addition to the conversation and painfully aware of it.

She saw Pete's eyes sparkle as he gazed upon the handsome stranger. He listened smilingly to all she said. The woman was familiar with all his affairs, asked him about mutual friends, and knew the amount of his salary.

She paid no attention to Maggie, looking toward her once or twice and apparently seeing the wall beyond.

The mere boy was sulky. In the beginning he had welcomed the additions with acclamations.

'Let's all have a drink! What'll you take, Nell? And you, Miss What's-your-name. Have a drink, Mr—, you, I mean.'

He had shown a sprightly desire to do the talking for the company and tell all about his family. In a loud voice he declaimed on various topics. He assumed a patronising air toward Pete. As Maggie was silent, he paid no attention to her. He made a great show of lavishing wealth upon the woman of brilliance and audacity.

'Do keep still, Freddie! You talk like a clock,' said the woman to him. She turned away and devoted her attention to Pete.

'We'll have many a good time together again, eh?'

'Sure, Mike,' said Pete, enthusiastic at once.

'Say,' whispered she, leaning forward, 'let's go over to Billie's and have a time.'

'Well, it's dis way! See?' said Pete. 'I got dis lady frien' here.'

'Oh, g'way with her,' argued the woman.

Pete appeared disturbed.

'All right,' said she, nodding her head at him. 'All right for you! We'll see the next time you ask me to go anywheres with you.'

Pete squirmed.

'Say,' he said, beseechingly, 'come wid me a minit an' I'll tell yer why.'

The woman waved her hand.

'Oh, that's all right, you needn't explain, you know. You wouldn't come merely because you wouldn't come, that's all.'

To Pete's visible distress she turned to the mere boy, bringing him speedily out of a terrific rage. He had been debating whether it would be the part of a man to pick a quarrel with Pete, or would he be justified in striking him savagely with his beer glass without warning. But he recovered himself when the woman turned to renew her smilings. He beamed upon her with an expression that was somewhat tipsy and inexpressibly tender.

'Say, shake that Bowery jay,' requested he, in a loud whisper.

'Freddie, you are so funny,' she replied.

Pete reached forward and touched the woman on the arm.

'Come out a minit while I tells yeh why I can't go wid yer. Yer doin' me dirt, Nell! I never taut ye'd do me dirt, Nell. Come on, will yer?' He spoke in tones of injury.

'Why, I don't see why I should be interested in your explanations,' said the woman, with a coldness that seemed to reduce Pete to a pulp.

His eyes pleaded with her. 'Come out a minit while I tells yeh. On d' level, now.'

The woman nodded slightly at Maggie and the mere boy, saying, ' 'Scuse me.'

The mere boy interrupted his loving smile and turned a shrivelling glare upon Pete. His boyish countenance flushed and he spoke in a whine to the woman:

'Oh, I say, Nellie, this ain't a square deal, you know. You aren't goin' to leave me and go off with that duffer, are you? I should think – '

'Why, you dear boy, of course I'm not,' cried the woman, affectionately. She bent over and whispered in his ear. He smiled again and settled in his chair as if resolved to wait patiently.

As the woman walked down between the rows of tables, Pete was at her shoulder talking earnestly, apparently in explanation. The woman waved her hands with studied airs of indifference. The doors swung behind them, leaving Maggie and the mere boy seated at the table.

Maggie was dazed. She could dimly perceive that something stupendous had happened. She wondered why Pete saw fit to remonstrate with the woman, pleading forgiveness with his eyes. She thought she noted an air of submission about her leonine Pete. She was astounded.

The mere boy occupied himself with cocktails and a cigar. He was tranquilly silent for half an hour. Then he bestirred himself and spoke.

'Well,' he said, sighing, 'I knew this was the way it would be. They got cold feet.' There was another stillness. The mere boy seemed to be musing.

'She was pulling m'leg. That's the whole amount of it,' he said, suddenly. 'It's a bloomin' shame the way that girl does. Why, I've spent over two dollars in drinks tonight. And she goes off with that plug-ugly, who looks as if he had been hit in the face with a coin die. I call it rocky treatment for a fellah like me. Here, waiter, bring me a cocktail, and make it strong.'

Maggie made no reply. She was watching the doors. 'It's a mean piece of business,' complained the mere boy. He explained to her how amazing it was that anybody should treat him in such a manner. 'But I'll get square with her, you bet. She won't get far ahead of yours truly, you know,' he added, winking. 'I'll tell her plainly that it was bloomin' mean business. And she won't come it over me with any of her "now-Freddie-dears". She thinks my name is Freddie, you know, but of course it ain't. I always tell these people some name like that, because if they got on to your right name they might use it sometime. Understand? Oh, they don't fool me much.'

Maggie was paying no attention, being intent upon the doors. The mere boy relapsed into a period of gloom, during which he exterminated a number of cocktails with a determined air, as if replying defiantly to fate. He occasionally broke forth into sentences composed of invectives joined together in a long chain.

The girl was still staring at the doors. After a time the mere boy began to see cobwebs just in front of his nose. He spurred himself into being agreeable and insisted upon her having a charlotte russe and a glass of beer.

'They's gone,' he remarked, 'they's gone.' He looked at her through the smoke wreaths. 'Shay, lil' girl, we mightish well make bes' of it. You ain't such bad-lookin' girl, y'know. Not half bad. Can't come up to Nell, though. No, can't do it! Well, I should shay not! Nell fine-lookin' girl! F—i—n—ine. You look bad longsider her, but by y'self ain't so bad. Have to do anyhow. Nell gone. O'ny you left. Not half bad, though.'

Maggie stood up.

'I'm going home,' she said.

The mere boy started.

'Eh? What? Home,' he cried, struck with amazement. 'I beg pardon, did hear say home?'

'I'm going home,' she repeated

'Great heavens! what hav'a struck?' demanded the mere boy of himself, stupefied.

In a semi-comatose state he conducted her on board an up-town car, ostentatiously paid her fare, leered kindly at her through the rear window, and fell off the steps.

❧ 15 ❧

A forlorn woman went along a lighted avenue. The street was filled with people desperately bound on missions. An endless crowd darted at the elevated station stairs, and the horse cars were thronged with owners of bundles.

The pace of the forlorn woman was slow. She was apparently searching for someone. She loitered near the doors of saloons and watched men emerge from them. She furtively scanned the faces in the rushing stream of pedestrians. Hurrying men, bent on catching some boat or train, jostled her elbows, failing to notice her, their thoughts fixed on distant dinners.

The forlorn woman had a peculiar face. Her smile was no smile. But when in repose her features had a shadowy look that was like a sardonic grin, as if someone had sketched with cruel forefinger indelible lines about her mouth.

Jimmie came strolling up the avenue. The woman encountered him with an aggrieved air.

'Oh, Jimmie, I've been lookin' all over for yehs – ' she began.

Jimmie made an impatient gesture and quickened his pace.

'Ah, don't bodder me!' he said with the savageness of a man whose life is pestered.

The woman followed him along the sidewalk in somewhat the manner of a suppliant.

'But, Jimmie,' she said, 'yehs told me yehs – '

Jimmie turned upon her fiercely as if resolved to make a last stand for comfort and peace.

'Say, Hattie, don' foller me from one end of deh city teh deh odder. Let up, will yehs! Give me a minute's res', can't yehs? Yehs makes me tired, allus taggin' me. See? Ain' yehs got no sense? Do yehs want people teh get on to me? Go chase yerself.'

The woman stepped closer and laid her fingers on his arm. 'But, look-a here – '

Jimmie snarled. 'Oh, go teh blazes!'

He darted into the front door of a convenient saloon and a moment later came out into the shadows that surrounded the side door. On the brilliantly lighted avenue he perceived the forlorn woman dodging about like a scout. Jimmie laughed with an air of relief and went away.

When he arrived home he found his mother clamouring. Maggie had returned. She stood shivering beneath the torrent of her mother's wrath.

'Well, I'm damned!' said Jimmie in greeting.

His mother, tottering about the room, pointed a quivering forefinger.

'Look ut her, Jimmie, look ut her. Dere's yer sister, boy. Dere's yer sister. Look ut her! Look ut her!'

She screamed at Maggie with scoffing laughter.

The girl stood in the middle of the room. She edged about as if unable to find a place on the floor to put her feet.

'Ha, ha, ha!' bellowed the mother. 'Dere she stands! Ain' she purty? Look ut her! Ain' she sweet, deh beast? Look ut her! Ha, ha! look ut her!'

She lurched forward and put her red and seamed hands upon her daughter's face. She bent down and peered keenly up into the eyes of the girl.

'Oh, she's jes' dessame as she ever was, ain' she? She's her mudder's putty darlin' yit, ain' she? Look ut her, Jimmie. Come here and look ut her.'

The loud, tremendous railing of the mother brought the denizens of the Rum Alley tenement to their doors. Women came in the hallways. Children scurried to and fro.

'What's up? Dat Johnson party on anudder tear?'

'Naw! Young Mag's come home!'

'Git out!'

Through the open doors curious eyes stared in at Maggie. Children ventured into the room and ogled her as if they formed the front row at a theatre. Women, without, bent toward each other and whispered, nodding their heads with airs of profound philosophy.

A baby, overcome with curiosity concerning this object at which all were looking, sidled forward and touched her dress, cautiously, as if investigating a red-hot stove. Its mother's voice rang out like a warning trumpet. She rushed forward and grabbed her child, casting a terrible look of indignation at the girl.

Maggie's mother paced to and fro, addressing the doorful of eyes, expounding like a glib showman. Her voice rang through the building.

'Dere she stands,' she cried, wheeling suddenly and pointing with dramatic finger, 'Dere she stands! Lookut her! Ain' she a dindy? An' she was so good as to come home teh her mudder, she was! Ain' she a beaut'? Ain' she a dindy?'

The jeering cries ended in another burst of shrill laughter.

The girl seemed to awaken. 'Jimmie –'

He drew hastily back from her.

'Well, now, yer a t'ing, ain' yeh?' he said, his lips curling in scorn. Radiant virtue sat upon his brow and his repelling hands expressed horror of contamination.

Maggie turned and went.

The crowd at the door fell back precipitately. A baby falling down in front of the door wrenched a scream like that of a wounded animal from its mother. Another woman sprang forward and picked it up with a chivalrous air, as if rescuing a human being from an oncoming express train.

As the girl passed down through the hall, she went before open doors framing more eyes strangely microscopic, and sending broad beams of inquisitive light into the darkness of her path. On the second floor she met the gnarled old woman who possessed the music box.

'So,' she cried, ' 'ere yehs are back again, are yehs? An' dey've kicked yehs out? Well, come in an' stay wid me t'-night. I ain' got no moral standin'.'

From above came an unceasing babble of tongues, over all of which rang the mother's derisive laughter.

❧ 16 ❧

Pete did not consider that he had ruined Maggie. If he had thought that her soul could never smile again, he would have believed the mother and brother, who were pyrotechnic over the affair, to be responsible for it.

Besides, in his world, souls did not insist upon being able to smile. 'What d' hell?'

He felt a trifle entangled. It distressed him. Revelations and scenes might bring upon him the wrath of the owner of the saloon, who insisted upon respectability of an advanced type.

'What do dey wanna' raise such a smoke about it fer?' demanded he of himself, disgusted with the attitude of the family. He saw no necessity that people should lose their equilibrium merely because their sister or their daughter had stayed away from home.

Searching about in his mind for possible reasons for their conduct, he came upon the conclusion that Maggie's motives were correct, but that the two others wished to snare him. He felt pursued.

The woman whom he had met in the hilarious hall showed a disposition to ridicule him.

'A little pale thing with no spirit,' she said. 'Did you note the expression of her eyes? There was something in them about pumpkin pie and virtue. That is a peculiar way the left corner of her mouth has of twitching, isn't it? Dear, dear, Pete, what are you coming to?'

Pete asserted at once that he never was very much interested in the girl. The woman interrupted him, laughing.

'Oh, it's not of the slightest consequence to me, my dear young man. You needn't draw maps for my benefit. Why should I be concerned about it?'

But Pete continued with his explanations. If he was laughed at for his tastes in women, he felt obliged to say that they were only temporary or indifferent ones.

The morning after Maggie had departed from home Pete stood behind the bar. He was immaculate in white jacket and apron and his hair was plastered over his brow with infinite correctness. No customers were in the place. Pete was twisting his napkined fist slowly in a beer glass, softly whistling to himself, and occasionally holding the object of his attention between his eyes and a few weak beams of sunlight that found their way over the thick screens and into the shaded rooms.

With lingering thoughts of the woman of brilliance and audacity, the bartender raised his head and stared through the varying cracks between the swaying bamboo doors. Suddenly the whistling pucker faded from his lips. He saw Maggie walking slowly past. He gave a great start, fearing for the previously mentioned eminent respectability of the place.

He threw a swift, nervous glance about him, all at once feeling guilty. No one was in the room.

He went hastily over to the side door. Opening it and looking out, he perceived Maggie standing, as if undecided, at the corner. She was searching the place with her eyes.

As she turned her face toward him, Pete beckoned to her hurriedly, intent upon returning with speed to a position behind the bar, and to the atmosphere of respectability upon which the proprietor insisted.

Maggie came to him, the anxious look disappearing from her face and a smile wreathing her lips.

'Oh, Pete –' she began brightly.

The bartender made a violent gesture of impatience.

'Oh, say,' cried he vehemently. 'What d' yeh wanna hang aroun' here fer? Do yer wanna git me inteh trouble?' he demanded with an air of injury.

Astonishment swept over the girl's features. 'Why, Pete! yehs tol' me –'

Pete's glance expressed profound irritation. His countenance reddened with the anger of a man whose respectability is being threatened.

'Say, yehs makes me tired! See? What d' yeh wanna tag aroun' atter me fer? Yeh'll do me dirt wid d' ol' man and dey'll be trouble! If he sees a woman roun' here he'll go crazy an' I'll lose me job! See? Ain' yehs got no sense? Don' be allus bodderin' me. See? Yer brudder came in here an' made trouble an' d' ol' man hada put up fer it! An' now I'm done! See? I'm done.'

The girl's eyes stared into his face. 'Pete, don't yeh remem –'

'Oh, go ahn!' interrupted Pete anticipating.

The girl seemed to have a struggle with herself. She was apparently bewildered and could not find speech. Finally she asked in a low voice, 'But where kin I go?'

The question exasperated Pete beyond the powers of endurance. It was a direct attempt to give him some responsibility in a matter that did not concern him. In his indignation he volunteered information.

'Oh, go to hell!' cried he. He slammed the door furiously and returned, with an air of relief, to his respectability.

Maggie went away.

She wandered aimlessly for several blocks. She stopped once and asked aloud a question of herself: 'Who?'

A man who was passing near her shoulder humorously took the questioning word as intended for him

'Eh? What? Who? Nobody! I didn't say anything,' he laughingly said, and continued his way.

Soon the girl discovered that if she walked with such apparent aimlessness, some men looked at her with calculating eyes. She quickened her step, frightened. As a protection, she adopted a demeanour of intentness as if going somewhere.

After a time she left rattling avenues and passed between rows of houses with sternness and stolidity stamped upon their features. She hung her head, for she felt their eyes grimly upon her.

Suddenly she came upon a stout gentleman in a silk hat and a chaste black coat, whose decorous row of buttons reached from his chin to his knees. The girl had heard of the grace of God and she decided to approach this man.

His beaming, chubby face was a picture of benevolence and kindheartedness. His eyes shone goodwill.

But as the girl timidly accosted him, he made convulsive movement and saved his respectability by a vigorous side step. He did not risk it to save a soul. For how was he to know that there was a soul before him that needed saving?

❦ 17 ❧

Upon a wet evening, several months after the last chapter, two interminable rows of cars, pulled by slipping horses, jangled along a prominent side street. A dozen cabs, with coat-enshrouded drivers, clattered to and fro. Electric lights, whirring softly, shed a blurred radiance. A flower dealer, his feet tapping impatiently, his nose and his wares glistening with raindrops, stood behind an array of roses and chrysanthemums. Two or three theatres emptied a crowd upon the storm-swept pavements. Men pulled their hats over their eyebrows and raised their collars to their ears. Women shrugged impatient shoulders in their warm cloaks and stopped to arrange their skirts for a walk through the storm. People who had been constrained to comparative silence for two hours burst into a roar of conversation, their hearts still kindling from the glowings of the stage.

The pavements became tossing seas of umbrellas. Men stepped forth to hail cabs or cars, raising their fingers in varied forms of polite request or imperative demand. An endless procession wended toward elevated stations. An atmosphere of pleasure and prosperity seemed to hang over the throng, born, perhaps, of good clothes and of two hours in a place of forgetfulness.

In the mingled light and gloom of an adjacent park, a handful of wet wanderers, in attitudes of chronic dejection, were scattered among the benches.

A girl of the painted cohorts of the city went along the street. She threw changing glances at men who passed her, giving smiling invitations to those of rural or untaught pattern and usually seeming sedately unconscious of the men with a metropolitan seal upon their faces.

Crossing glittering avenues, she went into the throng emerging from the places of forgetfulness. She hurried forward through the crowd as if intent upon reaching a distant home, bending forward in her handsome cloak, daintily lifting her skirts, and picking for her well-shod feet the dryer spots upon the pavements.

The restless doors of saloons, clashing to and fro, disclosed animated rows of men before bars and hurrying barkeepers.

A concert-hall gave to the street faint sounds of swift, machine-like music, as if a group of phantom musicians were hastening.

A tall young man, smoking a cigarette with a sublime air, strolled near the girl. He had on evening dress, a moustache, a chrysanthemum, and a look of *ennui*, all of which he kept carefully under his eye. Seeing the girl walk on as if such a young man as he was not in existence, he looked back transfixed with interest. He stared glassily for a moment, but gave a slight convulsive start when he discerned that she was neither new, Parisian, nor theatrical. He wheeled about hastily and turned his stare into the air, like a sailor with a searchlight.

A stout gentleman, with pompous and philanthropic whiskers, went stolidly by, the broad of his back sneering at the girl.

A belated man in business clothes, and in haste to catch a car, bounced against her shoulder. 'Hi, there, Mary, I beg your pardon! Brace up, old girl.' He grasped her arm to steady her, and then was away running down the middle of the street.

The girl walked on out of the realm of restaurants and saloons. She passed more glittering avenues and went into darker blocks than those where the crowd travelled.

A young man in light overcoat and Derby hat received a glance shot keenly from the eyes of the girl. He stopped and looked at her, thrusting his hands in his pockets and making a mocking smile curl his lips. 'Come, now, old lady,' he said, 'you don't mean to tell me that you sized me up for a farmer?'

A labouring man marched along with bundles under his arms. To her remarks, he replied, 'It's a fine evenin', ain't it?'

She smiled squarely into the face of a boy who was hurrying by with his hands buried in his overcoat pockets, his blonde locks bobbing on his youthful temples, and a cheery smile of unconcern upon his lips. He turned his head and smiled back at her, waving his hands.

'Not this eve – some other eve!'

A drunken man, reeling in her pathway, began to roar at her. 'I ain' ga no money!' he shouted, in a dismal voice. He lurched on up the street, wailing to himself: 'I ain't ga no money. Ba' luck. Ain' ga no more money.'

The girl went into gloomy districts near the river, where the tall black factories shut in the street and only occasional broad beams of light fell across the pavements from saloons. In front of one of these places, whence came the sound of a violin vigorously scraped, the patter of feet on boards and the ring of loud laughter, there stood a man with blotched features.

Further on in the darkness she met a ragged being with shifting, bloodshot eyes and grimy hands.

She went into the blackness of the final block. The shutters of the tall buildings were closed like grim lips. The structure seemed to have eyes that looked over them, beyond them, at other things. Afar off the lights of the avenues glittered as if from an impossible distance. Street-car bells jingled with a sound of merriment.

At the feet of the tall buildings appeared the deathly black hue of the river. Some hidden factory sent up a yellow glare, that lit for a moment the waters lapping oilily against timbers. The varied sounds of life, made joyous by distance and seeming unapproachableness, came faintly and died away to a silence.

❦ 18 ❦

In a partitioned-off section of a saloon sat a man with a half-dozen women, gleefully laughing, hovering about him. The man had arrived at that stage of drunkenness where affection is felt for the universe.

'I'm good f'ler, girls,' he said, convincingly. 'I'm good f'ler. An'body treats me right, I allus trea's zem right! See?'

The women nodded their heads approvingly. 'To be sure,' they cried in hearty chorus. 'You're the kind of a man we like, Pete. You're outa sight! What yeh goin' to buy this time, dear?'

'An't'ing yehs wants!' said the man in an abandonment of good will. His countenance shone with the true spirit of benevolence. He was in the proper mood of missionaries. He would have fraternised with obscure Hottentots. And above all, he was overwhelmed in tenderness for his friends, who were all illustrious.

'An't'ing yehs wants!' repeated he, waving his hands with beneficent recklessness. 'I'm good f'ler, girls, an' if an'body treats me right I – here,' called he through an open door to a waiter, 'bring girls drinks. What 'ill yehs have, girls? An't'ing yehs want.'

The waiter glanced in with the disgusted look of the man who serves intoxicants for the man who takes too much of them. He nodded his head shortly at the order from each individual, and went.

'W're havin' great time,' said the man. 'I like you girls! Yer right sort! See?'

He spoke at length and with feeling concerning the excellences of his assembled friends.

'Don' try pull man's leg, but have a good time! Das right! Das way teh do! Now, if I sawght yehs tryin' work me fer drinks, wouldn' buy not'ing! But yer right sort! Yehs know how ter treat a f'ler, an' I stays by yehs 'til spen' las' cent! Das right! I'm good f'ler an' I knows when an'body treats me right!'

Between the times of the arrival and departure of the waiter, the man discoursed to the women on the tender regard he felt for all living things. He laid stress upon the purity of his motives in all dealings with men in the world and spoke of the fervour of his friendship for those who were amiable. Tears welled slowly from his eyes. His voice quavered when he spoke to his companions.

Once when the waiter was about to depart with an empty tray, the man drew a coin from his pocket and held it forth.

'Here,' said he, quite magnificently, 'here's quar'.'

The waiter kept his hands on his tray.

'I don't want yer money,' he said.

The other put forth the coin with tearful insistence.

'Here's quar'!' cried he, 'tak't! Yer goo' f'ler an' I wan' yehs tak't!'

'Come, come, now,' said the waiter, with the sullen air of a man who is forced into giving advice. 'Put yer mon in yer pocket! Yer loaded an' yehs on'y makes a fool of yerself.'

As the latter passed out of the door the man turned pathetically to the women.

'He don' know I'm goo' f'ler,' cried he, dismally.

'Never you mind, Pete, dear,' said the woman of brilliance and audacity, laying her hand with great affection upon his arm. 'Never you mind, old boy! We'll stay by you, dear!'

'Das ri'!' cried the man, his face lighting up at the soothing tones of the woman's voice. 'Das ri'; I'm goo' f'ler an' w'en anyone trea's me ri', I trea's zem ri'! Shee?'

'Sure!' cried the women. 'And we're not goin' back on you, old man.'

The man turned appealing eyes to the woman. He felt that if he could be convicted of a contemptible action he would die.

'Shay, Nell, I allus trea's yehs shsquare, didn' I? I allus been goo' f'ler wi' yehs, ain't I, Nell?'

'Sure you have, Pete,' assented the woman. She delivered an oration to her companions. 'Yessir, that's a fact. Pete's a square fellah, he is. He never goes back on a friend. He's the right kind an' we stay by him, don't we, girls?'

'Sure!' they exclaimed. Looking lovingly at him they raised their glasses and drank his health.

'Girlsh,' said the man, beseechingly, 'I allus trea's yehs ri', didn' I? I'm goo' f'ler, ain' I, girlsh?'

'Sure!' again they chorused.

'Well,' said he finally, 'le's have nozzer drink, zen.'

'That's right,' hailed a woman, 'that's right. Yer no bloomin' jay! Yer spends yer money like a man. Dat's right.'

The man pounded the table with his quivering fists.

'Yessir,' he cried, with deep earnestness, as if someone disputed him. 'I'm goo' f'ler, an' w'en anyone trea's me ri', I allus trea's – le's have nozzer drink.'

He began to beat the wood with his glass.

'Shay!' howled he, growing suddenly impatient. As the waiter did not then come, the man swelled with wrath.

'Shay!' howled he again.

The waiter appeared at the door.

'Bringsh drinksh,' said the man.

The waiter disappeared with the orders.

'Zat f'ler fool!' cried the man. 'He insul' me! I'm ge'man! Can' stan' be insul'! I'm goin' lickim when comes!'

'No, no!' cried the women, crowding about and trying to subdue him. 'He's all right! He didn't mean anything! Let it go! He's a good fellah!'

'Din' he insul' me?' asked the man earnestly.

'No,' said they. 'Of course he didn't! He's all right!'

'Sure he didn' insul' me?' demanded the man, with deep anxiety in his voice.

'No, no! We know him! He's a good fellah. He didn't mean anything.'

'Well, zen,' said the man resolutely, 'I'm go' 'pol'gise!'

When the waiter came, the man struggled to the middle of the floor.

'Girlsh shed you insul' me! I shay – lie! I 'pol'gise!'

'All right,' said the waiter.

The man sat down. He felt a sleepy but strong desire to straighten things out and have a perfect understanding with everybody.

'Nell, I allus trea's yeh shsquare, din' I? Yeh likes me, don' yehs, Nell? I'm goo' f'ler?'

'Sure!' said the woman.

'Yeh knows I'm stuck on yehs, don' yehs, Nell?'

'Sure!' she repeated, carelessly.

Overwhelmed by a spasm of drunken adoration, he drew two or three bills from his pocket, and with the trembling fingers of an offering priest, laid them on the table before the woman.

'Yehs knows yehs kin have all I got, 'cause I'm stuck on yehs, Nell, I I'm stuck on yehs, Nell – buy drinksh – we're havin' great time – w'en anyone trea's me ri' – I – Nell – we're havin' heluva – time.'

Presently he went to sleep with his swollen face fallen forward on his chest.

The women drank and laughed, not heeding the slumbering man in the corner. Finally he lurched forward and fell groaning to the floor.

The women screamed in disgust and drew back their skirts.

'Come ahn!' cried one, starting up angrily, 'let's get out of here.'

The woman of brilliance and audacity stayed behind, taking up the bills and stuffing them into a deep, irregularly shaped pocket. A guttural snore from the recumbent man caused her to turn and look down at him.

She laughed. 'What a fool!' she said, and went.

The smoke from the lamps settled heavily down in the little compartment, obscuring the way out. The smell of oil, stifling in its intensity, pervaded the air. The wine from an overturned glass dripped softly down upon the blotches on the man's neck.

❧ 19 ❧

In a room a woman sat at a table eating like a fat monk in a picture.

A soiled, unshaven man pushed open the door and entered.

'Well,' said he, 'Mag's dead.'

'What?' said the woman, her mouth filled with bread.

'Mag's dead,' repeated the man.

'Deh blazes she is!' said the woman. She continued her meal. When she finished her coffee she began to weep.

'I kin remember when her two feet was no bigger dan yer thumb, and she weared worsted boots,' moaned she.

'Well, whata dat?' said the man.

'I kin remember when she weared worsted boots,' she cried.

The neighbours began to gather in the hall, staring in at the weeping woman as if watching the contortions of a dying dog. A dozen women entered and lamented with her. Under their busy hands the room took on that appalling appearance of neatness and order with which death is greeted.

Suddenly the door opened and a woman in a black gown rushed in with outstretched arms. 'Ah, poor Mary!' she cried, and tenderly embraced the moaning one.

'Ah, what ter'ble affliction is dis!' continued she. Her vocabulary was derived from mission churches. 'Me poor Mary, how I feel fer yehs! Ah, what a ter'ble affliction is a disobed'ent chile.'

Her good, motherly face was wet with tears. She trembled in eagerness to express her sympathy. The mourner sat with bowed head, rocking her body heavily to and fro, and crying out in a high, strained voice that sounded like a dirge on some forlorn pipe.

'I kin remember when she weared worsted boots an' her two feets was no bigger dan yer stumb an' she weared worsted boots, Miss Smith,' she cried, raising her streaming eyes.

'Ah, me poor Mary!' sobbed the woman in black. With low, coddling cries, she sank on her knees by the mourner's chair, and put her arms about her. The other women began to groan in different keys.

'Yer poor misguided chil' is gone now, Mary, an' let us hope its fer deh bes'. Yeh'll fergive her now, Mary, won't yehs, dear, all her disobed'ence? All her t'ankless behaviour to her mudder an' all her badness? She's gone where her ter'ble sins will be judged.'

The woman in black raised her face and paused. The inevitable sunlight came streaming in at the window and shed a ghastly cheerfulness upon the faded hues of the room. Two or three of the spectators were sniffling, and one was weeping loudly. The mourner arose and staggered into the other room. In a moment she emerged with a pair of faded baby shoes held in the hollow of her hand.

'I kin remember when she used to wear dem!' cried she. The women burst anew into cries as if they had all been stabbed. The mourner turned to the soiled and unshaven man.

'Jimmie, boy, go git yer sister! Go git yer sister an' we'll put deh boots on her feets!'

'Dey won't fit her now, yeh fool,' said the man.

'Go git yer sister, Jimmie!' shrieked the woman, confronting him fiercely.

The man swore sullenly. He went over to a corner and slowly began to put on his coat. He took his hat and went out, with a dragging, reluctant step.

The woman in black came forward and again besought the mourner.

'Yeh'll fergive her, Mary! Yeh'll fergive yer bad, bad chil'! Her life was a curse an' her days were black an' yeh'll fergive yer bad girl? She's gone where her sins will be judged.'

'She's gone where her sins will be judged!' cried the other women, like a choir at a funeral.

'Deh Lord gives and deh Lord takes away,' said the woman in black, raising her eyes to the sunbeams.

'Deh Lord gives and deh Lord takes away,' responded the others.

'Yeh'll fergive her, Mary?' pleaded the woman in black. The mourner essayed to speak but her voice gave way. She shook her great shoulders frantically, in an agony of grief. The tears seemed to scald her face. Finally her voice came and arose in a scream of pain.

'Oh, yes, I'll fergive her! I'll fergive her!'

The Monster

❦ I ❧

Little Jim was, for the time, engine Number 36, and he was making the run between Syracuse and Rochester. He was fourteen minutes behind time, and the throttle was wide open. In consequence, when he swung around the curve at the flower-bed, a wheel of his cart destroyed a peony. Number 36 slowed down at once and looked guiltily at his father, who was mowing the lawn. The doctor had his back to this accident, and he continued to pace slowly to and fro, pushing the mower.

Jim dropped the tongue of the cart. He looked at his father and at the broken flower. Finally he went to the peony and tried to stand it on its pins, resuscitated, but the spine of it was hurt, and it would only hang limply from his hand. Jim could do no reparation. He looked again towards his father.

He went on to the lawn, very slowly, and kicking wretchedly at the turf. Presently his father came along with the whirring machine, while the sweet, new grass blades spun from the knives. In a low voice, Jim said, 'Pa!'

The doctor was shaving this lawn as if it were a priest's chin. All during the season he had worked at it in the coolness and peace of the evenings after supper. Even in the shadow of the cherry-trees the grass was strong and healthy. Jim raised his voice a trifle. 'Pa!'

The doctor paused, and with the howl of the machine no longer occupying the sense, one could hear the robins in the cherry-trees arranging their affairs. Jim's hands were behind his back, and sometimes his fingers clasped and unclasped. Again he said, 'Pa!' the child's fresh and rosy lip was lowered.

The doctor stared down at his son, thrusting his head forward and frowning attentively. 'What is it, Jimmie?'

'Pa!' repeated the child at length. Then he raised his finger and pointed at the flowerbed. 'There!'

'What?' said the doctor, frowning more. 'What is it, Jim?'

After a period of silence, during which the child may have undergone a severe mental tumult, he raised his finger and repeated his former word – 'There!' The father had respected this silence with perfect courtesy. Afterwards his glance carefully followed the direction indicated by the child's finger, but he could see nothing which explained to him. 'I don't understand what you mean, Jimmie,' he said.

It seemed that the importance of the whole thing had taken away the boy's vocabulary. He could only reiterate, 'There!'

The doctor mused upon the situation, but he could make nothing of it. At last he said, 'Come, show me.'

Together they crossed the lawn towards the flower-bed. At some yards from the broken peony Jimmie began to lag. 'There!' The word came almost breathlessly.

'Where?' said the doctor.

Jimmie kicked at the grass. 'There!' he replied.

The doctor was obliged to go forward alone. After some trouble he found the subject of the incident, the broken flower. Turning then, he saw the child lurking at the rear and scanning his countenance.

The father reflected. After a time he said, 'Jimmie, come here.' With an infinite modesty of demeanour the child came forward. 'Jimmie, how did this happen?'

The child answered, 'Now – I was playin' train – and – now – I runned over it.'

'You were doing what?'

'I was playin' train.'

The father reflected again. 'Well, Jimmie,' he said, slowly, 'I guess you had better not play train any more today. Do you think you had better?'

'No, sir,' said Jimmie.

During the delivery of the judgment the child had not faced his father, and afterwards he went away, with his head lowered, shuffling his feet,

❧ 2 ☙

It was apparent from Jimmie's manner that he felt some kind of desire to efface himself. He went down to the stable. Henry Johnson, the negro who cared for the doctor's horses, was sponging the buggy. He grinned fraternally when he saw Jimmie coming. These two were pals.

In regard to almost everything in life they seemed to have minds precisely alike. Of course there were points of emphatic divergence. For instance, it was plain from Henry's talk that he was a very handsome negro, and he was known to be a light, a weight, and an eminence in the suburb of the town, where lived the larger number of the negroes, and obviously this glory was over Jimmie's horizon; but he vaguely appreciated it and paid deference to Henry for it mainly because Henry appreciated it and deferred to himself. However, on all points of conduct as related to the doctor, who was the moon, they were in complete but unexpressed understanding. Whenever Jimmie became the victim of an eclipse he went to the stable to solace himself with Henry's crimes. Henry, with the elasticity of his race, could usually provide a sin to place himself on a footing with the disgraced one. Perhaps he would remember that he had forgotten to put the hitching-strap in the back of the buggy on some recent occasion, and had been reprimanded by the doctor. Then these two would commune subtly and without words concerning their moon, holding themselves sympathetically as people who had committed similar treasons. On the other hand, Henry would sometimes choose to absolutely repudiate this idea, and when Jimmie appeared in his shame would bully him most virtuously, preaching with assurance the precepts of the doctor's creed, and pointing out to Jimmie all his abominations. Jimmie did not discover that this was odious in his comrade. He accepted it and lived in its shadow with humility, merely trying to conciliate the saintly Henry with acts of deference. Won by this attitude, Henry would sometimes allow the child to enjoy the felicity of squeezing the sponge over a buggy-wheel, even when Jimmie was still gory from unspeakable deeds.

Whenever Henry dwelt for a time in sackcloth, Jimmie did not patronise him at all. This was a justice of his age, his condition. He did not know. Besides, Henry could drive a horse, and Jimmie had a full sense of this sublimity. Henry personally conducted the moon during the splendid journeys through the country roads, where farms spread on all sides, with sheep, cows, and other marvels abounding.

'Hello, Jim!' said Henry, poising his sponge. Water was dripping from the buggy. Sometimes the horses in the stalls stamped thunderingly on the pine floor. There was an atmosphere of hay and of harness.

For a minute Jimmie refused to take an interest in anything. He was very downcast. He could not even feel the wonders of wagon-washing. Henry, while at his work, narrowly observed him.

'Your pop done wallop yer, didn't he?' he said at last.

'No,' said Jimmie, defensively; 'he didn't.'

After this casual remark Henry continued his labour, with a scowl of occupation. Presently he said: 'I done tol' yer many's th' time not to go a-foolin' an' a-projjeckin' with them flowers. Yer pop don' like it nohow.' As a matter of fact, Henry had never mentioned flowers to the boy.

Jimmie preserved a gloomy silence, so Henry began to use seductive wiles in this affair of washing a wagon. It was not until he began to spin a wheel on the tree, and the sprinkling water flew everywhere, that the boy was visibly moved. He had been seated on the sill of the carriage-house door, but at the beginning of this ceremony he arose and circled towards the buggy, with an interest that slowly consumed the remembrance of a late disgrace.

Johnson could then display all the dignity of a man whose duty it was to protect Jimmie from a splashing. 'Look out, boy! look out! You done gwi' spile yer pants. I raikon your mommer don't 'low this foolishness, she know it. I ain't gwi' have you round yere spilin' yer pants, an' have Mis' Trescott light on me pressen'ly. 'Deed I ain't.'

He spoke with an air of great irritation, but he was not annoyed at all. This tone was merely a part of his importance. In reality he was always delighted to have the child there to witness the business of the stable. For one thing, Jimmie was invariably overcome with reverence when he was told how beautifully a harness was polished or a horse groomed. Henry explained each detail of this kind with unction, procuring great joy from the child's admiration.

❧ 3 ❧

After Johnson had taken his supper in the kitchen, he went to his loft in the carriage-house and dressed himself with much care. No belle of a court circle could bestow more mind on a toilet than did Johnson. On second thought, he was more like a priest arraying himself for some parade of the church. As he emerged from his room and sauntered down the carriage-drive, no one would have suspected him of ever having washed a buggy.

It was not altogether a matter of the lavender trousers, nor yet the straw hat with its bright silk band. The change was somewhere far in the interior of Henry. But there was no cake-walk hyperbole in it. He was simply a quiet, well-bred gentleman of position, wealth, and other necessary achievements out for an evening stroll, and he had never washed a wagon in his life.

In the morning, when in his working-clothes, he had met a friend – 'Hello, Pete!' 'Hello, Henry!' Now, in his effulgence, he encountered this same friend. His bow was not at all haughty. If it expressed anything, it expressed consummate generosity – 'Good-evenin', Misteh Washington.' Pete, who was very dirty, being at work in a potato-patch, responded in a mixture of abasement and appreciation – 'Good-evenin', Misteh Johnson.'

The shimmering blue of the electric arc lamps was strong in the main street of the town. At numerous points it was conquered by the orange glare of the outnumbering gaslights in the windows of shops. Through this radiant lane moved a crowd, which culminated in a throng before the post-office, awaiting the distribution of the evening mails. Occasionally there came into it a shrill electric street-car, the motor singing like a cageful of grasshoppers, and possessing a great gong that clanged forth both warnings and simple noise. At the little theatre, which was a varnish and red-plush miniature of one of the famous New York theatres, a company of strollers was to play *East Lynne*. The young men of the town were mainly gathered at the corners, in distinctive groups, which expressed various shades and lines of chumship, and had little to do with any social gradations. There they discussed everything with critical insight, passing the whole town in review as it swarmed in the street. When the gongs of the electric cars ceased for a moment to harry the ears, there could be heard the sound of the feet of the leisurely crowd on the bluestone pavement, and it was like the peaceful evening lashing at the shore of a lake. At the foot of the hill, where two lines of maples sentinelled the way, an electric lamp glowed high among the embowering branches, and made most wonderful shadow-etchings on the road below it.

When Johnson appeared amid the throng a member of one of the profane groups at a corner instantly telegraphed news of this extraordinary arrival to his companions. They hailed him. 'Hello, Henry! Going to walk for a cake tonight?'

'Ain't he smooth?'

'Why, you've got that cake right in your pocket, Henry!'

'Throw out your chest a little more.'

Henry was not ruffled in any way by these quiet admonitions and compliments. In reply he laughed a supremely good-natured, chuckling laugh, which nevertheless expressed an underground complacency of superior metal.

Young Griscom, the lawyer, was just emerging from Reifsnyder's barber shop, rubbing his chin contentedly. On the steps he dropped his hand and looked with wide eyes into the crowd. Suddenly he bolted back into the shop. 'Wow!' he cried to the parliament; 'you ought to see the coon that's coming!'

Reifsnyder and his assistant instantly poised their razors high and turned towards the window. Two belathered heads reared from the chairs. The electric shine in the street caused an effect like water to them who looked through the glass from the yellow glamour of Reifsnyder's shop. In fact, the people without resembled the inhabitants of a great aquarium that here had a square pane in it. Presently into this frame swam the graceful form of Henry Johnson.

'Chee!' said Reifsnyder. He and his assistant with one accord threw their obligations to the winds, and leaving their lathered victims helpless, advanced to the window. 'Ain't he a taisy?' said Reifsnyder, marvelling.

But the man in the first chair, with a grievance in his mind, had found a weapon. 'Why, that's only Henry Johnson, you blamed idiots! Come on now, Reif, and shave me. What do you think I am – a mummy?'

Reifsnyder turned, in a great excitement. 'I bait you any money that vas not Henry Johnson! Henry Johnson! Rats!' The scorn put into this last word made it an explosion. 'That man was a Pullman-car porter or someding. How could that be Henry Johnson?' he demanded, turbulently. 'You vas crazy.'

The man in the first chair faced the barber in a storm of indignation. 'Didn't I give him those lavender trousers?' he roared.

And young Griscom, who had remained attentively at the window, said: 'Yes, I guess that was Henry. It looked like him.'

'Oh, vell,' said Reifsnyder, returning to his business, 'if you think so! Oh, vell!' He implied that he was submitting for the sake of amiability.

Finally the man in the second chair, mumbling from a mouth made timid by adjacent lather, said: 'That was Henry Johnson all right. Why, he always dresses like that when he wants to make a front! He's the biggest dude in town – anybody knows that.'

'Chinger!' said Reifsnyder.

Henry was not at all oblivious of the wake of wondering ejaculation that streamed out behind him. On other occasions he had reaped this same joy, and he always had an eye for the demonstration. With a face beaming with happiness he turned away from the scene of his victories into a narrow side street, where the electric light still hung high, but only to exhibit a row of tumble-down houses leaning together like paralytics.

The saffron Miss Bella Farragut, in a calico frock, had been crouched on the front stoop, gossiping at long range, but she espied her approaching caller at a distance. She dashed around the corner of the house, galloping like a horse. Henry saw it all, but he preserved the polite demeanour of a guest when a waiter spills claret down his cuff. In this awkward situation he was simply perfect.

The duty of receiving Mr Johnson fell upon Mrs Farragut, because Bella, in another room, was scrambling wildly into her best gown. The fat old woman met him with a great ivory smile, sweeping back with the door, and bowing low. 'Walk in, Misteh Johnson, walk in. How is you dis ebenin', Misteh Johnson – how is you?'

Henry's face showed like a reflector as he bowed and bowed, bending almost from his head to his ankles. 'Good-evenin', Mis' Fa'gut; good-evenin'. How is you dis evenin'? Is all you' folks well, Mis' Fa'gut?'

After a great deal of kowtow, they were planted in two chairs opposite each other in the living-room. Here they exchanged the most tremendous civilities, until Miss Bella swept into the room, when there was more kowtow on all sides, and a smiling show of teeth that was like an illumination.

The cooking-stove was of course in this drawing-room, and on the fire was some kind of a long-winded stew. Mrs Farragut was obliged to arise and attend to it from time to time. Also young Sim came in and went to bed on his pallet in the corner. But to all these domesticities the three maintained an absolute dumbness. They bowed and smiled and ignored and imitated until a late hour, and if they had been the occupants of the most gorgeous salon in the world they could not have been more like three monkeys.

After Henry had gone, Bella, who encouraged herself in the appropriation of phrases, said, 'Oh, ma, isn't he divine?'

❧ 4 ❧

A Saturday evening was a sign always for a larger crowd to parade the thoroughfare. In summer the band played until ten o'clock in the little park. Most of the young men of the town affected to be superior to this band, even to despise it; but in the still and fragrant evenings they invariably turned out in force, because the girls were sure to attend this concert, strolling slowly over the grass, linked closely in pairs, or preferably in threes, in the curious public dependence upon one another which was their inheritance. There was no particular social aspect to this gathering, save that group regarded group with interest, but mainly in silence. Perhaps one girl would nudge another girl and suddenly say, 'Look! there goes Gertie Hodgson and her sister!' And they would appear to regard this as an event of importance.

On a particular evening a rather large company of young men were gathered on the sidewalk that edged the park. They remained thus beyond the borders of the festivities because of their dignity, which would not exactly allow them to appear in anything which was so much fun for the younger lads. These latter were careering madly through the crowd, precipitating minor accidents from time to time, but usually fleeing like mist swept by the wind before retribution could lay hands upon them.

The band played a waltz which involved a gift of prominence to the bass horn, and one of the young men on the sidewalk said that the music reminded him of the new engines on the hill pumping water into the reservoir. A similarity of this kind was not inconceivable, but the young man did not say it because he disliked the band's playing. He said it because it was fashionable to say that manner of thing concerning the band. However, over in the stand, Billie Harris, who played the snare-drum, was always surrounded by a throng of boys, who adored his every whack.

After the mails from New York and Rochester had been finally distributed, the crowd from the post-office added to the mass already in the park. The wind waved the leaves of the maples, and, high in the air, the blue-burning globes of the arc lamps caused the wonderful traceries of leaf shadows on the ground. When the light fell upon the upturned face of a girl, it caused it to glow with a wonderful pallor. A policeman came suddenly from the darkness and chased a gang of obstreperous little boys. They hooted him from a distance. The leader of the band had some of the mannerisms of the great musicians, and during a period of silence the crowd smiled when they saw him raise his hand to his brow, stroke it sentimentally, and glance upward with a look of poetic anguish. In the shivering light, which gave to the park an effect like a great vaulted hall, the throng swarmed, with a gentle murmur of dresses switching the turf, and with a steady hum of voices.

Suddenly, without preliminary bars, there arose from afar the great hoarse roar of a factory whistle. It raised and swelled to a sinister note, and then it sang on the night wind one long call that held the crowd in the park immovable, speechless. The band-master had been about to vehemently let fall his hand to start the band on a thundering career through a popular march, but, smitten by this giant voice from the night, his hand dropped slowly to his knee, and, his mouth agape, he looked at his men in silence. The cry died away to a wail and then to stillness. It released the muscles of the company of young men on the sidewalk, who had been like statues, posed eagerly, lithely, their ears turned. And then they wheeled upon each other simultaneously, and, in a single explosion, they shouted, 'One!'

Again the sound swelled in the night and roared its long ominous cry, and as it died away the crowd of young men wheeled upon each other and, in chorus, yelled, 'Two!'

There was a moment of breathless waiting. Then they bawled, 'Second district!' In a flash the company of indolent and cynical young men had vanished like a snowball disrupted by dynamite.

❧ 5 ☙

Jake Rogers was the first man to reach the home of Tuscarora Hose Company Number Six. He had wrenched his key from his pocket as he tore down the street, and he jumped at the spring-lock like a demon. As the doors flew back before his hands he leaped and kicked the wedges from a pair of wheels, loosened a tongue from its clasp, and in the glare of the electric light which the town placed before each of its hose-houses the next comers beheld the spectacle of Jake Rogers bent like hickory in the manfulness of his pulling, and the heavy cart was moving slowly towards the doors. Four men joined him at the time, and as they swung with the cart out into the street, dark figures sped towards them from the ponderous shadows back of the electric lamps. Some set up the inevitable question, 'What district?'

'Second,' was replied to them in a compact howl. Tuscarora Hose Company Number Six swept on a perilous wheel into Niagara Avenue, and as the men, attached to the cart by the rope which had been paid out front the windlass under the tongue, pulled madly in their fervour and abandon, the gong under the axle clanged incitingly. And sometimes the same cry was heard, 'What district?'

'Second.'

On a grade Johnnie Thorpe fell, and exercising a singular muscular ability, rolled out in time from the track of the on-coming wheel, and arose, dishevelled and aggrieved, casting a look of mournful disenchantment upon the black crowd that poured after the machine. The cart seemed to be the apex of a dark wave that was whirling as if it had been a broken dam. Back of the lad were stretches of land, and in that direction front-doors were banged by men who hoarsely shouted out into the clamorous avenue, 'What district?'

At one of these houses a woman came to the door bearing a lamp, shielding her face from its rays with her hands. Across the cropped grass the avenue represented to her a kind of black torrent, upon which, nevertheless, fled numerous miraculous figures upon bicycles. She did not know that the towering light at the corner was continuing its nightly whine.

Suddenly a little boy somersaulted around the corner of the house as if he had been projected down a flight of stairs by a catapultian boot. He halted himself in front of the house by dint of a rather extraordinary evolution with his legs. 'Oh, ma,' he gasped, 'can I go? Can I, ma?'

She straightened with the coldness of the exterior mother-judgment, although the hand that held the lamp trembled slightly. 'No, Willie; you had better come to bed.'

Instantly he began to buck and fume like a mustang. 'Oh, ma,' he cried, contorting himself – 'oh, ma, can't I go? Please, ma, can't I go? Can't I go, ma?'

'It's half-past nine now, Willie.'

He ended by wailing out a compromise: 'Well, just down to the corner, ma? Just down to the corner?'

From the avenue came the sound of rushing men who wildly shouted. Somebody had grappled the bell-rope in the Methodist church, and now over the town rang this solemn and terrible voice, speaking from the clouds. Moved from its peaceful business, this bell gained a new spirit in the portentous night, and it swung the heart to and fro, up and down, with each peal of it.

'Just down to the corner, ma?'

'Willie, it's half-past nine now.'

❦ 6 ❦

The outlines of the house of Dr Trescott had faded quietly into the evening, hiding a shape such as we call Queen Anne against the pall of the blackened sky. The neighbourhood was at this time so quiet, and seemed so devoid of obstructions, that Hannigan's dog thought it a good opportunity to prowl in forbidden precincts, and so came and pawed Trescott's lawn, growling, and considering himself a formidable beast. Later, Peter Washington strolled past the house and whistled, but there was no dim light shining from Henry's loft, and presently Peter went his way. The rays from the street, creeping in silvery waves over the grass, caused the row of shrubs along the drive to throw a clear, bold shade.

A wisp of smoke came from one of the windows at the end of the house and drifted quietly into the branches of a cherry-tree. Its companions followed it in slowly increasing numbers, and finally there was a current controlled by invisible banks which poured into the fruit-laden boughs of the cherry-tree. It was no more to be noted than if a troop of dim and silent grey monkeys had been climbing a grapevine into the clouds.

After a moment the window brightened as if the four panes of it had been stained with blood, and a quick ear might have been led to imagine the fire-imps calling and calling, clan joining clan, gathering to the colours. From the street, however, the house maintained its dark quiet, insisting to a passer-by that it was the safe dwelling of people who chose to retire early to tranquil dreams. No one could have heard this low droning of the gathering clans.

Suddenly the panes of the red window tinkled and crashed to the ground, and at other windows there suddenly reared other flames, like bloody spectres at the apertures of a haunted house. This outbreak had been well planned, as if by professional revolutionists.

A man's voice suddenly shouted: 'Fire! Fire! Fire!' Hannigan had flung his pipe frenziedly from him because his lungs demanded room. He tumbled down from his perch, swung over the fence, and ran shouting towards the front-door of the Trescotts'. Then he hammered on the door, using his fists as if they were mallets. Mrs Trescott instantly came to one of the windows on the second floor. Afterwards she knew she had been about to say, 'The doctor is not at home, but if you will leave your name, I will let him know as soon as he comes.'

Hannigan's bawling was for a minute incoherent, but she understood that it was not about croup.

'What?' she said, raising the window swiftly.

'Your house is on fire! You're all ablaze! Move quick if – ' His cries were resounding in the street as if it were a cave of echoes. Many feet pattered swiftly on the stones. There was one man who ran with an almost fabulous speed. He wore lavender trousers. A straw hat with a bright silk band was held half crumpled in his hand.

As Henry reached the front-door, Hannigan had just broken the lock with a kick. A thick cloud of smoke poured over them, and Henry, ducking his head, rushed into it. From Hannigan's clamour he knew only one thing, but it turned him blue with horror. In the hall a lick of flame had found the cord that supported 'Signing the Declaration'. The engraving slumped suddenly down at one end, and then dropped to the floor, where it burst with the sound of a bomb. The fire was already roaring like a winter wind among the pines.

At the head of the stairs Mrs Trescott was waving her arms as if they were two reeds. 'Jimmie! Save Jimmie!' she screamed in Henry's face. He plunged past her and disappeared, taking the long-familiar routes among these upper chambers, where he had once held office as a sort of second assistant housemaid.

Hannigan had followed him up the stairs, and grappled the arm of the maniacal woman there. His face was black with rage. 'You must come down,' he bellowed.

She would only scream at him in reply: 'Jimmie! Jimmie! Save Jimmie!' But he dragged her forth while she babbled at him.

As they swung out into the open air a man ran across the lawn, and seizing a shutter, pulled it from its hinges and flung it far out upon the grass. Then he frantically attacked the other shutters one by one. It was a kind of temporary insanity.

'Here, you,' howled Hannigan, 'hold Mrs Trescott – And stop – '

The news had been telegraphed by a twist of the wrist of a neighbour who had gone to the fire-box at the corner, and the time when Hannigan and his charge struggled out of the house was the time when the whistle roared its hoarse night call, smiting the crowd in the park, causing the leader of the band, who was about to order the first triumphal clang of a military march, to let his hand drop slowly to his knees.

❦ 7 ❧

Henry pawed awkwardly through the smoke in the upper halls. He had attempted to guide himself by the walls, but they were too hot. The paper was crimpling, and he expected at any moment to have a flame burst from under his hands.

'Jimmie!'

He did not call very loud, as if in fear that the humming flames below would overhear him.

'Jimmie! Oh, Jimmie!'

Stumbling and panting, he speedily reached the entrance to Jimmie's room and flung open the door. The little chamber had no smoke in it at all. It was faintly illuminated by a beautiful rosy light reflected circuitously from the flames that were consuming the house. The boy had apparently just been aroused by the noise. He sat in his bed, his lips apart, his eyes wide, while upon his little white-robed figure played caressingly the light from the fire. As the door flew open he had before him this apparition of his pal, a terror-stricken negro, all tousled and with wool scorching, who leaped upon him and bore him up in a blanket as if the whole affair were a case of kidnapping by a dreadful robber chief. Without waiting to go through the usual short but complete process of wrinkling up his face, Jimmie let out a gorgeous bawl, which resembled the expression of a calf's deepest terror. As Johnson, bearing him, reeled into the smoke of the hall, he flung his arms about his neck and buried his face in the blanket. He called twice in muffled tones: 'Mam-ma! Mam-ma!'

When Johnson came to the top of the stairs with his burden, he took a quick step backward. Through the smoke that rolled to him he could see that the lower hall was all ablaze. He cried out then in a howl that resembled Jimmie's former achievement. His legs gained a frightful faculty of bending sideways. Swinging about precariously on these reedy legs, he made his way back slowly, back along the upper hall. From the way of him then, he had given up almost all idea of escaping from the burning house, and with it the desire. He was submitting, submitting because of his fathers, bending his mind in a most perfect slavery to this conflagration.

He now clutched Jimmie as unconsciously as when, running toward the house, he had clutched the hat with the bright silk band.

Suddenly he remembered a little private staircase which led from a bedroom to an apartment which the doctor had fitted up as a laboratory and work-house, where he used some of his leisure, and also hours when he might have been sleeping, in devoting himself to experiments which came in the way of his study and interest.

When Johnson recalled this stairway the submission to the blaze departed instantly. He had been perfectly familiar with it, but his confusion had destroyed the memory of it.

In his sudden momentary apathy there had been little that resembled fear, but now, as a way of safety came to him, the old frantic terror caught him. He was no longer creature to the flames, and he was afraid of the battle with them. It was a singular and swift set of alternations in which he feared twice without submission, and submitted once without fear.

'Jimmie!' he wailed, as he staggered on his way. He wished this little inanimate body at his breast to participate in his tremblings. But the child had lain limp and still during these headlong charges and countercharges, and no sign came from him.

Johnson passed through two rooms and came to the head of the stairs. As he opened the door great billows of smoke poured out, but gripping Jimmie closer, he plunged down through them. All manner of odours assailed him during this flight. They seemed to be alive with envy, hatred, and malice. At the entrance to the laboratory he confronted a strange spectacle. The room was like a garden in the region where might be burning flowers. Flames of violet, crimson, green, blue, orange, and purple were blooming everywhere. There was one blaze that was precisely the hue of a delicate coral. In another place was a mass that lay merely in phosphorescent inaction like a pile of emeralds. But all these marvels were to be seen dimly through clouds of heaving, turning, deadly smoke.

Johnson halted for a moment on the threshold. He cried out again in the negro wail that had in it the sadness of the swamps. Then he rushed across the room. An orange-coloured flame leaped like a panther at the lavender trousers. This animal bit deeply into Johnson. There was an explosion at one side, and suddenly before him there reared a delicate, trembling sapphire shape like a fairy lady. With a quiet smile she blocked his path and doomed him and Jimmie. Johnson shrieked, and then ducked in the manner of his race in fights. He aimed to pass under the left guard of the sapphire lady. But she was swifter than eagles, and her talons caught in him as he plunged past her. Bowing his head as if his neck had been struck, Johnson lurched forward, twisting this way and that way. He fell on his back. The still form in the blanket flung from his arms, rolled to the edge of the floor and beneath the window.

Johnson had fallen with his head at the base of an old-fashioned desk. There was a row of jars upon the top of this desk. For the most part, they were silent amid this rioting, but there was one which seemed to hold a scintillant and writhing serpent.

Suddenly the glass splintered, and a ruby-red snakelike thing poured its thick length out upon the top of the old desk. It coiled and hesitated, and then began to swim a languorous way down the mahogany slant. At the angle it waved its sizzling molten head to and fro over the closed eyes of the man beneath it. Then, in a moment, with a mystic impulse, it moved again, and the red snake flowed directly down into Johnson's upturned face.

Afterwards the trail of this creature seemed to reek, and amid flames and low explosions drops like red-hot jewels pattered softly down it at leisurely intervals.

~ 8 ~

Suddenly all roads led to Dr Trescott's. The whole town flowed towards one point. Chippeway Hose Company Number One toiled desperately up Bridge Street Hill even as the Tuscaroras came in an impetuous sweep down Niagara Avenue. Meanwhile the machine of the hook-and-ladder experts from across the creek was spinning on its way. The chief of the fire department had been playing poker in the rear room of Whiteley's cigar-store, but at the first breath of the alarm he sprang through the door like a man escaping with the kitty.

In Whilomville, on these occasions, there was always a number of people who instantly turned their attention to the bells in the churches and schoolhouses. The bells not only emphasised the alarm, but it was the habit to send these sounds rolling across the sky in a stirring brazen uproar until the flames were practically vanquished. There was also a kind of rivalry as to which bell should be made to produce the greatest din. Even the Valley Church, four miles away among the farms, had heard the voices of its brethren, and immediately added a quaint little yelp.

Dr Trescott had been driving homeward, slowly smoking a cigar, and feeling glad that this last case was now in complete obedience to him, like a wild animal that he had subdued, when he heard the long whistle, and chirped to his horse under the unlicensed but perfectly distinct impression that a fire had broken out in Oakhurst, a new and rather high-flying suburb of the town which was at least two miles from his own home. But in the second blast and in the ensuing silence he read the designation of his own district. He was then only a few blocks from his house. He took out the whip and laid it lightly on the mare. Surprised and frightened at this extraordinary action, she leaped forward, and as the reins straightened like steel bands, the doctor leaned backward a trifle. When the mare whirled him up to the closed gate he was wondering whose house could be afire. The man who had rung the signal-box yelled something at him, but he already knew. He left the mare to her will.

In front of his door was a maniacal woman in a wrapper. 'Ned!' she screamed at sight of him. 'Jimmie! Save Jimmie!'

Trescott had grown hard and chill. 'Where?' he said. 'Where?'

Mrs Trescott's voice began to bubble. 'Up – up – up – ' She pointed at the second-storey windows.

Hannigan was already shouting: 'Don't go in that way! You can't go in that way!'

Trescott ran around the corner of the house and disappeared from them. He knew from the view he had taken of the main hall that it would be impossible to ascend from there. His hopes were fastened now to the stairway which led from the laboratory. The door which opened from this room out upon the lawn was fastened with a bolt and lock, but he kicked close to the lock and then close to the bolt. The door with a loud crash flew back. The doctor recoiled from the roll of smoke, and then bending low, he stepped into the garden of burning flowers. On the floor his stinging eyes could make out a form in a smouldering blanket near the window. Then, as he carried his son towards the door, he saw that the whole lawn seemed now alive with men and boys, the leaders in the great charge that the whole town was making. They seized him and his burden, and overpowered him in wet blankets and water.

But Hannigan was howling: 'Johnson is in there yet! Henry Johnson is in there yet! He went in after the kid! Johnson is in there yet!'

These cries penetrated to the sleepy senses of Trescott, and he struggled with his captors, swearing, unknown to him and to them, all the deep blasphemies of his medical-student days. He rose to his feet and went again towards the door of the laboratory. They endeavoured to restrain him, although they were much affrighted at him.

But a young man who was a brakeman on the railway, and lived in one of the rear streets near the Trescotts, had gone into the laboratory and brought forth a thing which he laid on the grass.

❧ 9 ❧

There were hoarse commands from in front of the house. 'Turn on your water, Five!' 'Let 'er go, One!' The gathering crowd swayed this way and that way. The flames, towering high, cast a wild red light on their faces. There came the clangour of a gong from along some adjacent street. The crowd exclaimed at it. 'Here comes Number Three!' 'That's Three a-comin'!' A panting and irregular mob dashed into view, dragging a hose-cart. A cry of exultation arose from the little boys. 'Here's Three!' The lads welcomed Never-Die Hose Company Number Three as if it was composed of a chariot dragged by a band of gods. The perspiring citizens flung themselves into the fray. The boys danced in impish joy at the displays of prowess. They acclaimed the approach of Number Two. They welcomed Number Four with cheers. They were so deeply moved by this whole affair that they bitterly guyed the late appearance of the hook and ladder company, whose heavy apparatus had almost stalled them on the Bridge Street hill. The lads hated and feared a fire, of course. They did not particularly want to have anybody's house burn, but still it was fine to see the gathering of the companies, and amid a great noise to watch their heroes perform all manner of prodigies.

They were divided into parties over the worth of different companies, and supported their creeds with no small violence. For instance, in that part of the little city where Number Four had its home it would be most daring for a boy to contend the superiority of any other company.

Likewise, in another quarter, where a strange boy was asked which fire company was the best in Whilomville, he was expected to answer 'Number One'. 'Feuds, which the boys forgot and remembered according to chance or the importance of some recent event, existed all through the town.

They did not care much for John Shipley, the chief of the department. It was true that he went to a fire with the speed of a falling angel, but when there he invariably lapsed into a certain still mood, which was almost a preoccupation, moving leisurely around the burning structure and surveying it, puffing meanwhile at a cigar. This quiet man, who even when life was in danger seldom raised his voice, was not much to their fancy. Now old Sykes Huntington, when he was chief, used to bellow continually like a bull and gesticulate in a sort of delirium. He was much finer as a spectacle than this Shipley, who viewed a fire with the same steadiness that he viewed a raise in a large jackpot. The greater number of the boys could never understand why the members of these companies persisted in re-electing Shipley, although they often pretended to understand it, because 'My father says' was a very formidable phrase in argument, and the fathers seemed almost unanimous in advocating Shipley.

At this time there was considerable discussion as to which company had gotten the first stream of water on the fire. Most of the boys claimed that Number Five owned that distinction, but there was a determined minority who contended for Number One. Boys who were the blood adherents of other companies were obliged to choose between the two on this occasion, and the talk waxed warm.

But a great rumour went among the crowds. It was told with hushed voices. Afterwards a reverent silence fell even upon the boys. Jimmie Trescott and Henry Johnson had been burned to death, and Dr Trescott himself had been most savagely hurt. The crowd did not even feel the police pushing at them. They raised their eyes, shining now with awe, towards the high flames.

The man who had information was at his best. In low tones he described the whole affair. 'That was the kid's room – in the corner there. He had measles or somethin', and this coon – Johnson – was a-settin' up with 'im, and Johnson got sleepy or somethin' and upset the lamp, and the doctor he was down in his office, and he came running up, and they all got burned together till they dragged 'em out.'

Another man, always preserved for the deliverance of the final judgment, was saying: 'Oh, they'll die sure. Burned to flinders. No chance. Hull lot of 'em. Anybody can see.' The crowd concentrated its gaze still more closely upon these flags of fire which waved joyfully against the black sky. The bells of the town were clashing unceasingly.

A little procession moved across the lawn and towards the street. There were three cots, borne by twelve of the firemen. The police moved sternly, but it needed no effort of theirs to open a lane for this slow cortège. The men who bore the cots were well known to the crowd, but in this solemn parade during the ringing of the bells and the shouting, and with the red glare upon the sky, they seemed utterly foreign, and Whilomville paid them a deep respect. Each man in this stretcher party had gained a reflected majesty. They were footmen to death, and the crowd made subtle obeisance to this august dignity derived from three prospective graves. One woman turned away with a shriek at sight of the covered body on the first stretcher, and people faced her suddenly in silent and mournful indignation. Otherwise there was barely a sound as these twelve important men with measured tread carried their burdens through the throng.

The little boys no longer discussed the merits of the different fire companies. For the greater part they had been routed. Only the more courageous viewed closely the three figures veiled in yellow blankets.

❧ 10 ❧

Old Judge Denning Hagenthorpe, who lived nearly opposite the Trescotts, had thrown his door wide open to receive the afflicted family. When it was publicly learned that the doctor and his son and the negro were still alive, it required a specially detailed policeman to prevent people from scaling the front porch and interviewing these sorely wounded. One old lady appeared with a miraculous poultice, and she quoted most damning Scripture to the officer when he said that she could not pass him. Throughout the night some lads old enough to be given privileges or to compel them from their mothers remained vigilantly upon the kerb in anticipation of a death or some such event. The reporter of the *Morning Tribune* rode thither on his bicycle every hour until three o'clock.

Six of the ten doctors in Whilomville attended at Judge Hagenthorpe's house.

Almost at once they were able to know that Trescott's burns were not vitally important. The child would possibly be scarred badly, but his life was undoubtedly safe. As for the negro Henry Johnson, he could not live. His body was frightfully seared, but more than that, he now had no face. His face had simply been burned away.

Trescott was always asking news of the two other patients. In the morning he seemed fresh and strong, so they told him that Johnson was doomed. They then saw him stir on the bed, and sprang quickly to see if the bandages needed readjusting. In the sudden glance he threw from one to another he impressed them as being both leonine and impracticable.

The morning paper announced the death of Henry Johnson. It contained a long interview with Edward J. Hannigan, in which the latter described in full the performance of Johnson at the fire. There was also an editorial built from all the best words in the vocabulary of the staff. The town halted in its accustomed road of thought, and turned a reverent attention to the memory of this hostler. In the breasts of many people was the regret that they had not known enough to give him a hand and a lift when he was alive, and they judged themselves stupid and ungenerous for this failure.

The name of Henry Johnson became suddenly the title of a saint to the little boys. The one who thought of it first could, by quoting it in an argument, at once overthrow his antagonist, whether it applied to the subject or whether it did not.

> 'Nigger, nigger, never die,
> Black face and shiny eye.'

Boys who had called this odious couplet in the rear of Johnson's march buried the fact at the bottom of their hearts.

Later in the day Miss Bella Farragut, of No. 7 Watermelon Alley, announced that she had been engaged to marry Mr Henry Johnson.

❦ II ❧

The old judge had a cane with an ivory head. He could never think at his best until he was leaning slightly on this stick and smoothing the white top with slow movements of his hands. It was also to him a kind of narcotic. If by any chance he mislaid it, he grew at once very irritable, and was likely to speak sharply to his sister, whose mental incapacity he had patiently endured for thirty years in the old mansion on Ontario Street. She was not at all aware of her brother's opinion of her endowments, and so it might be said that the judge had successfully dissembled for more than a quarter of a century, only risking the truth at the times when his cane was lost.

On a particular day the judge sat in his armchair on the porch. The sunshine sprinkled through the lilac-bushes and poured great coins on the boards. The sparrows disputed in the trees that lined the pavements. The judge mused deeply, while his hands gently caressed the ivory head of his cane.

Finally he arose and entered the house, his brow still furrowed in a thoughtful frown. His stick thumped solemnly in regular beats. On the second floor he entered a room where Dr Trescott was working about the bedside of Henry Johnson. The bandages on the negro's head allowed only one thing to appear, an eye, which unwinkingly stared at the judge. The latter spoke to Trescott on the condition of the patient. Afterward he evidently had something further to say, but he seemed to be kept from it by the scrutiny of the unwinking eye, at which he furtively glanced from time to time.

When Jimmie Trescott was sufficiently recovered, his mother had taken him to pay a visit to his grandparents in Connecticut. The doctor had remained to take care of his patients, but as a matter of truth he spent most of his time at Judge Hagenthorpe's house, where lay Henry Johnson. Here he slept and ate almost every meal in the long nights and days of his vigil.

At dinner, and away from the magic of the unwinking eye, the judge said, suddenly, 'Trescott, do you think it is – ' As Trescott paused expectantly, the judge fingered his knife. He said, thoughtfully, 'No one wants to advance such ideas, but somehow I think that that poor fellow ought to die.'

There was in Trescott's face at once a look of recognition, as if in this tangent of the judge he saw an old problem. He merely sighed and answered, 'Who knows?' The words were spoken in a deep tone that gave them an elusive kind of significance.

The judge retreated to the cold manner of the bench. 'Perhaps we may not talk with propriety of this kind of action, but I am induced to say that you are performing a questionable charity in preserving this negro's life. As near as I can understand, he will hereafter be a monster, a perfect monster, and probably with an affected brain. No man can observe you as I have observed you and not know that it was a matter of conscience with you, but I am afraid, my friend, that it is one of the blunders of virtue.' The judge had delivered his views with his habitual oratory. The last three words he spoke with a particular emphasis, as if the phrase was his discovery.

The doctor made a weary gesture. 'He saved my boy's life.'

'Yes,' said the judge, swiftly – 'yes, I know!'

'And what am I to do?' said Trescott, his eyes suddenly lighting like an outburst from smouldering peat. 'What am I to do? He gave himself for – for Jimmie. What am I to do for him?'

The judge abased himself completely before these words. He lowered his eyes for a moment. He picked at his cucumbers.

Presently he braced himself straightly in his chair. 'He will be your creation, you understand. He is purely your creation. Nature has very evidently given him up. He is dead. You are restoring him to life. You are making him, and he will be a monster, and with no mind.'

'He will be what you like, judge,' cried Trescott, in sudden, polite fury. 'He will be anything, but, by God! he saved my boy.'

The judge interrupted in a voice trembling with emotion: 'Trescott! Trescott! Don't I know?'

Trescott had subsided to a sullen mood. 'Yes, you know,' he answered, acidly; 'but you don't know all about your own boy being saved from death.' This was a perfectly childish allusion to the judge's bachelorhood. Trescott knew that the remark was infantile, but he seemed to take desperate delight in it.

But it passed the judge completely. It was not his spot.

'I am puzzled,' said he, in profound thought. 'I don't know what to say.'

Trescott had become repentant. 'Don't think I don't appreciate what you say, judge. But – '

'Of course!' responded the judge, quickly. 'Of course.'

'It – ' began Trescott.

'Of course,' said the judge.

In silence they resumed their dinner.

'Well,' said the judge, ultimately, 'it is hard for a man to know what to do.'

'It is,' said the doctor, fervidly.

There was another silence. It was broken by the judge:

'Look here, Trescott; I don't want you to think – '

'No, certainly not,' answered the doctor, earnestly.

'Well, I don't want you to think I would say anything to – It was only that I thought that I might be able to suggest to you that – perhaps – the affair was a little dubious.'

With an appearance of suddenly disclosing his real mental perturbation, the doctor said: 'Well, what would you do? Would you kill him?' he asked, abruptly and sternly.

'Trescott, you fool,' said the old man, gently.

'Oh, well, I know, judge, but then – ' He turned red, and spoke with new violence: 'Say, he saved my boy – do you see? He saved my boy.'

'You bet he did,' cried the judge, with enthusiasm. 'You bet he did.' And they remained for a time gazing at each other, their faces illuminated with memories of a certain deed.

After another silence, the judge said, 'It is hard for a man to know what to do.'

❦ 12 ❦

Late one evening Trescott, returning from a professional call, paused his buggy at the Hagenthorpe gate. He tied the mare to the old tin-covered post, and entered the house. Ultimately he appeared with a companion – a man who walked slowly and carefully, as if he were learning. He was wrapped to the heels in an old-fashioned ulster. They entered the buggy and drove away.

After a silence only broken by the swift and musical humming of the wheels on the smooth road, Trescott spoke. 'Henry,' he said, 'I've got you a home here with old Alek Williams. You will have everything you want to eat and a good place to sleep, and I hope you will get along there all right. I will pay all your expenses, and come to see you as often as I can. If you don't get along, I want you to let me know as soon as possible, and then we will do what we can to make it better.'

The dark figure at the doctor's side answered with a cheerful laugh. 'These buggy wheels don' look like I washed 'em yesterday, docteh,' he said.

Trescott hesitated for a moment, and then went on insistently, 'I am taking you to Alek Williams, Henry, and I – '

The figure chuckled again. 'No, 'deed! No, seh! Alek Williams don' know a hoss! 'Deed he don't. He don' know a hoss from a pig.' The laugh that followed was like the rattle of pebbles.

Trescott turned and looked sternly and coldly at the dim form in the gloom from the buggy-top. 'Henry,' he said, 'I didn't say anything about horses. I was saying – '

'Hoss? Hoss?' said the quavering voice from these near shadows. 'Hoss? 'Deed I don' know all erbout a hoss! 'Deed I don't.' There was a satirical chuckle.

At the end of three miles the mare slackened and the doctor leaned forward, peering, while holding tight reins. The wheels of the buggy bumped often over out-cropping boulders. A window shone forth, a simple square of topaz on a great black hillside. Four dogs charged the buggy with ferocity, and when it did not promptly retreat, they circled courageously around the flanks, baying. A door opened near the window in the hillside, and a man came and stood on a beach of yellow light.

'Yah! yah! You Roveh! You Susie! Come yah! Come yah this minit!'

Trescott called across the dark sea of grass, 'Hello, Alek!'

'Hello!'

'Come down here and show me where to drive.'

The man plunged from the beach into the surf, and Trescott could then only trace his course by the fervid and polite ejaculations of a host who was somewhere approaching. Presently Williams took the mare by the head, and uttering cries of welcome and scolding the swarming dogs, led the equipage towards the lights. When they halted at the door and Trescott was climbing out, Williams cried, 'Will she stand, docteh?'

'She'll stand all right, but you better hold her for a minute. Now, Henry.' The doctor turned and held both arms to the dark figure. It crawled to him painfully like a man going down a ladder. Williams took the mare away to be tied to a little tree, and when he returned he found them awaiting him in the gloom beyond the rays from the door.

He burst out then like a siphon pressed by a nervous thumb. 'Hennery! Hennery, ma ol' frien'. Well, if I ain' glade. If I ain' glade!'

Trescott had taken the silent shape by the arm and led it forward into the full revelation of the light. 'Well, now, Alek, you can take Henry and put him to bed, and in the morning I will – '

Near the end of this sentence old Williams had come front to front with Johnson. He gasped for a second, and then yelled the yell of a man stabbed in the heart.

For a fraction of a moment Trescott seemed to be looking for epithets. Then he roared: 'You old black chump! You old black – Shut up! Shut up! Do you hear?'

Williams obeyed instantly in the matter of his screams, but he continued in a lowered voice: 'Ma Lode amassy! Who'd ever think? Ma Lode amassy!'

Trescott spoke again in the manner of a commander of a battalion. 'Alek!'

The old negro again surrendered, but to himself he repeated in a whisper, 'Ma Lode!' He was aghast and trembling.

As these three points of widening shadows approached the golden doorway a hale old negress appeared there, bowing. 'Good-evenin', docteh! Good-evenin'! Come in! come in!' She had evidently just retired from a tempestuous struggle to place the room in order, but she was now bowing rapidly. She made the effort of a person swimming.

'Don't trouble yourself, Mary,' said Trescott, entering. 'I've brought Henry for you to take care of, and all you've got to do is to carry out what I tell you.' Learning that he was not followed, he faced the door, and said, 'Come in, Henry.'

Johnson entered. 'Whee!' shrieked Mrs Williams. She almost achieved a back somersault. Six young members of the tribe of Williams made a simultaneous plunge for a position behind the stove, and formed a wailing heap.

❦ 13 ❧

'You know very well that you and your family lived usually on less than three dollars a week, and now that Dr Trescott pays you five dollars a week for Johnson's board, you live like millionaires. You haven't done a stroke of work since Johnson began to board with you – everybody knows that – and so what are you kicking about?'

The judge sat in his chair on the porch, fondling his cane, and gazing down at old Williams, who stood under the lilac-bushes. 'Yes, I know, jedge,' said the negro, wagging his head in a puzzled manner. ' 'Tain't like as if I didn't 'preciate what the docteh done, but – but – well, yeh see, jedge,' he added, gaining a new impetus, 'it's – it's hard wuk. This ol' man nev' did wuk so hard. Lode, no.'

'Don't talk such nonsense, Alek,' spoke the judge, sharply. 'You have never really worked in your life – anyhow, enough to support a family of sparrows, and now when you are in a more prosperous condition than ever before, you come around talking like an old fool.'

The negro began to scratch his head. 'Yeh see, jedge,' he said at last, 'my ol' 'ooman she cain't 'ceive no lady callahs, nohow.'

'Hang lady callers!' said the judge, irascibly. 'If you have flour in the barrel and meat in the pot, your wife can get along without receiving lady callers, can't she?'

'But they won't come ainyhow, jedge,' replied Williams, with an air of still deeper stupefaction. 'Noner ma wife's frien's ner noner ma frien's 'll come near ma res'dence.'

'Well, let them stay home if they are such silly people.'

The old negro seemed to be seeking a way to elude this argument, but evidently finding none, he was about to shuffle meekly off. He halted, however. 'Jedge,' said he, 'ma ol' 'ooman's near driv' abstracted.'

'Your old woman is an idiot,' responded the judge.

Williams came very close and peered solemnly through a branch of lilac. 'Jedge,' he whispered, 'the chillens.'

'What about them?'

Dropping his voice to funereal depths, Williams said, 'They – they cain't eat.'

'Can't eat!' scoffed the judge, loudly. 'Can't eat! You must think I am as big an old fool as you are. Can't eat – the little rascals! What's to prevent them from eating?'

In answer, Williams said, with mournful emphasis, 'Hennery.' Moved with a kind of satisfaction at his tragic use of the name, he remained staring at the judge for a sign of its effect.

The judge made a gesture of irritation. 'Come, now, you old scoundrel, don't beat around the bush any more. What are you up to? What do you want? Speak out like a man, and don't give me any more of this tiresome rigamarole.'

'I ain't er-beatin' round 'bout nuffin, jedge,' replied Williams, indignantly. 'No, seh; I say whatter got to say right out. 'Deed I do.'

'Well, say it, then.'

'Jedge,' began the negro, taking off his hat and switching his knee with it, 'Lode knows I'd do jes 'bout as much fer five dollehs er week as ainy cul'd man, but – but this yere business is awful, jedge. I raikon 'ain't been no sleep in – in my house sence docteh done fetch 'im.'

'Well, what do you propose to do about it?'

Williams lifted his eyes from the ground and gazed off through the trees. 'Raikon I got good appetite, an' sleep jes like er dog, but he – he's done broke me all up. 'Tain't no good, nohow. I wake up in the night; I hear 'im, mebbe, er-whimperin' an' er-whimperin', an' I sneak an' I sneak until I try th' do' to see if he locked in. An' he keep me er-puzzlin' an' er-quakin' all night long. Don't know how 'll do in th' winter. Can't let 'im out where th' chillen is. He'll done freeze where he is now.' Williams spoke these sentences as if he were talking to himself. After a silence of deep reflection he continued: 'Folks go round sayin' he ain't Hennery Johnson at all. They say he's er devil!'

'What?' cried the judge.

'Yesseh,' repeated Williams, in tones of injury, as if his veracity had been challenged. 'Yesseh. I'm er-tellin' it to yeh straight, jedge. Plenty cul'd people folks up my way say it is a devil.'

'Well, you don't think so yourself, do you?'

'No. 'Tain't no devil. It's Hennery Johnson.'

'Well, then, what is the matter with you? You don't care what a lot of foolish people say. Go on 'tending to your business, and pay no attention to such idle nonsense.'

' 'Tis nonsense, jedge; but he *looks* like er devil.'

'What do you care what he looks like?' demanded the judge.

'Ma rent is two dollehs and er half er month,' said Williams, slowly.

'It might just as well be ten thousand dollars a month,' responded the judge. 'You never pay it, anyhow.'

'Then, anoth' thing,' continued Williams, in his reflective tone. 'If he was all right in his haid I could stan' it; but, jedge, he's crazier 'n er loon. Then when he looks like er devil, an' done skears all ma frien's away, an' ma chillens cain't eat, an' ma ole 'ooman jes raisin' Cain all the time, an' ma rent two dollehs an' er half er month, an' him not right in his haid, it seems like five dollehs er week – '

The judge's stick came down sharply and suddenly upon the floor of the porch. 'There,' he said, 'I thought that was what you were driving at.'

Williams began swinging his head from side to side in the strange racial mannerism. 'Now hol' on a minnet, jedge,' he said, defensively. ' 'Tain't like as if I didn't 'preciate what the docteh done. 'Tain't that. Docteh Trescott is er kind man, an' 'tain't like as if I didn't 'preciate what he done; but – but – '

'But what? You are getting painful, Alek. Now tell me this: did you ever have five dollars a week regularly before in your life?'

Williams at once drew himself up with great dignity, but in the pause after that question he drooped gradually to another attitude. In the end he answered, heroically: 'No, jedge, I 'ain't. An' 'tain't like as if I was er-sayin' five dollehs wasn't er lot er money for a man like me. But, jedge, what er man oughter git fer this kinder wuk is er salary. Yesseh, jedge,' he repeated, with a great impressive gesture; 'fer this kinder wuk er man oughter git er Salary.' He laid a terrible emphasis upon the final word.

The judge laughed. 'I know Dr Trescott's mind concerning this affair, Alek; and if you are dissatisfied with your boarder, he is quite ready to move him to some other place; so, if you care to leave word with me that you are tired of the arrangement and wish it changed, he will come and take Johnson away.'

Williams scratched his head again in deep perplexity. 'Five dollehs is er big price fer bo'd, but 'tain't no big price fer the bo'd of er crazy man,' he said, finally.

'What do you think you ought to get?' asked the judge.

'Well,' answered Alek, in the manner of one deep in a balancing of the scales, 'he looks like er devil, an' done skears e'rybody, an' ma chillens cain't eat, an' I cain't sleep, an' he ain't right in his haid, an' – '

'You told me all those things.'

After scratching his wool, and beating his knee with his hat, and gazing off through the trees and down at the ground, Williams said, as he kicked nervously at the gravel, 'Well, jedge, I think it is wuth – ' He stuttered.

'Worth what?'

'Six dollehs,' answered Williams, in a desperate outburst.

The judge lay back in his great armchair and went through all the motions of a man laughing heartily, but he made no sound save a slight cough. Williams had been watching him with apprehension.

'Well,' said the judge, 'do you call six dollars a salary?'

'No, seh,' promptly responded Williams. ' 'Tain't a salary. No, 'deed! 'Tain't a salary.' He looked with some anger upon the man who questioned his intelligence in this way.

'Well, supposing your children can't eat?'

'I – '

'And supposing he looks like a devil? And supposing all those things continue? Would you be satisfied with six dollars a week?'

Recollections seemed to throng in Williams's mind at these interrogations, and he answered dubiously. 'Of co'se a man who ain't right in his haid, an' looks like er devil – But six dollehs – ' After these two attempts at a sentence Williams suddenly appeared as an orator, with a great shiny palm waving in the air. 'I tell yeh, jedge, six dollehs is six dollehs, but if I git six dollehs for bo'ding Hennery Johnson, I uhns it! I uhns it!'

'I don't doubt that you earn six dollars for every week's work you do,' said the judge.

'Well, if I bo'd Hennery Johnson fer six dollehs er week, I uhns it! I uhns it!' cried Williams, wildly.

ᘓ 14 ᘔ

Reifsnyder's assistant had gone to his supper, and the owner of the shop was trying to placate four men who wished to be shaved at once. Reifsnyder was very garrulous – a fact which made him rather remarkable among barbers, who, as a class, are austerely speechless, having been taught silence by the hammering reiteration of a tradition. It is the customers who talk in the ordinary event.

As Reifsnyder waved his razor down the cheek of a man in the chair, he turned often to cool the impatience of the others with pleasant talk, which they did not particularly heed.

'Oh, he should have let him die,' said Bainbridge, a railway engineer, finally replying to one of the barber's orations. 'Shut up, Reif, and go on with your business!'

Instead, Reifsnyder paused shaving entirely, and turned to front the speaker. 'Let him die?' he demanded. 'How vas that? How can you let a man die?'

'By letting him die, you chump,' said the engineer. The others laughed a little, and Reifsnyder turned at once to his work, sullenly, as a man overwhelmed by the derision of numbers.

'How vas that?' he grumbled later. 'How can you let a man die when he vas done so much for you?'

' "When he vas done so much for you?" ' repeated Bainbridge. 'You better shave some people. How vas that? Maybe this ain't a barber shop?'

A man hitherto silent now said, 'If I had been the doctor, I would have done the same thing.'

'Of course,' said Reifsnyder. 'Any man vould do it. Any man that vas not like you, you – old – flint-hearted – fish.' He had sought the final words with painful care, and he delivered the collection triumphantly at Bainbridge. The engineer laughed.

The man in the chair now lifted himself higher, while Reifsnyder began an elaborate ceremony of anointing and combing his hair. Now free to join comfortably in the talk, the man said: 'They say he is the most terrible thing in the world. Young Johnnie Bernard – that drives the grocery wagon – saw him up at Alek Williams's shanty, and he says he couldn't eat anything for two days.'

'Chee!' said Reifsnyder.

'Well, what makes him so terrible?' asked another.

'Because he hasn't got any face,' replied the barber and the engineer in duet.

'Hasn't got any face!' repeated the man. 'How can he do without any face?'

> 'He has no face in the front of his head,
> In the place where his face ought to grow.'

Bainbridge sang these lines pathetically as he arose and hung his hat on a hook. The man in the chair was about to abdicate in his favour. 'Get a gait on you now,' he said to Reifsnyder. 'I go out at 7.31.'

As the barber foamed the lather on the cheeks of the engineer he seemed to be thinking heavily. Then suddenly he burst out. 'How would you like to be with no face?' he cried to the assemblage.

'Oh, if I had to have a face like yours – ' answered one customer.

Bainbridge's voice came from a sea of lather. 'You're kicking because if losing faces became popular, you'd have to go out of business.'

'I don't think it will become so much popular,' said Reifsnyder.

'Not if it's got to be taken off in the way his was taken off,' said another man. 'I'd rather keep mine, if you don't mind.'

'I guess so!' cried the barber. 'Just think!'

The shaving of Bainbridge had arrived at a time of comparative liberty for him. 'I wonder what the doctor says to himself?' he observed. 'He may be sorry he made him live.'

'It was the only thing he could do,' replied a man. The others seemed to agree with him.

'Supposing you were in his place,' said one, 'and Johnson had saved your kid. What would you do?'

'Certainly!'

'Of course! You would do anything on earth for him. You'd take all the trouble in the world for him. And spend your last dollar on him. Well, then?'

'I wonder how it feels to be without any face?' said Reifsnyder, musingly.

The man who had previously spoken, feeling that he had expressed himself well, repeated the whole thing. 'You would do anything on earth for him. You'd take all the trouble in the world for him. And spend your last dollar on him. Well, then?'

'No, but look,' said Reifsnyder; 'supposing you don't got a face!'

ᕦ 15 ᕤ

As soon as Williams was hidden from the view of the old judge he began to gesture and talk to himself. An elation had evidently penetrated to his vitals, and caused him to dilate as if he had been filled with gas. He snapped his fingers in the air, and whistled fragments of triumphal music. At times, in his progress towards his shanty, he indulged in a shuffling movement that was really a dance. It was to be learned from the intermediate monologue that he had emerged from his trials laurelled and proud. He was the unconquerable Alexander Williams. Nothing could exceed the bold self-reliance of his manner. His kingly stride, his heroic song, the derisive flourish of his hands – all betokened a man who had successfully defied the world.

On his way he saw Zeke Paterson coming to town. They hailed each other at a distance of fifty yards.

'How do, Broth' Paterson?'

'How do, Broth' Williams?'

They were both deacons.

'Is you' folks well, Broth' Paterson?'

'Middlin', middlin'. How's you' folks, Broth' Williams?'

Neither of them had slowed his pace in the smallest degree. They had simply begun this talk when a considerable space separated them, continued it as they passed, and added polite questions as they drifted steadily apart. Williams's mind seemed to be a balloon. He had been so inflated that he had not noticed that Paterson had definitely shied into the dry ditch as they came to the point of ordinary contact.

Afterwards, as he went a lonely way, he burst out again in song and pantomimic celebration of his estate. His feet moved in prancing steps.

When he came in sight of his cabin, the fields were bathed in a blue dusk, and the light in the window was pale. Cavorting and gesticulating, he gazed joyfully for some moments upon this light. Then suddenly another idea seemed to attack his mind, and he stopped, with an air of being suddenly dampened. In the end he approached his home as if it were the fortress of an enemy.

Some dogs disputed his advance for a loud moment, and then discovering their lord, slunk away embarrassed. His reproaches were addressed to them in muffled tones.

Arriving at the door, he pushed it open with the timidity of a new thief. He thrust his head cautiously sideways, and his eyes met the eyes of his wife, who sat by the table, the lamplight defining a half of her face. ' 'Sh!' he said, uselessly. His glance travelled swiftly to the inner door which shielded the one bedchamber. The pickaninnies, strewn upon the floor of the living-room, were softly snoring. After a hearty meal they had promptly dispersed themselves about the place and gone to sleep. ' 'Sh!' said Williams again to his motionless and silent wife. He had allowed only his head to appear. His wife, with one hand upon the edge of the table and the other at her knee, was regarding him with wide eyes and parted lips as if he were a spectre. She looked to be one who was living in terror, and even the familiar face at the door had thrilled her because it had come suddenly.

Williams broke the tense silence. 'Is he all right?' he whispered, waving his eyes towards the inner door. Following his glance timorously, his wife nodded, and in a low tone answered:

'I raikon he's done gone t' sleep.'

Williams then slunk noiselessly across his threshold.

He lifted a chair, and with infinite care placed it so that it faced the dreaded inner door. His wife moved slightly, so as to also squarely face it. A silence came upon them in which they seemed to be waiting for a calamity, pealing and deadly.

Williams finally coughed behind his hand. His wife started, and looked upon him in alarm. ' 'Pears like he done gwine keep quiet ternight,' he breathed. They continually pointed their speech and their looks at the inner door, paying it the homage due to a corpse or a phantom. Another long stillness followed this sentence. Their eyes shone white and wide. A wagon rattled down the distant road. From their chairs they looked at the window, and the effect of the light in the cabin was a presentation of an intensely black and solemn night. The old woman adopted the attitude used always in church at funerals. At times she seemed to be upon the point of breaking out in prayer.

'He mighty quiet ternight,' whispered Williams. 'Was he good terday?' For answer his wife raised her eyes to the ceiling in the supplication of Job. Williams moved restlessly. Finally he tiptoed to the door. He knelt slowly and without a sound, and placed his ear near the key-hole. Hearing a noise behind him, he turned quickly. His wife was staring at him aghast. She stood in front of the stove, and her arms were spread out in the natural movement to protect all her sleeping ducklings.

But Williams arose without having touched the door. 'I raikon he er-sleep,' he said, fingering his wool. He debated with himself for some time. During this interval his wife remained, a great fat statue of a mother shielding her children.

It was plain that his mind was swept suddenly by a wave of temerity. With a sounding step he moved towards the door. His fingers were almost upon the knob when he swiftly ducked and dodged away, clapping his hands to the back of his head. It was as if the portal had threatened him. There was a little tumult near the stove, where Mrs Williams's desperate retreat had involved her feet with the prostrate children.

After the panic Williams bore traces of a feeling of shame. He returned to the charge. He firmly grasped the knob with his left hand, and with his other hand turned the key in the lock. He pushed the door, and as it swung portentously open he sprang nimbly to one side like the fearful slave liberating the lion. Near the stove a group had formed, the terror stricken mother, with her arms stretched, and the aroused children clinging frenziedly to her skirts.

The light streamed after the swinging door, and disclosed a room six feet one way and six feet the other way. It was small enough to enable the radiance to lay it plain. Williams peered warily around the corner made by the door-post.

Suddenly he advanced, retired, and advanced again with a howl. His palsied family had expected him to spring backward, and at his howl they heaped themselves wondrously. But Williams simply stood in the little room emitting his howls before an open window. 'He's gone! He's gone! He's gone!' His eye and his hand had speedily proved the fact. He had even thrown open a little cupboard.

Presently he came flying out. He grabbed his hat, and hurled the outer door back upon its hinges. Then he tumbled headlong into the night. He was yelling: 'Docteh Trescott! Docteh Trescott!' He ran wildly through the fields, and galloped in the direction of town. He continued to call to Trescott, as if the latter was within easy hearing. It was as if Trescott was poised in the contemplative sky over the running negro, and could heed this reaching voice – 'Docteh Trescott!'

In the cabin, Mrs Williams, supported by relays from the battalion of children, stood quaking watch until the truth of daylight came as a reinforcement and made them arrogant, strutting, swashbuckler children, and a mother who proclaimed her illimitable courage.

❦ 16 ❦

Theresa Page was giving a party. It was the outcome of a long series of arguments addressed to her mother, which had been overheard in part by her father. He had at last said five words, 'Oh, let her have it.' The mother had then gladly capitulated.

Theresa had written nineteen invitations, and distributed them at recess to her schoolmates. Later her mother had composed five large cakes, and still later a vast amount of lemonade.

So the nine little girls and the ten little boys sat quite primly in the dining-room, while Theresa and her mother plied them with cake and lemonade, and also with ice-cream. This primness sat now quite strangely upon them. It was owing to the presence of Mrs Page. Previously in the parlour alone with their games they had overturned a chair; the boys had let more or less of their hoodlum spirit shine forth. But when circumstances could be possibly magnified to warrant it, the girls made the boys victims of an insufferable pride, snubbing them mercilessly. So in the dining-room they resembled a class at Sunday school, if it were not for the subterranean smiles, gestures, rebuffs, and poutings which stamped the affair as a children's party.

Two little girls of this subdued gathering were planted in a settle with their backs to the broad window. They were beaming lovingly upon each other with an effect of scorning the boys.

Hearing a noise behind her at the window, one little girl turned to face it. Instantly she screamed and sprang away, covering her face with her hands. 'What was it? What was it?' cried everyone in a roar. Some slight movement of the eyes of the weeping and shuddering child informed the company that she had been frightened by an appearance at the window. At once they all faced the imperturbable window, and for a moment there was a silence. An astute lad made an immediate census of the other lads. The prank of slipping out and looming spectrally at a window was too venerable. But the little boys were all present and astonished.

As they recovered their minds they uttered warlike cries, and through a side door sallied rapidly out against the terror. They vied with each other in daring.

None wished particularly to encounter a dragon in the darkness of the garden, but there could be no faltering when the fair ones in the dining-room were present. Calling to each other in stern voices, they went dragooning over the lawn, attacking the shadows with ferocity; but still with the caution of reasonable beings. They found, however, nothing new to the peace of the night. Of course there was a lad who told a great lie. He described a grim figure, bending low and slinking off along the fence. He gave a number of details, rendering his lie more splendid by a repetition of certain forms which he recalled from romances. For instance, he insisted that he had heard the creature emit a hollow laugh.

Inside the house the little girl who had raised the alarm was still shuddering and weeping. With the utmost difficulty was she brought to a state approximating calmness by Mrs Page. Then she wanted to go home at once.

Page entered the house at this time. He had exiled himself until he concluded that this children's party was finished and gone. He was obliged to escort the little girl home because she screamed again when they opened the door and she saw the night.

She was not coherent even to her mother. Was it a man? She didn't know. It was simply a thing, a dreadful thing.

❧ 17 ❧

In Watermelon Alley the Farraguts were spending their evening as usual on the little rickety porch. Sometimes they howled gossip to other people on other rickety porches. The thin wail of a baby arose from a near house. A man had a terrific altercation with his wife, to which the alley paid no attention at all.

There appeared suddenly before the Farraguts a monster making a low and sweeping bow. There was an instant's pause, and then occurred something that resembled the effect of an upheaval of the earth's surface. The old woman hurled herself backward with a dreadful cry. Young Sim had been perched gracefully on a railing. At sight of the monster he simply fell over it to the ground. He made no sound, his eyes stuck out, his nerveless hands tried to grapple the rail to prevent a tumble, and then he vanished. Bella, blubbering, and with her hair suddenly and mysteriously dishevelled, was crawling on her hands and knees fearsomely up the steps.

Standing before this wreck of a family gathering, the monster continued to bow. It even raised a deprecatory claw. 'Don' make no botheration 'bout me, Miss Fa'gut,' it said, politely. 'No, 'deed. I jes drap in ter ax if yer well this evenin', Miss Fa'gut. Don' make no botheration. No, 'deed. I gwine ax you to go to er daince with me, Miss Fa'gut. I ax you if I can have the magnifercent gratitude of you' company on that 'casion, Miss Fa'gut.'

The girl cast a miserable glance behind her. She was still crawling away. On the ground beside the porch young Sim raised a strange bleat, which expressed both his fright and his lack of wind. Presently the monster, with a fashionable amble, ascended the steps after the girl.

She grovelled in a corner of the room as the creature took a chair. It seated itself very elegantly on the edge. It held an old cap in both hands. 'Don' make no botheration, Miss Fa'gut. Don' make no botherations. No, 'deed. I jes drap in ter ax you if you won' do me the proud of acceptin' ma humble invitation to er daince, Miss Fa'gut.'

She shielded her eyes with her arms and tried to crawl past it, but the genial monster blocked the way. 'I jes drap in ter ax you 'bout er daince, Miss Fa'gut. I ax you if I kin have the magnifercent gratitude of you' company on that 'casion, Miss Fa'gut.'

In a last outbreak of despair, the girl, shuddering and wailing, threw herself face downward on the floor, while the monster sat on the edge of the chair gabbling courteous invitations, and holding the old hat daintily to his stomach.

At the back of the house, Mrs Farragut, who was of enormous weight, and who for eight years had done little more than sit in an armchair and describe her various ailments, had with speed and agility scaled a high board fence.

❧ 18 ❧

The black mass in the middle of Trescott's property was hardly allowed to cool before the builders were at work on another house. It had sprung upward at a fabulous rate. It was like a magical composition born of the ashes. The doctor's office was the first part to be completed, and he had already moved in his new books and instruments and medicines.

Trescott sat before his desk when the chief of police arrived. 'Well, we found him,' said the latter.

'Did you?' cried the doctor. 'Where?'

'Shambling around the streets at daylight this morning. I'll be blamed if I can figure on where he passed the night.'

'Where is he now?'

'Oh, we jugged him. I didn't know what else to do with him. That's what I want you to tell me. Of course we can't keep him. No charge could be made, you know.'

'I'll come down and get him.'

The official grinned retrospectively. 'Must say he had a fine career while he was out. First thing he did was to break up a children's party at Page's. Then he went to Watermelon Alley. Whoo! He stampeded the whole outfit. Men, women, and children running pell-mell, and yelling. They say one old woman broke her leg, or something, shinning over a fence. Then he went right out on the main street, and an Irish girl threw a fit, and there was a sort of a riot. He began to run, and a big crowd chased him, firing rocks. But he gave them the slip somehow down there by the foundry and in the railroad yard. We looked for him all night, but couldn't find him.'

'Was he hurt any? Did anybody hit him with a stone?'

'Guess there isn't much of him to hurt any more, is there? Guess he's been hurt up to the limit. No. They never touched him. Of course nobody really wanted to hit him, but you know how a crowd gets. It's like – it's like – '

'Yes, I know.'

For a moment the chief of the police looked reflectively at the floor. Then he spoke hesitatingly. 'You know Jake Winter's little girl was the one that he scared at the party. She is pretty sick, they say.'

'Is she? Why, they didn't call me. I always attend the Winter family.'

'No? Didn't they?' asked the chief, slowly. 'Well – you know – Winter is – well, Winter has gone clean crazy over this business. He wanted – he wanted to have you arrested.'

'Have me arrested? The idiot! What in the name of wonder could he have me arrested for?'

'Of course. He is a fool. I told him to keep his trap shut. But then you know how he'll go all over town yapping about the thing. I thought I'd better tip you.'

'Oh, he is of no consequence; but then, of course, I'm obliged to you, Sam.'

'That's all right. Well, you'll be down tonight and take him out, eh?

You'll get a good welcome from the jailer. He don't like his job for a cent. He says you can have your man whenever you want him. He's got no use for him.'

'But what is this business of Winter's about having me arrested?'

'Oh, it's a lot of chin about your having no right to allow this – this – this man to be at large. But I told him to tend to his own business. Only I thought I'd better let you know. And I might as well say right now, doctor, that there is a good deal of talk about this thing. If I were you, I'd come to the jail pretty late at night, because there is likely to be a crowd around the door, and I'd bring a – er – mask, or some kind of a veil, anyhow.'

❧ 19 ❧

Martha Goodwin was single, and well along into the thin years. She lived with her married sister in Whilomville. She performed nearly all the housework in exchange for the privilege of existence. Everyone tacitly recognised her labour as a form of penance for the early end of her betrothed, who had died of smallpox, which he had not caught from her.

But despite the strenuous and unceasing workaday of her life, she was a woman of great mind. She had adamantine opinions upon the situation in Armenia, the condition of women in China, the flirtation between Mrs Minster of Niagara Avenue and young Griscom, the conflict in the Bible class of the Baptist Sunday school, the duty of the United States towards the Cuban insurgents, and many other colossal matters. Her fullest experience of violence was gained on an occasion when she had seen a hound clubbed, but in the plan which she had made for the reform of the world she advocated drastic measures. For instance, she contended that all the Turks should be pushed into the sea and drowned, and that Mrs Minster and young Griscom should be hanged side by side on twin gallows. In fact, this woman of peace, who had seen only peace, argued constantly for a creed of illimitable ferocity. She was invulnerable on these questions, because eventually she overrode all opponents with a sniff. This sniff was an active force. It was to her antagonists like a bang over the head, and none was known to recover from this expression of exalted contempt. It left them windless and conquered. They never again came forward as candidates for suppression. And Martha walked her kitchen with a stern brow, an invincible being like Napoleon.

Nevertheless her acquaintances, from the pain of their defeats, had been long in secret revolt. It was in no wise a conspiracy, because they did not care to state their open rebellion, but nevertheless it was understood that any woman who could not coincide with one of Martha's contentions was entitled to the support of others in the small circle. It amounted to an arrangement by which all were required to disbelieve any theory for which Martha fought. This, however, did not prevent them from speaking of her mind with profound respect.

Two people bore the brunt of her ability. Her sister Kate was visibly afraid of her, while Carrie Dungen sailed across from her kitchen to sit respectfully at Martha's feet and learn the business of the world. To be sure, afterwards, under another sun, she always laughed at Martha and pretended to deride her ideas, but in the presence of the sovereign she always remained silent or admiring. Kate, the sister, was of no consequence at all. Her principal delusion was that she did all the work in the upstairs rooms of the house, while Martha did it downstairs. The truth was seen only by the husband, who treated Martha with a kindness that was half banter, half deference. Martha herself had no suspicion that she was the only pillar of the domestic edifice. The situation was without definitions. Martha made definitions, but she devoted them entirely to the Armenians and Griscom and the Chinese and other subjects. Her dreams, which in early days had been of love of meadows and the shade of trees, of the face of a man, were now involved otherwise, and they were companioned in the kitchen curiously, Cuba, the hot-water kettle, Armenia, the washing of the dishes, and the whole thing being jumbled. In regard to social misdemeanours, she who was simply the mausoleum of a dead passion was probably the most savage critic in town. This unknown woman, hidden in a kitchen as in a well, was sure to have a considerable effect of the one kind or the other in the life of the town. Every time it moved a yard, she had personally contributed an inch. She could hammer so stoutly upon the door of a proposition that it would break from its hinges and fall upon her, but at any rate it moved. She was an engine, and the fact that she did not know that she was an engine contributed largely to the effect. One reason that she was formidable was that she did not even imagine that she was formidable. She remained a weak, innocent, and pig-headed creature, who alone would defy the universe if she thought the universe merited this proceeding.

One day Carrie Dungen came across from her kitchen with speed. She had a great deal of grist. 'Oh,' she cried, 'Henry Johnson got away from where they was keeping him, and came to town last night, and scared everybody almost to death.'

Martha was shining a dish-pan, polishing madly. No reasonable person could see cause for this operation, because the pan already glistened like silver. 'Well!' she ejaculated. She imparted to the word a deep meaning. 'This, my prophecy, has come to pass.' It was a habit.

The overplus of information was choking Carrie. Before she could go on she was obliged to struggle for a moment. 'And, oh, little Sadie Winter is awful sick, and they say Jake Winter was around this morning trying to get Dr Trescott arrested. And poor old Mrs Farragut sprained her ankle in trying to climb a fence. And there's a crowd around the jail all the time. They put Henry in jail because they didn't know what else to do with him, I guess. They say he is perfectly terrible.'

Martha finally released the dish-pan and confronted the headlong speaker. 'Well!' she said again, poising a great brown rag. Kate had heard the excited newcomer, and drifted down from the novel in her room. She was a shivery little woman. Her shoulder-blades seemed to be two panes of ice, for she was constantly shrugging and shrugging. 'Serves him right if he was to lose all his patients,' she said suddenly, in bloodthirsty tones. She snipped her words out as if her lips were scissors.

'Well, he's likely to,' shouted Carrie Dungen. 'Don't a lot of people say that they won't have him any more? If you're sick and nervous, Dr Trescott would scare the life out of you, wouldn't he? He would me. I'd keep thinking.'

Martha, stalking to and fro, sometimes surveyed the two other women with a contemplative frown.

🙚 20 🙚

After the return from Connecticut, little Jimmie was at first much afraid of the monster who lived in the room over the carriage-house. He could not identify it in any way. Gradually, however, his fear dwindled under the influence of a weird fascination. He sidled into closer and closer relations with it.

One time the monster was seated on a box behind the stable basking in the rays of the afternoon sun. A heavy crêpe veil was swathed about its head.

Little Jimmie and many companions came around the corner of the stable. They were all in what was popularly known as the baby class, and consequently escaped from school a half-hour before the other children. They halted abruptly at sight of the figure on the box. Jimmie waved his hand with the air of a proprietor.

'There he is,' he said.

'O-o-o!' murmured all the little boys – 'o-o-o!' They shrank back, and grouped according to courage or experience, as at the sound the monster slowly turned its head. Jimmie had remained in the van alone. 'Don't be afraid! I won't let him hurt you,' he said, delighted.

'Huh!' they replied, contemptuously. 'We ain't afraid.'

Jimmie seemed to reap all the joys of the owner and exhibitor of one of the world's marvels, while his audience remained at a distance – awed and entranced, fearful and envious.

One of them addressed Jimmie gloomily. 'Bet you dassent walk right up to him.' He was an older boy than Jimmie, and habitually oppressed him to a small degree. This new social elevation of the smaller lad probably seemed revolutionary to him.

'Huh!' said Jimmie, with deep scorn. 'Dassent I? Dassent I, hey? Dassent I?'

The group was immensely excited. It turned its eyes upon the boy that Jimmie addressed. 'No, you dassent,' he said, stolidly, facing a moral defeat. He could see that Jimmie was resolved. 'No, you dassent,' he repeated, doggedly.

'Ho?' cried Jimmie. 'You just watch! – you just watch!'

Amid a silence he turned and marched towards the monster. But possibly the palpable wariness of his companions had an effect upon him that weighed more than his previous experience, for suddenly, when near to the monster, he halted dubiously. But his playmates immediately uttered a derisive shout, and it seemed to force him forward. He went to the monster and laid his hand delicately on its shoulder. 'Hello, Henry,' he said, in a voice that trembled a trifle. The monster was crooning a weird line of negro melody that was scarcely more than a thread of sound, and it paid no heed to the boy.

Jimmie strutted back to his companions. They acclaimed him and hooted his opponent. Amid this clamour the larger boy with difficulty preserved a dignified attitude.

'I dassent, dassent I?' said Jimmie to him. 'Now, you're so smart, let's see you do it!'

This challenge brought forth renewed taunts from the others. The larger boy puffed out his cheeks. 'Well, I ain't afraid,' he explained, sullenly. He had made a mistake in diplomacy, and now his small enemies were tumbling his prestige all about his ears. They crowed like roosters and bleated like lambs, and made many other noises which were supposed to bury him in ridicule and dishonour. 'Well, I ain't afraid,' he continued to explain through the din.

Jimmie, the hero of the mob, was pitiless. 'You ain't afraid, hey?' he sneered. 'If you ain't afraid, go do it, then.'

'Well, I would if I wanted to,' the other retorted. His eyes wore an expression of profound misery, but he preserved steadily other portions of a pot-valiant air. He suddenly faced one of his persecutors. 'If you're so smart, why don't you go do it?' This persecutor sank promptly through the group to the rear. The incident gave the badgered one a breathing-spell, and for a moment even turned the derision in another direction. He took advantage of his interval. 'I'll do it if anybody else will,' he announced, swaggering to and fro.

Candidates for the adventure did not come forward. To defend themselves from this counter-charge, the other boys again set up their crowing and bleating. For a while they would hear nothing from him. Each time he opened his lips their chorus of noises made oratory impossible. But at last he was able to repeat that he would volunteer to dare as much in the affair as any other boy.

'Well, you go first,' they shouted.

But Jimmie intervened to once more lead the populace against the large boy. 'You're mighty brave, ain't you?' he said to him. 'You dared me to do it, and I did – didn't I? Now who's afraid?' The others cheered this view loudly, and they instantly resumed the baiting of the large boy.

He shamefacedly scratched his left shin with his right foot. 'Well, I ain't afraid.' He cast an eye at the monster. 'Well, I ain't afraid.' With a glare of hatred at his squalling tormentors, he finally announced a grim intention. 'Well, I'll do it, then, since you're so fresh. Now!'

The mob subsided as with a formidable countenance he turned towards the impassive figure on the box. The advance was also a regular progression from high daring to craven hesitation. At last, when some yards from the monster, the lad came to a full halt, as if he had encountered a stone wall. The observant little boys in the distance promptly hooted. Stung again by these cries, the lad sneaked two yards forward. He was crouched like a young cat ready for a backward spring. The crowd at the rear, beginning to respect this display, uttered some encouraging cries. Suddenly the lad gathered himself together, made a white and desperate rush forward, touched the monster's shoulder with a far-outstretched finger, and sped away, while his laughter rang out wild, shrill, and exultant.

The crowd of boys reverenced him at once, and began to throng into his camp, and look at him, and be his admirers. Jimmie was discomfited for a moment, but he and the larger boy, without agreement or word of any kind, seemed to recognise a truce, and they swiftly combined and began to parade before the others.

'Why, it's just as easy as nothing,' puffed the larger boy. 'Ain't it, Jim?'

' 'Course,' blew Jimmie. 'Why, it's as e-e-easy.'

They were people of another class. If they had been decorated for courage on twelve battlefields, they could not have made the other boys more ashamed of the situation.

Meanwhile they condescended to explain the emotions of the excursion, expressing unqualified contempt for anyone who could hang back. 'Why, it ain't nothin'. He won't do nothin' to you,' they told the others, in tones of exasperation.

One of the very smallest boys in the party showed signs of a wistful desire to distinguish himself, and they turned their attention to him, pushing at his shoulders while he swung away from them, and hesitated dreamily. He was eventually induced to make furtive expedition, but it was only for a few yards. Then he paused, motionless, gazing with open mouth. The vociferous entreaties of Jimmie and the large boy had no power over him.

Mrs Hannigan had come out on her back porch with a pail of water. From this coign she had a view of the secluded portion of the Trescott grounds that was behind the stable. She perceived the group of boys, and the monster on the box. She shaded her eyes with her hand to benefit her vision. She screeched then as if she was being murdered. 'Eddie! Eddie! You come home this minute!'

Her son querulously demanded, 'Aw, what for?'

'You come home this minute. Do you hear?'

The other boys seemed to think this visitation upon one of their number required them to preserve for a time the hang-dog air of a collection of culprits, and they remained in guilty silence until the little Hannigan, wrathfully protesting, was pushed through the door of his home. Mrs Hannigan cast a piercing glance over the group, stared with a bitter face at the Trescott house, as if this new and handsome edifice was insulting her, and then followed her son.

There was wavering in the party. An inroad by one mother always caused them to carefully sweep the horizon to see if there were more coming. 'This is my yard,' said Jimmie, proudly. 'We don't have to go home.'

The monster on the box had turned its black crêpe countenance towards the sky, and was waving its arms in time to a religious chant. 'Look at him now,' cried a little boy. They turned, and were transfixed by the solemnity and mystery of the indefinable gestures. The wail of the melody was mournful and slow. They drew back. It seemed to spellbind them with the power of a funeral. They were so absorbed that they did not hear the doctor's buggy drive up to the stable. Trescott got out, tied his horse, and approached the group. Jimmie saw him first, and at his look of dismay the others wheeled.

'What's all this, Jimmie?' asked Trescott, in surprise.

The lad advanced to the front of his companions, halted, and said nothing. Trescott's face gloomed slightly as he scanned the scene.

'What were you doing, Jimmie?'

'We was playin',' answered Jimmie, huskily.

'Playing at what?'

'Just playin'.'

Trescott looked gravely at the other boys, and asked them to please go home. They proceeded to the street much in the manner of frustrated and revealed assassins. The crime of trespass on another boy's place was still a crime when they had only accepted the other boy's cordial invitation, and they were used to being sent out of all manner of gardens upon the sudden appearance of a father or a mother. Jimmie had wretchedly watched the departure of his companions. It involved the loss of his position as a lad who controlled the privileges of his father's grounds, but then he knew that in the beginning he had no right to ask so many boys to be his guests.

Once on the sidewalk, however, they speedily forgot their shame as trespassers, and the large boy launched forth in a description of his success in the late trial of courage. As they went rapidly up the street, the little boy who had made the furtive expedition cried out confidently from the rear, 'Yes, and I went almost up to him, didn't I, Willie?'

The large boy crushed him in a few words. 'Huh!' he scoffed. 'You only went a little way. I went clear up to him.'

The pace of the other boys was so manly that the tiny thing had to trot, and he remained at the rear, getting entangled in their legs in his attempts to reach the front rank and become of some importance, dodging this way and that way, and always piping out his little claim to glory.

❧ 21 ❧

'By the way, Grace,' said Trescott, looking into the dining-room from his office door, 'I wish you would send Jimmie to me before school-time.'

When Jimmie came, he advanced so quietly that Trescott did not at first note him. 'Oh,' he said, wheeling from a cabinet, 'here you are, young man.'

'Yes, sir.'

Trescott dropped into his chair and tapped the desk with a thoughtful finger. 'Jimmie, what were you doing in the back garden yesterday – you and the other boys – to Henry?'

'We weren't doing anything, pa.'

Trescott looked sternly into the raised eyes of his son. 'Are you sure you were not annoying him in any way? Now what were you doing, exactly?'

'Why, we – why, we – now – Willie Dalzel said I dassent go right up to him, and I did; and then he did; and then – the other boys were 'fraid; and then – you comed.'

Trescott groaned deeply. His countenance was so clouded in sorrow that the lad, bewildered by the mystery of it, burst suddenly forth in dismal lamentations. 'There, there. Don't cry, Jim,' said Trescott, going round the desk. 'Only – ' He sat in a great leather reading-chair, and took the boy on his knee. 'Only I want to explain to you – '

After Jimmie had gone to school, and as Trescott was about to start on his round of morning calls, a message arrived from Dr Moser. It set forth that the latter's sister was dying in the old homestead, twenty miles away up the valley, and asked Trescott to care for his patients for the day at least. There was also in the envelope a little history of each case and of what had already been done. Trescott replied to the messenger that he would gladly assent to the arrangement.

He noted that the first name on Moser's list was Winter, but this did not seem to strike him as an important fact. When its turn came, he rang the Winter bell. 'Good-morning, Mrs Winter,' he said, cheerfully, as the door was opened. 'Dr Moser has been obliged to leave town today, and he has asked me to come in his stead. How is the little girl this morning?'

Mrs Winter had regarded him in stony surprise. At last she said: 'Come in! I'll see my husband.' She bolted into the house. Trescott entered the hall, and turned to the left into the sitting-room.

Presently Winter shuffled through the door. His eyes flashed towards Trescott. He did not betray any desire to advance far into the room. 'What do you want?' he said.

'What do I want? What do I want?' repeated Trescott, lifting his head suddenly. He had heard an utterly new challenge in the night of the jungle.

'Yes, that's what I want to know,' snapped Winter. 'What do you want?'

Trescott was silent for a moment. He consulted Moser's memoranda. 'I see that your little girl's case is a trifle serious,' he remarked. 'I would advise you to call a physician soon. I will leave you a copy of Dr Moser's record to give to anyone you may call.' He paused to transcribe the record on a page of his notebook. Tearing out the leaf, he extended it to Winter as he moved towards the door. The latter shrank against the wall. His head was hanging as he reached for the paper. This caused him to grasp air, and so Trescott simply let the paper flutter to the feet of the other man.

'Good-morning,' said Trescott from the hall. This placid retreat seemed to suddenly arouse Winter to ferocity. It was as if he had then recalled all the truths which he had formulated to hurl at Trescott. So he followed him into the hall, and down the hall to the door, and through the door to the porch, barking in fiery rage from a respectful distance. As Trescott imperturbably turned the mare's head down the road, Winter stood on the porch, still yelping. He was like a little dog.

⤳ 22 ⤶

'Have you heard the news?' cried Carrie Dungen, as she sped towards Martha's kitchen. 'Have you heard the news?' Her eyes were shining with delight.

'No,' answered Martha's sister Kate, bending forward eagerly. 'What was it? What was it?'

Carrie appeared triumphantly in the open door. 'Oh, there's been an awful scene between Dr Trescott and Jake Winter. I never thought that Jake Winter had any pluck at all, but this morning he told the doctor just what he thought of him.'

'Well, what did he think of him?' asked Martha.

'Oh, he called him everything. Mrs Howarth heard it through her front blinds. It was terrible, she says. It's all over town now. Everybody knows it.'

'Didn't the doctor answer back?'

'No! Mrs Howarth – she says he never said a word. He just walked down to his buggy and got in, and drove off as co-o-o-l. But Jake gave him jinks, by all accounts.'

'But what did he say?' cried Kate, shrill and excited. She was evidently at some kind of a feast.

'Oh, he told him that Sadie had never been well since that night Henry Johnson frightened her at Theresa Page's party, and he held him responsible, and how dared he cross his threshold – and – and – and – '

'And what?' said Martha.

'Did he swear at him?' said Kate, in fearsome glee.

'No – not much. He did swear at him a little, but not more than a man does anyhow when he is real mad, Mrs Howarth says.'

'O-oh!' breathed Kate. 'And did he call him any names?'

Martha, at her work, had been for a time in deep thought. She now interrupted the others. 'It don't seem as if Sadie Winter had been sick since that time Henry Johnson got loose. She's been to school almost the whole time since then, hasn't she?'

They combined upon her in immediate indignation. 'School? School? I should say not. Don't think for a moment. School!'

Martha wheeled from the sink. She held an iron spoon, and it seemed as if she was going to attack them. 'Sadie Winter has passed here many a morning since then carrying her school-bag. Where was she going? To a wedding?'

The others, long accustomed to a mental tyranny, speedily surrendered.

'Did she?' stammered Kate. 'I never saw her.'

Carrie Dungen made a weak gesture.

'If I had been Dr Trescott,' exclaimed Martha, loudly, 'I'd have knocked that miserable Jake Winter's head off.'

Kate and Carrie, exchanging glances, made an alliance in the air. 'I don't see why you say that, Martha,' replied Carrie, with considerable boldness, gaining support and sympathy from Kate's smile. 'I don't see how anybody can be blamed for getting angry when their little girl gets almost scared to death and gets sick from it, and all that. Besides, everybody says – '

'Oh, I don't care what everybody says,' said Martha.

'Well, you can't go against the whole town,' answered Carrie, in sudden sharp defiance.

'No, Martha, you can't go against the whole town,' piped Kate, following her leader rapidly.

' "The whole town",' cried Martha. 'I'd like to know what you call "the whole town". Do you call these silly people who are scared of Henry Johnson "the whole town"?'

'Why, Martha,' said Carrie, in a reasoning tone, 'you talk as if you wouldn't be scared of him!'

'No more would I,' retorted Martha.

'O-oh, Martha, how you talk!' said Kate. 'Why, the idea! Everybody's afraid of him.'

Carrie was grinning. 'You've never seen him, have you?' she asked, seductively.

'No,' admitted Martha.

'Well, then, how do you know that you wouldn't be scared?'

Martha confronted her. 'Have you ever seen him? No? Well, then, how do you know you *would* be scared?'

The allied forces broke out in chorus: 'But, Martha, everybody says so. Everybody says so.'

'Everybody says what?'

'Everybody that's seen him say they were frightened almost to death. 'Tisn't only women, but it's men too. It's awful.'

Martha wagged her head solemnly. 'I'd try not to be afraid of him.'

'But supposing you could not help it?' said Kate.

'Yes, and look here,' cried Carrie. 'I'll tell you another thing. The Hannigans are going to move out of the house next door.'

'On account of him?' demanded Martha.

Carrie nodded. 'Mrs Hannigan says so herself.'

'Well, of all things!' ejaculated Martha. 'Going to move, eh? You don't say so! Where they going to move to?'

'Down on Orchard Avenue.'

'Well, of all things! Nice house?'

'I don't know about that. I haven't heard. But there's lots of nice houses on Orchard.'

'Yes, but they're all taken,' said Kate. 'There isn't a vacant house on Orchard Avenue.'

'Oh yes, there is,' said Martha. 'The old Hampstead house is vacant.'

'Oh, of course,' said Kate. 'But then I don't believe Mrs Hannigan would like it there. I wonder where they can be going to move to?'

'I'm sure I don't know,' sighed Martha. 'It must be to some place we don't know about.'

'Well,' said Carrie Dungen, after a general reflective silence, 'it's easy enough to find out, anyhow.'

'Who knows – around here?' asked Kate.

'Why, Mrs Smith, and there she is in her garden,' said Carrie, jumping to her feet. As she dashed out of the door, Kate and Martha crowded at the window. Carrie's voice rang out from near the steps. 'Mrs Smith! Mrs Smith! Do you know where the Hannigans are going to move to?'

❧ 23 ☙

The autumn smote the leaves, and the trees of Whilomville were panoplied in crimson and yellow. The winds grew stronger, and in the melancholy purple of the nights the home shine of a window became a finer thing. The little boys, watching the sear and sorrowful leaves drifting down from the maples, dreamed of the near time when they could heap bushels in the streets and burn them during the abrupt evenings.

Three men walked down the Niagara Avenue. As they approached Judge Hagenthorpe's house he came down his walk to meet them in the manner of one who has been waiting.

'Are you ready, judge?' one said.

'All ready,' he answered.

The four then walked to Trescott's house. He received them in his office, where he had been reading. He seemed surprised at this visit of four very active and influential citizens, but he had nothing to say of it.

After they were all seated, Trescott looked expectantly from one face to another. There was a little silence. It was broken by John Twelve, the wholesale grocer, who was worth $400,000, and reported to be worth over a million.

'Well, doctor,' he said, with a short laugh, 'I suppose we might as well admit at once that we've come to interfere in something which is none of our business.'

'Why, what is it?' asked Trescott, again looking from one face to another. He seemed to appeal particularly to Judge Hagenthorpe, but the old man had his chin lowered musingly to his cane, and would not look at him.

'It's about what nobody talks of – much,' said Twelve. 'It's about Henry Johnson.'

Trescott squared himself in his chair. 'Yes?' he said.

Having delivered himself of the title, Twelve seemed to become more easy. 'Yes,' he answered, blandly, 'we wanted to talk to you about it.'

'Yes?' said Trescott.

Twelve abruptly advanced on the main attack. 'Now see here, Trescott, we like you, and we have come to talk right out about this business. It may be none of our affairs and all that, and as for me, I don't mind if you tell me so; but I am not going to keep quiet and see you ruin yourself. And that's how we all feel.'

'I am not ruining myself,' answered Trescott.

'No, maybe you are not exactly ruining yourself,' said Twelve, slowly, 'but you are doing yourself a great deal of harm. You have changed from being the leading doctor in town to about the last one. It is mainly because there are always a large number of people who are very thoughtless fools, of course, but then that doesn't change the condition.'

A man who had not heretofore spoken said, solemnly, 'It's the women.'

'Well, what I want to say is this,' resumed Twelve: 'Even if there are a lot of fools in the world, we can't see any reason why you should ruin yourself by opposing them. You can't teach them anything, you know.'

'I am not trying to teach them anything.' Trescott smiled wearily. 'I – It is a matter of – well – '

'And there are a good many of us that admire you for it immensely,' interrupted Twelve; 'but that isn't going to change the minds of all those ninnies.'

'It's the women,' stated the advocate of this view again.

'Well, what I want to say is this,' said Twelve. 'We want you to get out of this trouble and strike your old gait again. You are simply killing your practice through your infernal pig-headedness. Now this thing is out of the ordinary, but there must be ways to – to beat the game somehow, you see. So we've talked it over – about a dozen of us – and, as I say, if you want to tell us to mind our own business, why, go ahead; but we've talked it over, and we've come to the conclusion that the only way to go is to get Johnson a place somewhere off up the valley, and – '

Trescott wearily gestured. 'You don't know, my friend. Everybody is so afraid of him, they can't even give him good care. Nobody can attend to him as I do myself.'

'But I have a little no-good farm up beyond Clarence Mountain that I was going to give to Henry,' cried Twelve, aggrieved. 'And if you – and if you – if you – through your house burning down, or anything – why, all the boys were prepared to take him right off your hands, and – and – '

Trescott arose and went to the window. He turned his back upon them. They sat waiting in silence. When he returned he kept his face in the shadow. 'No, John Twelve,' he said, 'it can't be done.'

There was another stillness. Suddenly a man stirred on his chair.

'Well, then, a public institution – ' he began.

'No,' said Trescott; 'public institutions are all very good, but he is not going to one.'

In the background of the group old Judge Hagenthorpe was thoughtfully smoothing the polished ivory head of his cane.

❧ 24 ❧

Trescott loudly stamped the snow from his feet and shook the flakes from his shoulders. When he entered the house he went at once to the dining-room, and then to the sitting-room. Jimmie was there, reading painfully in a large book concerning giraffes and tigers and crocodiles.

'Where is your mother, Jimmie?' asked Trescott.

'I don't know, pa,' answered the boy. 'I think she is upstairs.'

Trescott went to the foot of the stairs and called, but there came no answer. Seeing that the door of the little drawing-room was open, he entered. The room was bathed in the half-light that came from the four dull panes of mica in the front of the great stove. As his eyes grew used to the shadows he saw his wife curled in an armchair. He went to her. 'Why, Grace,' he said, 'didn't you hear me calling you?'

She made no answer, and as he bent over the chair he heard her trying to smother a sob in the cushion.

'Grace!' he cried. 'You're crying!'

She raised her face. 'I've got a headache, a dreadful headache, Ned.'

'A headache?' he repeated, in surprise and incredulity.

He pulled a chair close to hers. Later, as he cast his eye over the zone of light shed by the dull red panes, he saw that a low table had been drawn close to the stove, and that it was burdened with many small cups and plates of uncut tea-cake. He remembered that the day was Wednesday, and that his wife received on Wednesdays.

'Who was here today, Gracie?' he asked.

From his shoulder there came a mumble, 'Mrs Twelve.'

'Was she – um,' he said. 'Why – didn't Anna Hagenthorpe come over?'

The mumble from his shoulder continued, 'She wasn't well enough.'

Glancing down at the cups, Trescott mechanically counted them. There were fifteen of them. 'There, there,' he said. 'Don't cry, Grace. Don't cry.'

The wind was whining round the house, and the snow beat aslant upon the windows. Sometimes the coal in the stove settled with a crumbling sound, and the four panes of mica flashed a sudden new crimson. As he sat holding her head on his shoulder, Trescott found himself occasionally trying to count the cups. There were fifteen of them.

The Blue Hotel

The Palace Hotel at Fort Romper was painted a light blue, a shade that is on the legs of a kind of heron, causing the bird to declare its position against any background. The Palace Hotel, then, was always screaming and howling in a way that made the dazzling winter landscape of Nebraska seem only a grey swampish hush. It stood alone on the prairie, and when the snow was falling the town two hundred yards away was not visible. But when the traveller alighted at the railway station he was obliged to pass the Palace Hotel before he could come upon the company of low clapboard houses which composed Fort Romper, and it was not to be thought that any traveller could pass the Palace Hotel without looking at it. Pat Scully, the proprietor, had proved himself a master of strategy when he chose his paints. It is true that on clear days, when the great trans-continental expresses, long lines of swaying Pullmans, swept through Fort Romper, passengers were overcome at the sight, and the cult that knows the brown-reds and the subdivisions of the dark greens of the East expressed shame, pity, horror, in a laugh. But to the citizens of this prairie town and to the people who would naturally stop there, Pat Scully had performed a feat. With this opulence and splendour, these creeds, classes, egotisms, that streamed through Romper on the rails day after day, they had no colour in common.

As if the displayed delights of such a blue hotel were not sufficiently enticing, it was Scully's habit to go every morning and evening to meet the leisurely trains that stopped at Romper and work his seductions upon any man that he might see wavering, gripsack in hand.

One morning, when a snow-crusted engine dragged its long string of freight cars and its one passenger coach to the station, Scully performed the marvel of catching three men. One was a shaky and quick-eyed Swede, with a great shining cheap valise; one was a tall bronzed cowboy, who was on his way to a ranch near the Dakota line; one was a little silent man from the East, who didn't look it, and didn't announce it. Scully practically made them prisoners. He was so nimble and merry and kindly that each probably felt it would be the height of brutality to try to escape. They trudged off over the creaking board sidewalks in the wake of the eager little Irishman. He wore a heavy fur cap squeezed tightly down on his head. It caused his two red ears to stick out stiffly, as if they were made of tin.

At last, Scully, elaborately, with boisterous hospitality, conducted them through the portals of the blue hotel. The room which they entered was small. It seemed to be merely a proper temple for an enormous stove, which, in the centre, was humming with godlike violence. At various points on its surface the iron had become luminous and glowed yellow from the heat. Beside the stove Scully's son Johnnie was playing High-Five with an old farmer who had whiskers both grey and sandy. They were quarrelling. Frequently the old farmer turned his face towards a box of sawdust – coloured brown from tobacco juice – that was behind the stove, and spat with an air of great impatience and irritation. With a loud flourish of words Scully destroyed the game of cards, and bustled his son upstairs with part of the baggage of the new guests. He himself conducted them to three basins of the coldest water in the world. The cowboy and the Easterner burnished themselves fiery-red with this water, until it seemed to be some kind of a metal polish. The Swede, however, merely dipped his fingers gingerly and with trepidation. It was notable that throughout this series of small ceremonies the three travellers were made to feel that Scully was very benevolent. He was conferring great favours upon them. He handed the towel from one to the other with an air of philanthropic impulse.

Afterwards they went to the first room, and, sitting about the stove, listened to Scully's officious clamour at his daughters, who were preparing the midday meal. They reflected in the silence of experienced men who tread carefully amid new people. Nevertheless, the old farmer, stationary, invincible in his chair near the warmest part of the stove, turned his face from the sawdust box frequently and addressed a glowing commonplace to the strangers. Usually he was answered in short but adequate sentences by either the cowboy or the Easterner. The Swede said nothing. He seemed to be occupied in making furtive estimates of each man in the room. One might have thought that he had the sense of silly suspicion which comes to guilt. He resembled a badly frightened man.

Later, at dinner, he spoke a little, addressing his conversation entirely to Scully. He volunteered that he had come from New York, where for ten years he had worked as a tailor. These facts seemed to strike Scully as fascinating, and afterwards he volunteered that he had lived at Romper for fourteen years. The Swede asked about the crops and the price of labour. He seemed barely to listen to Scully's extended replies. His eyes continued to rove from man to man.

Finally, with a laugh and a wink, he said that some of these Western communities were very dangerous; and after his statement he straightened his legs under the table, tilted his head, and laughed again, loudly. It was plain that the demonstration had no meaning to the others. They looked at him wondering and in silence.

⤳ 2 ⤳

As the men trooped heavily back into the front-room, the two little windows presented views of a turmoiling sea of snow. The huge arms of the wind were making attempts – mighty, circular, futile – to embrace the flakes as they sped. A gate-post like a still man with a blanched face stood aghast amid this profligate fury. In a hearty voice Scully announced the presence of a blizzard. The guests of the blue hotel, lighting their pipes, assented with grunts of lazy masculine contentment. No island of the sea could be exempt in the degree of this little room with its humming stove. Johnnie, son of Scully, in a tone which defined his opinion of his ability as a card-player, challenged the old farmer of both grey and sandy whiskers to a game of High-Five. The farmer agreed with a contemptuous and bitter scoff. They sat close to the stove, and squared their knees under a wide board. The cowboy and the Easterner watched the game with interest. The Swede remained near the window, aloof, but with a countenance that showed signs of an inexplicable excitement.

The play of Johnnie and the grey-beard was suddenly ended by another quarrel. The old man arose while casting a look of heated scorn at his adversary. He slowly buttoned his coat, and then stalked with fabulous dignity from the room. In the discreet silence of all other men the Swede laughed. His laughter rang somehow childish. Men by this time had begun to look at him askance, as if they wished to inquire what ailed him.

A new game was formed jocosely. The cowboy volunteered to become the partner of Johnnie, and they all then turned to ask the Swede to throw in his lot with the little Easterner. He asked some questions about the game, and, learning that it wore many names, and that he had played it when it was under an alias, he accepted the invitation. He strode towards the men nervously, as if he expected to be assaulted. Finally, seated, he gazed from face to face and laughed shrilly. This laugh was so strange that the Easterner looked up quickly, the cowboy sat intent and with his mouth open, and Johnnie paused, holding the cards with still fingers.

Afterwards there was a short silence. Then Johnnie said, 'Well, let's get at it. Come on now!' They pulled their chairs forward until their knees were bunched under the board. They began to play, and their interest in the game caused the others to forget the manner of the Swede.

The cowboy was a board-whacker. Each time that he held superior cards he whanged them, one by one, with exceeding force, down upon the improvised table, and took the tricks with a glowing air of prowess and pride that sent thrills of indignation into the hearts of his opponents. A game with a board-whacker in it is sure to become intense. The countenances of the Easterner and the Swede were miserable whenever the cowboy thundered down his aces and kings, while Johnnie, his eyes gleaming with joy, chuckled and chuckled.

Because of the absorbing play none considered the strange ways of the Swede. They paid strict heed to the game. Finally, during a lull caused by a new deal, the Swede suddenly addressed Johnnie: 'I suppose there have been a good many men killed in this room.' The jaws of the others dropped and they looked at him.

'What in hell are you talking about?' said Johnnie.

The Swede laughed again his blatant laugh, full of a kind of false courage and defiance. 'Oh, you know what I mean all right,' he answered.

'I'm a liar if I do!' Johnnie protested. The card was halted, and the men stared at the Swede. Johnnie evidently felt that as the son of the proprietor he should make a direct inquiry. 'Now, what might you be drivin' at, mister?' he asked. The Swede winked at him. It was a wink full of cunning. His fingers shook on the edge of the board. 'Oh, maybe you think I have been to nowheres. Maybe you think I'm a tenderfoot?'

'I don't know nothin' about you,' answered Johnnie, 'and I don't give a damn where you've been. All I got to say is that I don't know what you're driving at. There hain't never been nobody killed in this room.'

The cowboy, who had been steadily gazing at the Swede, then spoke: 'What's wrong with you, mister?'

Apparently it seemed to the Swede that he was formidably menaced. He shivered and turned white near the corners of his mouth. He sent an appealing glance in the direction of the little Easterner. During these moments he did not forget to wear his air of advanced pot-valour. 'They say they don't know what I mean,' he remarked mockingly to the Easterner.

The latter answered after prolonged and cautious reflection. 'I don't understand you,' he said, impassively.

The Swede made a movement then which announced that he thought he had encountered treachery from the only quarter where he had expected sympathy, if not help. 'Oh, I see you are all against me. I see – '

The cowboy was in a state of deep stupefaction. 'Say,' he cried, as he tumbled the deck violently down upon the board '– say, what are you gittin' at, hey?'

The Swede sprang up with the celerity of a man escaping from a snake on the floor. 'I don't want to fight!' he shouted. 'I don't want to fight!'

The cowboy stretched his long legs indolently and deliberately. His hands were in his pockets. He spat into the sawdust box. 'Well, who the hell thought you did?' he inquired.

The Swede backed rapidly towards a corner of the room. His hands were out protectingly in front of his chest, but he was making an obvious struggle to control his fright. 'Gentlemen,' he quavered, 'I suppose I am going to be killed before I can leave this house! I suppose I am going to be killed before I can leave this house!' In his eyes was the dying-swan look. Through the windows could be seen the snow turning blue in the shadow of dusk. The wind tore at the house and some loose thing beat regularly against the clapboards like a spirit tapping.

A door opened, and Scully himself entered. He paused in surprise as he noted the tragic attitude of the Swede. Then he said, 'What's the matter here?'

The Swede answered him swiftly and eagerly: 'These men are going to kill me.'

'Kill you!' ejaculated Scully. 'Kill you! What are you talkin'?'

The Swede made the gesture of a martyr.

Scully wheeled sternly upon his son. 'What is this, Johnnie?'

The lad had grown sullen. 'Damned if I know,' he answered. 'I can't make no sense to it.' He began to shuffle the cards, fluttering them together with an angry snap. 'He says a good many men have been killed in this room, or something like that. And he says he's goin' to be killed here too. I don't know what ails him. He's crazy, I shouldn't wonder.'

Scully then looked for explanation to the cowboy, but the cowboy simply shrugged his shoulders.

'Kill you?' said Scully again to the Swede. 'Kill you? Man, you're off your nut.'

'Oh, I know,' burst out the Swede. 'I know what will happen. Yes, I'm crazy – yes. Yes, of course, I'm crazy – yes. But I know one thing – ' There was a sort of sweat of misery and terror upon his face. 'I know I won't get out of here alive.'

The cowboy drew a deep breath, as if his mind was passing into the last stages of dissolution. 'Well, I'm dog-goned,' he whispered to himself.

Scully wheeled suddenly and faced his son. 'You've been troublin' this man!'

Johnnie's voice was loud with its burden of grievance. 'Why, good Gawd, I ain't done nothin' to 'im.'

The Swede broke in. 'Gentlemen, do not disturb yourselves. I will leave this house. I will go away because' – he accused them dramatically with his glance – 'because I do not want to be killed.'

Scully was furious with his son. 'Will you tell me what is the matter, you young divil? What's the matter, anyhow? Speak out!'

'Blame it!' cried Johnnie in despair, 'don't I tell you I don't know. He – he says we want to kill him, and that's all I know. I can't tell what ails him.'

The Swede continued to repeat: 'Never mind, Mr Scully; never mind. I will leave this house. I will go away, because I do not wish to be killed. Yes, of course, I am crazy – yes. But I know one thing! I will go away. I will leave this house. Never mind, Mr Scully; never mind. I will go away.'

'You will not go 'way,' said Scully. 'You will not go 'way until I hear the reason of this business. If anybody has troubled you I will take care of him. This is my house. You are under my roof, and I will not allow any peaceable man to be troubled here.' He cast a terrible eye upon Johnnie, the cowboy, and the Easterner.

'Never mind, Mr Scully; never mind. I will go away. I do not wish to be killed.' The Swede moved towards the door, which opened upon the stairs. It was evidently his intention to go at once for his baggage.

'No, no,' shouted Scully peremptorily; but the white-faced man slid by him and disappeared. 'Now,' said Scully severely, 'what does this mane?'

Johnnie and the cowboy cried together: 'Why, we didn't do nothin' to 'im!'

Scully's eyes were cold. 'No,' he said, 'you didn't?'

Johnnie swore a deep oath. 'Why, this is the wildest loon I ever see. We didn't do nothin' at all. We were jest sittin' here playin' cards, and he –'

The father suddenly spoke to the Easterner. 'Mr Blanc,' he asked, 'what has these boys been doin'?'

The Easterner reflected again. 'I didn't see anything wrong at all,' he said at last, slowly.

Scully began to howl. 'But what does it mane?' He stared ferociously at his son. 'I have a mind to lather you for this, me boy.'

Johnnie was frantic. 'Well, what have I done?' he bawled at his father.

❧ 3 ❧

'I think you are tongue-tied,' said Scully finally to his son, the cowboy, and the Easterner; and at the end of this scornful sentence he left the room.

Upstairs the Swede was swiftly fastening the straps of his great valise. Once his back happened to be half turned towards the door, and, hearing a noise there, he wheeled and sprang up, uttering a loud cry. Scully's wrinkled visage showed grimly in the light of the small lamp he carried. This yellow effulgence, streaming upward, coloured only his prominent features, and left his eyes, for instance, in mysterious shadow. He resembled a murderer.

'Man! man!' he exclaimed, 'have you gone daffy?'

'Oh, no! Oh, no!' rejoined the other. 'There are people in this world who know pretty nearly as much as you do – understand?'

For a moment they stood gazing at each other. Upon the Swede's deathly pale cheeks were two spots brightly crimson and sharply edged, as if they had been carefully painted. Scully placed the light on the table and sat himself on the edge of the bed. He spoke ruminatively. 'By cracky, I never heard of such a thing in my life. It's a complete muddle. I can't, for the soul of me, think how you ever got this idea into your head.' Presently he lifted his eyes and asked: 'And did you sure think they were going to kill you?'

The Swede scanned the old man as if he wished to see into his mind. 'I did,' he said at last. He obviously suspected that this answer might precipitate an outbreak. As he pulled on a strap his whole arm shook, the elbow wavering like a bit of paper.

Scully banged his hand impressively on the foot-board of the bed. 'Why, man, we're goin' to have a line of ilictric street-cars in this town next spring.'

' "A line of electric street-cars," ' repeated the Swede, stupidly.

'And,' said Scully, 'there's a new railroad goin' to be built down from Broken Arm to here. Not to mintion the four churches and the smashin' big brick schoolhouse. Then there's the big factory, too. Why, in two years Romper 'll be a met-tro-*pol*-is.'

Having finished the preparation of his baggage, the Swede straightened himself. 'Mr Scully,' he said, with sudden hardihood, 'how much do I owe you?'

'You don't owe me anythin',' said the old man, angrily.

'Yes, I do,' retorted the Swede. He took seventy-five cents from his pocket and tendered it to Scully; but the latter snapped his fingers in disdainful refusal. However, it happened that they both stood gazing in a strange fashion at the three silver pieces on the Swede's open palm.

'I'll not take your money,' said Scully at last. 'Not after what's been goin' on here.' Then a plan seemed to strike him. 'Here,' he cried, picking up his lamp and moving towards the door. 'Here! Come with me a minute.'

'No,' said the Swede, in overwhelming alarm.

'Yes,' urged the old man. 'Come on! want you to come and see a picter – just across the hall – in my room.'

The Swede must have concluded that his hour was come. His jaw dropped and his teeth showed like a dead man's. He ultimately followed Scully across the corridor, but he had the step of one hung in chains.

Scully flashed the light high on the wall of his own chamber. There was revealed a ridiculous photograph of a little girl. She was leaning against a balustrade of gorgeous decoration, and the formidable bang to her hair was prominent. The figure was as graceful as an upright sled-stake, and, withal, it was of the hue of lead. 'There,' said Scully, tenderly, 'that's the picter of my little girl that died. Her name was Carrie. She had the purtiest hair you ever saw! I was that fond of her, she – '

Turning then, he saw that the Swede was not contemplating the picture at all, but, instead, was keeping keen watch on the gloom in the rear.

'Look, man!' cried Scully, heartily. 'That's the picter of my little gal that died. Her name was Carrie. And then here's the picter of my oldest boy, Michael. He's a lawyer in Lincoln, an' doin' well. I gave that boy a grand eddycation, and I'm glad for it now. He's a fine boy. Look at 'im now. Ain't he bold as blazes, him there in Lincoln, an honoured an' respicted gintleman. An honoured an' respicted gintleman,' concluded Scully with a flourish. And, so saying, he smote the Swede jovially on the back.

The Swede faintly smiled.

'Now,' said the old man, 'there's only one more thing.' He dropped suddenly to the floor and thrust his head beneath the bed. The Swede could hear his muffled voice. 'I'd keep it under me piller if it wasn't for that boy Johnnie. Then there's the old woman – Where is it now? I never put it twice in the same place. Ah, now come out with you!'

Presently he backed clumsily from under the bed, dragging with him an old coat rolled into a bundle. 'I've fetched him,' he muttered. Kneeling on the floor, he unrolled the coat and extracted from its heart a large yellow-brown whiskey bottle.

His first manœuvre was to hold the bottle up to the light. Reassured, apparently, that nobody had been tampering with it, he thrust it with a generous movement towards the Swede.

The weak-kneed Swede was about to eagerly clutch this element of strength, but he suddenly jerked his hand away and cast a look of horror upon Scully.

'Drink,' said the old man affectionately. He had risen to his feet, and now stood facing the Swede.

There was a silence. Then again Scully said: 'Drink!'

The Swede laughed wildly. He grabbed the bottle, put it to his mouth, and as his lips curled absurdly around the opening and his throat worked, he kept his glance, burning with hatred, upon the old man's face.

꩜ 4 ꩜

After the departure of Scully the three men with the card-board still upon their knees, preserved for a long time an astounded silence. Then Johnnie said: 'That's the dog-dangest Swede I ever see.'

'He ain't no Swede,' said the cowboy, scornfully.

'Well, what is he then?' cried Johnnie. 'What is he then?'

'It's my opinion,' replied the cowboy deliberately, 'he's some kind of a Dutchman.' It was a venerable custom of the country to entitle as Swedes all light-haired men who spoke with a heavy tongue. In consequence the idea of the cowboy was not without its daring. 'Yes, sir,' he repeated. 'It's my opinion this feller is some kind of a Dutchman.'

'Well, he says he's a Swede, anyhow,' muttered Johnnie, sulkily. He turned to the Easterner: 'What do you think, Mr Blanc?'

'Oh, I don't know,' replied the Easterner.

'Well, what do you think makes him act that way?' asked the cowboy.

'Why, he's frightened.' The Easterner knocked his pipe against a rim of the stove. 'He's clear frightened out of his boots.'

'What at?' cried Johnnie and cowboy together.

The Easterner reflected over his answer.

'What at?' cried the others again.

'Oh, I don't know, but it seems to me this man has been reading dime-novels, and he thinks he's right out in the middle of it – the shootin' and stabbin' and all.'

'But,' said the cowboy, deeply scandalised, 'this ain't Wyoming, ner none of them places. This is Nebrasker.'

'Yes,' added Johnnie, 'an' why don't he wait till he gits *out West*?'

The travelled Easterner laughed. 'It isn't different there even – not in these days. But he thinks he's right in the middle of hell.'

Johnnie and the cowboy mused long.

'It's awful funny,' remarked Johnnie at last.

'Yes,' said the cowboy. 'This is a queer game. I hope we don't git snowed in, because then we'd have to stand this here man bein' around with us all the time. That wouldn't be no good.'

'I wish pop would throw him out,' said Johnnie.

Presently they heard a loud stamping on the stairs, accompanied by ringing jokes in the voice of old Scully, and laughter, evidently from the Swede. The men around the stove stared vacantly at each other. 'Gosh!' said the cowboy. The door flew open, and old Scully, flushed and anecdotal, came into the room. He was jabbering at the Swede, who followed him, laughing bravely. It was the entry of two roisterers from a banquet-hall.

'Come now,' said Scully sharply to the three seated men, 'move up and give us a chance at the stove.' The cowboy and the Easterner obediently sidled their chairs to make room for the newcomers. Johnnie, however, simply arranged himself in a more indolent attitude, and then remained motionless.

'Come! Git over, there,' said Scully.

'Plenty of room on the other side of the stove,' said Johnnie.

'Do you think we want to sit in the draught?' roared the father.

But the Swede here interposed with a grandeur of confidence. 'No, no. Let the boy sit where he likes,' he cried in a bullying voice to the father.

'All right! All right!' said Scully, deferentially. The cowboy and the Easterner exchanged glances of wonder.

The five chairs were formed in a crescent about one side of the stove. The Swede began to talk; he talked arrogantly, profanely, angrily. Johnnie, the cowboy, and the Easterner maintained a morose silence, while old Scully appeared to be receptive and eager, breaking in constantly with sympathetic ejaculations.

Finally the Swede announced that he was thirsty. He moved in his chair, and said that he would go for a drink of water.

'I'll git it for you,' cried Scully at once.

'No,' said the Swede, contemptuously. 'I'll get it for myself.' He arose and stalked with the air of an owner off into the executive parts of the hotel.

As soon as the Swede was out of hearing Scully sprang to his feet and whispered intensely to the others: 'Upstairs he thought I was tryin' to poison 'im.'

'Say,' said Johnnie, 'this makes me sick. Why don't you throw 'im out in the snow?'

'Why, he's all right now,' declared Scully. 'It was only that he was from the East, and he thought this was a tough place. That's all. He's all right now.'

The cowboy looked with admiration upon the Easterner. 'You were straight,' he said. 'You were on to that there Dutchman.'

'Well,' said Johnnie to his father, 'he may be all right now, but I don't see it. Other time he was scared, but now he's too fresh.'

Scully's speech was always a combination of Irish brogue and idiom, Western twang and idiom, and scraps of curiously formal diction taken from the story-books and newspapers. He now hurled a strange mass of language at the head of his son. 'What do I keep? What do I keep? What do I keep?' he demanded, in a voice of thunder. He slapped his knee impressively, to indicate that he himself was going to make reply, and that all should heed. 'I keep a hotel,' he shouted. 'A hotel, do you mind? A guest under my roof has sacred privileges. He is to be intimidated by none. Not one word shall he hear that would prijudice him in favour of goin' away. I'll not have it. There's no place in this here town where they can say they iver took in a guest of mine because he was afraid to stay here.' He wheeled suddenly upon the cowboy and the Easterner. 'Am I right?'

'Yes, Mr Scully,' said the cowboy, 'I think you're right.'

'Yes, Mr Scully,' said the Easterner, 'I think you're right.'

~§ 5 §~

At six-o'clock supper, the Swede fizzed like a fire-wheel. He sometimes seemed on the point of bursting into riotous song, and in all his madness he was encouraged by old Scully. The Easterner was encased in reserve; the cowboy sat in wide-mouthed amazement, forgetting to eat, while Johnnie wrathily demolished great plates of food. The daughters of the house, when they were obliged to replenish the biscuits, approached as warily as Indians, and, having succeeded in their purpose, fled with ill-concealed trepidation. The Swede domineered the whole feast, and he gave it the appearance of a cruel bacchanal. He seemed to have grown suddenly taller; he gazed, brutally disdainful, into every face. His voice rang through the room. Once when he jabbed out harpoon-fashion with his fork to pinion a biscuit, the weapon nearly impaled the hand of the Easterner which had been stretched quietly out for the same biscuit.

After supper, as the men filed towards the other room, the Swede smote Scully ruthlessly on the shoulder. 'Well, old boy, that was a good, square meal.' Johnnie looked hopefully at his father; he knew that shoulder was tender from an old fall; and, indeed, it appeared for a moment as if Scully was going to flame out over the matter, but in the end he smiled a sickly smile and remained silent. The others understood from his manner that he was admitting his responsibility for the Swede's new viewpoint.

Johnnie, however, addressed his parent in an aside. 'Why don't you license somebody to kick you downstairs?' Scully scowled darkly by way of reply.

When they were gathered about the stove, the Swede insisted on another game of High-Five. Scully gently deprecated the plan at first, but the Swede turned a wolfish glare upon him. The old man subsided, and the Swede canvassed the others. In his tone there was always a

great threat. The cowboy and the Easterner both remarked indifferently that they would play. Scully said that he would presently have to
go to meet the 6.58 train, and so the Swede turned menacingly upon
Johnnie. For a moment their glances crossed like blades, and then
Johnnie smiled and said, 'Yes, I'll play.'

They formed a square, with the little board on their knees. The
Easterner and the Swede were again partners. As the play went on, it
was noticeable that the cowboy was not board-whacking as usual.
Meanwhile, Scully, near the lamp, had put on his spectacles and, with
an appearance curiously like an old priest, was reading a newspaper. In
time he went out to meet the 6.58 train, and, despite his precautions, a
gust of polar wind whirled into the room as he opened the door.
Besides scattering the cards, it chilled the players to the marrow. The
Swede cursed frightfully. When Scully returned, his entrance disturbed
a cosy and friendly scene. The Swede again cursed. But presently they
were once more intent, their heads bent forward and their hands
moving swiftly. The Swede had adopted the fashion of board-whacking.

Scully took up his paper and for a long time remained immersed in
matters which were extraordinarily remote from him. The lamp
burned badly, and once he stopped to adjust the wick. The newspaper,
as he turned from page to page, rustled with a slow and comfortable
sound. Then suddenly he heard three terrible words: 'You are cheatin'!'

Such scenes often prove that there can be little of dramatic import in
environment. Any room can present a tragic front; any room can be
comic. This little den was now hideous as a torture-chamber. The new
faces of the men themselves had changed it upon the instant. The
Swede held a huge fist in front of Johnnie's face, while the latter looked
steadily over it into the blazing orbs of his accuser. The Easterner had
grown pallid; the cowboy's jaw had dropped in that expression of
bovine amazement which was one of his important mannerisms. After
the three words, the first sound in the room was made by Scully's paper
as it floated forgotten to his feet. His spectacles had also fallen from his
nose, but by a clutch he had saved them in air. His hand, grasping the
spectacles, now remained poised awkwardly and near his shoulder. He
stared at the card-players.

Probably the silence was while a second elapsed. Then, if the floor
had been suddenly twitched out from under the men they could not
have moved quicker. The five had projected themselves headlong
towards a common point. It happened that Johnnie, in rising to hurl
himself upon the Swede, had stumbled slightly because of his curiously
instinctive care for the cards and the board. The loss of the moment

allowed time for the arrival of Scully, and also allowed the cowboy time to give the Swede a great push which sent him staggering back. The men found tongue together, and hoarse shouts of rage, appeal, or fear burst from every throat. The cowboy pushed and jostled feverishly at the Swede, and the Easterner and Scully clung wildly to Johnnie; but, through the smoky air, above the swaying bodies of the peace-compellers, the eyes of the two warriors ever sought each other in glances of challenge that were at once hot and steely.

Of course the board had been overturned, and now the whole company of cards was scattered over the floor, where the boots of the men trampled the fat and painted kings and queens as they gazed with their silly eyes at the war that was waging above them.

Scully's voice was dominating the yells. 'Stop now! Stop, I say! Stop, now –'

Johnnie, as he struggled to burst through the rank formed by Scully and the Easterner, was crying, 'Well, he says I cheated! He says I cheated! I won't allow no man to say I cheated! If he says I cheated, he's a – !'

The cowboy was telling the Swede, 'Quit, now! Quit, d'ye hear –'

The screams of the Swede never ceased: 'He did cheat! I saw him! I saw him –'

As for the Easterner, he was importuning in a voice that was not heeded: 'Wait a moment, can't you? Oh, wait a moment. What's the good of a fight over a game of cards? Wait a moment –'

In this tumult no complete sentences were clear. 'Cheat' – 'Quit' – 'He says' – these fragments pierced the uproar and rang out sharply. It was remarkable that, whereas Scully undoubtedly made the most noise, he was the least heard of any of the riotous band.

Then suddenly there was a great cessation. It was as if each man had paused for breath; and although the room was still lighted with the anger of men, it could be seen that there was no danger of immediate conflict, and at once Johnnie, shouldering his way forward, almost succeeded in confronting the Swede. 'What did you say I cheated for? What did you say I cheated for? I don't cheat, and I won't let no man say I do!'

The Swede said, 'I saw you! I saw you!'

'Well,' cried Johnnie, 'I'll fight any man what says I cheat!'

'No, you won't,' said the cowboy. 'Not here.'

'Ah, be still, can't you?' said Scully, coming between them.

The quiet was sufficient to allow the Easterner's voice to be heard. He was repeating, 'Oh, wait a moment, can't you? What's the good of a fight over a game of cards? Wait a moment!'

Johnnie, his red face appearing above his father's shoulder, hailed the Swede again. 'Did you say I cheated?'

The Swede showed his teeth. 'Yes.'

'Then,' said Johnnie, 'we must fight.'

'Yes, fight,' roared the Swede. He was like a demoniac. 'Yes, fight! I'll show you what kind of a man I am! I'll show you who you want to fight! Maybe you think I can't fight! Maybe you think I can't! I'll show you, you skin, you card-sharp! Yes, you cheated! You cheated! You cheated!'

'Well, let's go at it, then, mister,' said Johnnie, coolly.

The cowboy's brow was beaded with sweat from his efforts in intercepting all sorts of raids. He turned in despair to Scully. 'What are you goin' to do now?'

A change had come over the Celtic visage of the old man. He now seemed all eagerness; his eyes glowed.

'We'll let them fight,' he answered, stalwartly. 'I can't put up with it any longer. I've stood this damned Swede till I'm sick. We'll let them fight.'

❦ 6 ❦

The men prepared to go out of doors. The Easterner was so nervous that he had great difficulty in getting his arms into the sleeves of his new leather coat. As the cowboy drew his fur cap down over his ears his hands trembled. In fact, Johnnie and old Scully were the only ones who displayed no agitation. These preliminaries were conducted without words.

Scully threw open the door. 'Well, come on,' he said. Instantly a terrific wind caused the flame of the lamp to struggle at its wick, while a puff of black smoke sprang from the chimney-top. The stove was in mid-current of the blast, and its voice swelled to equal the roar of the storm. Some of the scarred and bedabbled cards were caught up from the floor and dashed helplessly against the farther wall. The men lowered their heads and plunged into the tempest as into a sea.

No snow was falling, but great whirls and clouds of flakes, swept up from the ground by the frantic winds, were streaming southward with the speed of bullets. The covered land was blue with the sheen of an unearthly satin, and there was no other hue save where, at the low, black railway station – which seemed incredibly distant – one light gleamed like a tiny jewel. As the men floundered into a thigh-deep drift, it was known that the Swede was bawling out something. Scully went to him, put a hand on his shoulder and projected an ear. 'What's that you say?' he shouted.

'I say,' bawled the Swede again, 'I won't stand much show against this gang. I know you'll all pitch on me.'

Scully smote him reproachfully on the arm. 'Tut, man!' he yelled. The wind tore the words from Scully's lips and scattered them far alee.

'You are all a gang of – ' boomed the Swede, but the storm also seized the remainder of this sentence.

Immediately turning their backs upon the wind, the men had swung around a corner to the sheltered side of the hotel. It was the function of the little house to preserve here, amid this great devastation of snow, an irregular V-shape of heavily encrusted grass, which crackled beneath the feet. One could imagine the great drifts piled against the windward side. When the party reached the comparative peace of this spot it was found that the Swede was still bellowing.

'Oh, I know what kind of a thing this is! I know you'll all pitch on me. I can't lick you all!'

Scully turned upon him panther fashion. 'You'll not have to whip all of us. You'll have to whip my son Johnnie. An' the man what troubles you durin' that time will have me to dale with.'

The arrangements were swiftly made. The two men faced each other, obedient to the harsh commands of Scully, whose face, in the subtly luminous gloom, could be seen set in the austere impersonal lines that are pictured on the countenances of the Roman veterans. The Easterner's teeth were chattering, and he was hopping up and down like a mechanical toy. The cowboy stood rock-like.

The contestants had not stripped off any clothing. Each was in his ordinary attire. Their fists were up, and they eyed each other in a calm that had the elements of leonine cruelty in it.

During this pause, the Easterner's mind, like a film, took lasting impressions of three men – the iron-nerved master of the ceremony; the Swede, pale, motionless, terrible; and Johnnie, serene yet ferocious, brutish yet heroic. The entire prelude had in it a tragedy greater than the tragedy of action, and this aspect was accentuated by the long, mellow cry of the blizzard, as it sped the tumbling and wailing flakes into the black abyss of the south.

'Now!' said Scully.

The two combatants leaped forward and crashed together like

bullocks. There was heard the cushioned sound of blows, and of a curse squeezing out from between the tight teeth of one.

As for the spectators, the Easterner's pent-up breath exploded from him with a pop of relief, absolute relief from the tension of the preliminaries. The cowboy bounded into the air with a yowl. Scully was immovable as from supreme amazement and fear at the fury of the fight which he himself had permitted and arranged.

For a time the encounter in the darkness was such a perplexity of flying arms that it presented no more detail than would a swiftly revolving wheel. Occasionally a face, as if illumined by a flash of light, would shine out, ghastly and marked with pink spots. A moment later, the men might have been known as shadows, if it were not for the involuntary utterance of oaths that came from them in whispers.

Suddenly a holocaust of warlike desire caught the cowboy, and he bolted forward with the speed of a bronco. 'Go it, Johnnie! go it! Kill him! Kill him!'

Scully confronted him. 'Kape back,' he said; and by his glance the cowboy could tell that this man was Johnnie's father.

To the Easterner there was a monotony of unchangeable fighting that was an abomination. This confused mingling was eternal to his sense, which was concentrated in a longing for the end, the priceless end. Once the fighters lurched near him, and as he scrambled hastily backward he heard them breathe like men on the rack.

'Kill him, Johnnie! Kill him! Kill him! Kill him!' The cowboy's face was contorted like one of those agony masks in museums.

'Keep still,' said Scully, icily.

Then there was a sudden loud grunt, incomplete, cut short, and Johnnie's body swung away from the Swede and fell with sickening heaviness to the grass. The cowboy was barely in time to prevent the mad Swede from flinging himself upon his prone adversary. 'No, you don't,' said the cowboy, interposing an arm. 'Wait a second.'

Scully was at his son's side. 'Johnnie! Johnnie, me boy!' His voice had a quality of melancholy tenderness. 'Johnnie! Can you go on with it?' He looked anxiously down into the bloody, pulpy face of his son.

There was a moment of silence, and then Johnnie answered in his ordinary voice, 'Yes, I – it – yes.'

Assisted by his father he struggled to his feet. 'Wait a bit now till you git your wind,' said the old man.

A few paces away the cowboy was lecturing the Swede. 'No, you don't! Wait a second!'

The Easterner was plucking at Scully's sleeve. 'Oh, this is enough,' he pleaded. 'This is enough! Let it go as it stands. This is enough!'

'Bill,' said Scully, 'git out of the road.' The cowboy stepped aside. 'Now.' The combatants were actuated by a new caution as they advanced towards collision. They glared at each other, and then the Swede aimed a lightning blow that carried with it his entire weight. Johnnie was evidently half stupid from weakness, but he miraculously dodged, and his fist sent the over-balanced Swede sprawling.

The cowboy, Scully, and the Easterner burst into a cheer that was like a chorus of triumphant soldiery, but before its conclusion the Swede had scuffled agilely to his feet and come in berserk abandon at his foe. There was another perplexity of flying arms, and Johnnie's body again swung away and fell, even as a bundle might fall from a roof. The Swede instantly staggered to a little wind-waved tree and leaned upon it, breathing like an engine, while his savage and flame-lit eyes roamed from face to face as the men bent over Johnnie. There was a splendour of isolation in his situation at this time which the Easterner felt once when, lifting his eyes from the man on the ground, he beheld that mysterious and lonely figure, waiting.

'Are you any good yet, Johnnie?' asked Scully in a broken voice.

The son gasped and opened his eyes languidly. After a moment he answered, 'No – I ain't – any good – any – more.' Then, from shame and bodily ill, he began to weep, the tears furrowing down through the bloodstains on his face. 'He was too – too – too heavy for me.'

Scully straightened and addressed the waiting figure. 'Stranger,' he said, evenly, 'it's all up with our side.' Then his voice changed into that vibrant huskiness which is commonly the tone of the most simple and deadly announcements. 'Johnnie is whipped.'

Without replying, the victor moved off on the route to the front door of the hotel.

The cowboy was formulating new and unspellable blasphemies. The Easterner was startled to find that they were out in a wind that seemed to come direct from the shadowed arctic floes. He heard again the wail of the snow as it was flung to its grave in the south. He knew now that all this time the cold had been sinking into him deeper and deeper, and he wondered that he had not perished. He felt indifferent to the condition of the vanquished man.

'Johnnie, can you walk?' asked Scully.

'Did I hurt – hurt him any?' asked the son.

'Can you walk, boy? Can you walk?'

Johnnie's voice was suddenly strong. There was a robust impatience in it. 'I asked you whether I hurt him any!'

'Yes, yes, Johnnie,' answered the cowboy, consolingly; 'he's hurt a good deal.'

They raised him from the ground, and as soon as he was on his feet he went tottering off, rebuffing all attempts at assistance. When the party rounded the corner they were fairly blinded by the pelting of the snow. It burned their faces like fire. The cowboy carried Johnnie through the drift to the door. As they entered some cards again rose from the floor and beat against the wall.

The Easterner rushed to the stove. He was so profoundly chilled that he almost dared to embrace the glowing iron. The Swede was not in the room. Johnnie sank into a chair, and, folding his arms on his knees, buried his face in them. Scully, warming one foot and then the other at a rim of the stove, muttered to himself with Celtic mournfulness. The cowboy had removed his fur cap, and with a dazed and rueful air he was running one hand through his tousled locks. From overhead they could hear the creaking of boards, as the Swede tramped here and there in his room.

The sad quiet was broken by the sudden flinging open of a door that led towards the kitchen. It was instantly followed by an inrush of women. They precipitated themselves upon Johnnie amid a chorus of lamentation. Before they carried their prey off to the kitchen, there to be bathed and harangued with that mixture of sympathy and abuse which is a feat of their sex, the mother straightened herself and fixed old Scully with an eye of stern reproach. 'Shame be upon you, Patrick Scully!' she cried. 'Your own son, too. Shame be upon you!'

'There, now! Be quiet, now!' said the old man, weakly.

'Shame be upon you, Patrick Scully!' The girls, rallying to this slogan, sniffed disdainfully in the direction of those trembling accomplices, the cowboy and the Easterner. Presently they bore Johnnie away, and left the three men to dismal reflection.

❧ 7 ❧

'I'd like to fight this here Dutchman myself,' said the cowboy, breaking a long silence.

Scully wagged his head sadly. 'No, that wouldn't do. It wouldn't be right. It wouldn't be right.'

'Well, why wouldn't it?' argued the cowboy. 'I don't see no harm in it.'

'No,' answered Scully, with mournful heroism. 'It wouldn't be right. It was Johnnie's fight, and now we mustn't whip the man just because he whipped Johnnie.'

'Yes, that's true enough' said the cowboy; 'but – he better not get fresh with me, because I couldn't stand no more of it.'

'You'll not say a word to him,' commanded Scully, and even then they heard the tread of the Swede on the stairs. His entrance was made theatric. He swept the door back with a bang and swaggered to the middle of the room. No one looked at him. 'Well,' he cried, insolently, at Scully, 'I s'pose you'll tell me now how much I owe you?'

The old man remained stolid. 'You don't owe me nothin'.'

'Huh!' said the Swede, 'huh! Don't owe 'im nothin'.'

The cowboy addressed the Swede. 'Stranger, I don't see how you come to be so gay around here.'

Old Scully was instantly alert. 'Stop!' he shouted, holding his hand forth, fingers upward. 'Bill, you shut up!'

The cowboy spat carelessly into the sawdust-box. 'I didn't say a word, did I?' he asked.

'Mr Scully,' called the Swede, 'how much do I owe you?' It was seen that he was attired for departure, and that he had his valise in his hand.

'You don't owe me nothin',' repeated Scully in his same imperturbable way.

'Huh!' said the Swede. 'I guess you're right. I guess if it was any way at all, you'd owe me somethin'. That's what I guess.' He turned to the cowboy. ' "Kill him! Kill him! Kill him!" ' he mimicked, and then guffawed victoriously. ' "Kill him!" ' He was convulsed with ironical humour.

But he might have been jeering the dead. The three men were immovable and silent, staring with glassy eyes at the stove.

The Swede opened the door and passed into the storm, giving one derisive glance backward at the still group.

As soon as the door was closed, Scully and the cowboy leaped to their feet and began to curse. They trampled to and fro, waving their arms and smashing into the air with their fists. 'Oh, but that was a hard minute!' wailed Scully. 'That was a hard minute! Him there leerin' and scoffin'! One bang at his nose was worth forty dollars to me that minute! How did you stand it, Bill?'

'How did I stand it?' cried the cowboy in a quivering voice. 'How did I stand it? Oh!'

The old man burst into sudden brogue. 'I'd loike to take that Swade,' he wailed, 'and hould 'im down on a shtone flure and bate 'im to a jelly wid a shtick!'

The cowboy groaned in sympathy. 'I'd like to git him by the neck and ha-ammer him' – he brought his hand down on a chair with a noise like a pistol-shot – 'hammer that there Dutchman until he couldn't tell himself from a dead coyote!'

'I'd bate 'im until he – '

'I'd show *him* some things – '

And then together they raised a yearning, fanatic cry – 'Oh-o-oh! if we only could – '

'Yes!'

'Yes!'

'And then I'd – '

'O-o-oh!'

⤳ 8 ⤳

The Swede, tightly gripping his valise, tacked across the face of the storm as if he carried sails. He was following a line of little naked, gasping trees, which he knew must mark the way of the road. His face, fresh from the pounding of Johnnie's fists, felt more pleasure than pain in the wind and the driving snow. A number of square shapes loomed upon him finally, and he knew them as the houses of the main body of the town. He found a street and made travel along it, leaning heavily upon the wind whenever, at a corner, a terrific blast caught him.

He might have been in a deserted village. We picture the world as thick with conquering and elate humanity, but here, with the bugles of the tempest pealing, it was hard to imagine a peopled earth. One viewed the existence of man then as a marvel, and conceded a glamour of wonder to these lice which were caused to cling to a whirling, fire-smote, ice-locked, disease-stricken, space-lost bulb. The conceit of man was explained by this storm to be the very engine of life. One was a coxcomb not to die in it. However, the Swede found a saloon.

In front of it an indomitable red light was burning, and the snow-flakes were made blood-colour as they flew through the circumscribed territory of the lamp's shining. The Swede pushed open the door of the saloon and entered. A sanded expanse was before him, and at the end of it four men sat about a table drinking. Down one side of the room extended a radiant bar, and its guardian was leaning upon his elbows listening to the talk of the men at the table. The Swede dropped his valise upon the floor, and, smiling fraternally upon the barkeeper, said, 'Gimme some whiskey, will you?' The man placed a bottle, a whiskey-glass, and a glass of ice-thick water upon the bar. The Swede poured himself an abnormal portion of whiskey and drank it in three gulps. 'Pretty bad night,' remarked the bartender, indifferently. He was making the pretension of blindness which is usually a distinction of his class; but it could have been seen that he was furtively studying the half-erased bloodstains on the face of the Swede. 'Bad night,' he said again.

'Oh, it's good enough for me,' replied the Swede, hardily, as he poured himself some more whiskey. The barkeeper took his coin and manœuvred it through its reception by the highly nickelled cash-machine. A bell rang; a card labelled '20 cts' had appeared.

'No,' continued the Swede, 'this isn't too bad weather. It's good enough for me.'

'So?' murmured the barkeeper, languidly.

The copious drams made the Swede's eyes swim, and he breathed a trifle heavier. 'Yes, I like this weather. I like it. It suits me.' It was apparently his design to impart a deep significance to these words.

'So?' murmured the bartender again. He turned to gaze dreamily at the scroll-like birds and bird-like scrolls which had been drawn with soap upon the mirrors back of the bar.

'Well, I guess I'll take another drink,' said the Swede, presently. 'Have something?'

'No, thanks; I'm not drinkin',' answered the bartender. Afterwards he asked, 'How did you hurt your face?'

The Swede immediately began to boast loudly. 'Why, in a fight. I thumped the soul out of a man down here at Scully's hotel.'

The interest of the four men at the table was at last aroused.

'Who was it?' said one.

'Johnnie Scully,' blustered the Swede. 'Son of the man what runs it. He will be pretty near dead for some weeks, I can tell you. I made a nice thing of him, I did. He couldn't get up. They carried him in the house. Have a drink?'

Instantly the men in some subtle way encased themselves in reserve. 'No, thanks,' said one. The group was of curious formation. Two were prominent local businessmen; one was the district-attorney; and one was a professional gambler of the kind known as 'square'. But a scrutiny of the group would not have enabled an observer to pick the gambler from the men of more reputable pursuits. He was, in fact, a man so delicate in manner, when among people of fair class, and so judicious in his choice of victims, that in the strictly masculine part of the town's life he had come to be explicitly trusted and admired. People called him a thoroughbred. The fear and contempt with which his craft was regarded was undoubtedly the reason that his quiet dignity shone conspicuous above the quiet dignity of men who might be merely hatters, billiard-markers, or grocery-clerks. Beyond an occasional unwary traveller, who came by rail, this gambler was supposed to prey solely upon reckless and senile farmers, who, when flush with good crops, drove into town in all the pride and confidence of an absolutely invulnerable stupidity. Hearing at times in circuitous fashion of the despoilment of such a farmer, the important men of Romper invariably laughed in contempt of the victim, and, if they thought of the wolf at all, it was with a kind of pride at the knowledge that he would never dare think of attacking their wisdom and courage. Besides, it was popular that this gambler had a real wife and two real children in a neat cottage in a suburb, where he led an exemplary home life; and when anyone even suggested a discrepancy in his character, the crowd immediately vociferated descriptions of this virtuous family circle. Then men who led exemplary home lives, and men who did not lead exemplary home lives, all subsided in a bunch, remarking that there was nothing more to be said.

However, when a restriction was placed upon him – as, for instance, when a strong clique of members of the new Pollywog Club refused to permit him, even as a spectator, to appear in the rooms of the organisation – the candour and gentleness with which he accepted the judgment disarmed many of his foes and made his friends more desperately partisan. He invariably distinguished between himself and a respectable Romper man so quickly and frankly that his manner actually appeared to be a continual broadcast compliment.

And one must not forget to declare the fundamental fact of his entire position in Romper. It is irrefutable that in all affairs outside of his business, in all matters that occur eternally and commonly between man and man, this thieving card-player was so generous, so just, so moral, that, in a contest, he could have put to flight the consciences of nine-tenths of the citizens of Romper.

And so it happened that he was seated in this saloon with the two prominent local merchants and the district-attorney.

The Swede continued to drink raw whiskey, meanwhile babbling at the barkeeper and trying to induce him to indulge in potations. 'Come on. Have a drink. Come on. What – no? Well, have a little one, then. By gawd, I've whipped a man tonight, and I want to celebrate. I whipped him good, too. Gentlemen,' the Swede cried to the men at the table, 'have a drink?'

'Ssh!' said the barkeeper.

The group at the table, although furtively attentive, had been pretending to be deep in talk, but now a man lifted his eyes towards the Swede and said, shortly, 'Thanks. We don't want any more.'

At this reply the Swede ruffled out his chest like a rooster. 'Well,' he exploded, 'it seems I can't get anybody to drink with me in this town. Seems so, don't it? Well!'

' 'Ssh!' said the barkeeper.

'Say,' snarled the Swede, 'don't you try to shut me up. I won't have it. I'm a gentleman, and I want people to drink with me. And I want 'em to drink with me now. *Now* – do you understand?' He rapped the bar with his knuckles.

Years of experience had calloused the bartender. He merely grew sulky. 'I hear you,' he answered.

'Well,' cried the Swede, 'listen hard then. See those men over there? Well, they're going to drink with me, and don't you forget it. Now you watch.'

'Hi!' yelled the barkeeper, 'this won't do!'

'Why won't it?' demanded the Swede. He stalked over to the table, and by chance laid his hand upon the shoulder of the gambler. 'How about this?' he asked, wrathfully. 'I asked you to drink with me.'

The gambler simply twisted his head and spoke over his shoulder. 'My friend, I don't know you.'

'Oh, hell!' answered the Swede, 'come and have a drink.'

'Now, my boy,' advised the gambler, kindly, 'take your hand off my shoulder and go 'way and mind your own business.' He was a little, slim man, and it seemed strange to hear him use this tone of heroic patronage to the burly Swede. The other men at the table said nothing.

'What! You won't drink with me, you little dude? I'll make you then! I'll make you!' The Swede had grasped the gambler frenziedly at the throat, and was dragging him from his chair. The other men sprang up. The barkeeper dashed around the corner of his bar. There was a great tumult, and then was seen a long blade in the hand of the gambler. It shot forward, and a human body, this citadel of virtue, wisdom, power, was pierced as easily as if it had been a melon. The Swede fell with a cry of supreme astonishment.

The prominent merchants and the district-attorney must have at once tumbled out of the place backward. The bartender found himself hanging limply to the arm of a chair and gazing into the eyes of a murderer.

'Henry,' said the latter, as he wiped his knife on one of the towels that hung beneath the bar-rail, 'you tell 'em where to find me. I'll be home, waiting for 'em.' Then he vanished. A moment afterwards the barkeeper was in the street dinning through the storm for help, and, moreover, companionship.

The corpse of the Swede, alone in the saloon, had its eyes fixed upon a dreadful legend that dwelt atop of the cash-machine: 'This registers the amount of your purchase.'

❧ 9 ❧

Months later, the cowboy was frying pork over the stove of a little ranch near the Dakota line, when there was a quick thud of hoofs outside, and presently the Easterner entered with the letters and the papers.

'Well,' said the Easterner at once, 'the chap that killed the Swede has got three years. Wasn't much, was it?'

'He has? Three years?' The cowboy poised his pan of pork, while he ruminated upon the news. 'Three years. That ain't much.'

'No. It was a light sentence,' replied the Easterner as he unbuckled his spurs. 'Seems there was a good deal of sympathy for him in Romper.'

'If the bartender had been any good,' observed the cowboy, thoughtfully, 'he would have gone in and cracked that there Dutchman on the head with a bottle in the beginnin' of it and stopped all this here murderin'.'

'Yes, a thousand things might have happened,' said the Easterner, tartly.

The cowboy returned his pan of pork to the fire, but his philosophy continued. 'It's funny, ain't it? If he hadn't said Johnnie was cheatin' he'd be alive this minute. He was an awful fool. Game played for fun, too. Not for money. I believe he was crazy.'

'I feel sorry for that gambler,' said the Easterner.

'Oh, so do I,' said the cowboy. 'He don't deserve none of it for killin' who he did.'

'The Swede might not have been killed if everything had been square.'

'Might not have been killed?' exclaimed the cowboy. 'Everythin' square? Why, when he said that Johnnie was cheatin' and acted like such a jackass? And then in the saloon he fairly walked up to git hurt?' With these arguments the cowboy browbeat the Easterner and reduced him to rage.

'You're a fool!' cried the Easterner, viciously. 'You're a bigger jackass than the Swede by a million majority. Now let me tell you one thing. Let me tell you something. Listen! Johnnie *was* cheating!'

' "Johnnie",' said the cowboy, blankly. There was a minute of silence, and then he said, robustly, 'Why, no. The game was only for fun.'

'Fun or not,' said the Easterner, 'Johnnie was cheating. I saw him. I know it. I saw him. And I refused to stand up and be a man. I let the Swede fight it out alone. And you – you were simply puffing around the place and wanting to fight. And then old Scully himself! We are all in it! This poor gambler isn't even a noun. He is kind of an adverb. Every sin is the result of a collaboration. We, five of us, have collaborated in the murder of this Swede. Usually there are from a dozen to forty women really involved in every murder, but in this case it seems to be only five men – you, I, Johnnie, old Scully, and that fool of an unfortunate gambler came merely as a culmination, the apex of a human movement, and gets all the punishment.'

The cowboy, injured and rebellious, cried out blindly into this fog of mysterious theory: 'Well, I didn't do anythin', did I?'

His New Mittens

I

Little Horace was walking home from school, brilliantly decorated by a pair of new red mittens. A number of boys were snowballing gleefully in a field. They hailed him. 'Come on, Horace! We're having a battle.'

Horace was sad. 'No,' he said, 'I can't. I've got to go home.' At noon his mother had admonished him: 'Now, Horace, you come straight home as soon as school is out. Do you hear? And don't you get them nice new mittens all wet, either. Do you hear?' Also his aunt had said: 'I declare, Emily, it's a shame the way you allow that child to ruin his things.' She had meant mittens. To his mother, Horace had dutifully replied, 'Yes'm.' But he now loitered in the vicinity of the group of uproarious boys, who were yelling like hawks as the white balls flew.

Some of them immediately analysed this extraordinary hesitancy. 'Hah!' they paused to scoff, 'afraid of your new mittens, ain't you?' Some smaller boys, who were not yet so wise in discerning motives, applauded this attack with unreasonable vehemence. 'A-fray-ed of his mit-tens! A-fray-ed of his mit-tens.' They sang these lines to cruel and monotonous music which is as old perhaps as American childhood, and which it is the privilege of the emancipated adult to completely forget. 'A-fray-ed of his mit-tens!'

Horace cast a tortured glance towards his playmates, and then dropped his eyes to the snow at his feet. Presently he turned to the trunk of one of the great maple trees that lined the curb. He made a pretence of closely examining the rough and virile bark. To his mind, this familiar street of Whilomville seemed to grow dark in the thick shadow of shame. The trees and the houses were now palled in purple.

'A-fray-ed of his mittens!' The terrible music had in it a meaning from the moonlit war-drums of chanting cannibals.

At last Horace, with supreme effort, raised his head. ' 'Tain't them I care about,' he said, gruffly. 'I've got to go home. That's all.'

Whereupon each boy held his left forefinger as if it were a pencil and began to sharpen it derisively with his right forefinger. They came closer, and sang like a trained chorus, 'A-fray-ed of his mittens!'

When he raised his voice to deny the charge it was simply lost in the screams of the mob. He was alone, fronting all the traditions of boyhood held before him by inexorable representatives. To such a low state had he fallen that one lad, a mere baby, outflanked him and then struck him in the cheek with a heavy snowball. The act was acclaimed with loud jeers.

Horace turned to dart at his assailant, but there was an immediate demonstration on the other flank, and he found himself obliged to keep his face towards the hilarious crew of tormentors. The baby retreated in safety to the rear of the crowd, where he was received with fulsome compliments upon his daring. Horace retreated slowly up the walk. He continually tried to make them heed him, but the only sound was the chant, 'A-fray-ed of his mittens!' In this desperate withdrawal the beset and haggard boy suffered more than is the common lot of man.

Being a boy himself, he did not understand boys at all. He had, of course, the dismal conviction that they were going to dog him to his grave. But near the corner of the field they suddenly seemed to forget all about it. Indeed, they possessed only the malevolence of so many flitter-headed sparrows. The interest had swung capriciously to some other matter. In a moment they were off in the field again, carousing amid the snow. Some authoritative boy had probably said, 'Aw, come on!'

As the pursuit ceased, Horace ceased his retreat. He spent some time in what was evidently an attempt to adjust his self-respect, and then began to wander furtively down towards the group. He, too, had undergone an important change. Perhaps his sharp agony was only as durable as the malevolence of the others. In this boyish life obedience to some unformulated creed of manners was enforced with capricious but merciless rigour. However, they were, after all, his comrades, his friends.

They did not heed his return. They were engaged in an altercation. It had evidently been planned that this battle was between Indians and soldiers. The smaller and weaker boys had been induced to appear as Indians in the initial skirmish, but they were now very sick of it, and were reluctantly but steadfastly, affirming their desire for a change of caste. The larger boys had all won great distinction, devastating Indians materially, and they wished the war to go on as planned. They explained vociferously that it was proper for the soldiers always to thrash the Indians. The little boys did not pretend to deny the truth of this argument; they confined themselves to the simple statement that, in that case, they wished to be soldiers. Each little boy willingly appealed to the others to remain Indians, but as for himself he reiterated his desire to enlist as a soldier. The larger boys were in despair over this dearth of enthusiasm in the small Indians. They alternately wheedled and bullied, but they could not persuade the little boys, who were really suffering dreadful humiliation rather than submit to another onslaught of soldiers. They were called all the baby names that had the power of stinging deep into their pride, but they remained firm.

Then a formidable lad, a leader of reputation, one who could whip many boys that wore long trousers, suddenly blew out his cheeks and shouted, 'Well, all right then. I'll be an Indian myself. Now.' The little boys greeted with cheers this addition to their wearied ranks, and seemed then content. But matters were not mended in the least, because all of the personal following of the formidable lad, with the addition of every outsider, spontaneously forsook the flag and declared themselves Indians. There were now no soldiers. The Indians had carried everything unanimously. The formidable lad used his influence, but his influence could not shake the loyalty of his friends, who refused to fight under any colours but his colours.

Plainly there was nothing for it but to coerce the little ones. The formidable lad again became a soldier, and then graciously permitted to join him all the real fighting strength of the crowd, leaving behind a most forlorn band of little Indians. Then the soldiers attacked the Indians, exhorting them to opposition at the same time.

The Indians at first adopted a policy of hurried surrender, but this had no success, as none of the surrenders were accepted. They then turned to flee, bawling out protests. The ferocious soldiers pursued them amid shouts. The battle widened, developing all manner of marvellous detail.

Horace had turned towards home several times, but, as a matter of fact, this scene held him in a spell. It was fascinating beyond anything which the grown man understands. He had always in the back of his head a sense of guilt, even a sense of impending punishment for disobedience, but they could not weigh with the delirium of this snow-battle.

❧ 2 ❧

One of the raiding soldiers, espying Horace, called out in passing, 'A-fray-ed of his mittens!' Horace flinched at this renewal, and the other lad paused to taunt him again. Horace scooped some snow, moulded it into a ball, and flung it at the other. 'Ho!' cried the boy, 'you're an Indian, are you? Hey, fellers, here's an Indian that ain't been killed yet.' He and Horace engaged in a duel in which both were in such haste to mould snowballs that they had little time for aiming.

Horace once struck his opponent squarely in the chest. 'Hey,' he shouted, 'you're dead. You can't fight any more, Pete. I killed you. You're dead.'

The other boy flushed red, but he continued frantically to make ammunition. 'You never touched me!' he retorted, glowering. 'You never touched me! Where, now?' he added, defiantly. 'Where did you hit me?'

'On the coat! Right on your breast! You can't fight any more! You're dead!'

'You never!'

'I did, too! Hey, fellers, ain't he dead? hit 'im square!'

'He never!'

Nobody had seen the affair, but some of the boys took sides in absolute accordance with their friendship for one of the concerned parties. Horace's opponent went about contending, 'He never touched me! He never came near me! He never came near me!'

The formidable leader now came forward and accosted Horace. 'What was you? An Indian? Well, then, you're dead – that's all. He hit you. I saw him.'

'Me?' shrieked Horace. 'He never came within a mile of me – '

At that moment he heard his name called in a certain familiar tune of two notes, with the last note shrill and prolonged. He looked towards the sidewalk, and saw his mother standing there in her widow's weeds, with two brown paper parcels under her arm. A silence had fallen upon all the boys. Horace moved slowly towards his mother. She did not seem to note his approach; she was gazing austerely off through the naked branches of the maples where two crimson sunset bars lay on the deep blue sky.

At a distance of ten paces Horace made a desperate venture. 'Oh, ma,' he whined, 'can't I stay out for a while?'

'No,' she answered solemnly, 'you come with me.' Horace knew that profile; it was the inexorable profile. But he continued to plead, because it was not beyond his mind that a great show of suffering now might diminish his suffering later.

He did not dare to look back at his playmates. It was already a public scandal that he could not stay out as late as other boys, and he could imagine his standing now that he had been again dragged off by his mother in sight of the whole world. He was a profoundly miserable human being.

Aunt Martha opened the door for them. Light streamed about her straight skirt. 'Oh,' she said, 'so you found him on the road, eh? Well, I declare! It was about time!'

Horace slunk into the kitchen. The stove, straddling out on its four iron legs, was gently humming. Aunt Martha had evidently just lighted the lamp, for she went to it and began to twist the wick experimentally.

'Now,' said the mother, 'let's see them mittens.'

Horace's chin sank. The aspiration of the criminal, the passionate desire for an asylum from retribution, from justice, was aflame in his heart. 'I – I – don't – don't know where they are,' he gasped finally, as he passed his hand over his pockets.

'Horace,' intoned his mother, 'you are tellin' me a story!'

' 'Tain't a story,' he answered, just above his breath. He looked like a sheep-stealer.

His mother held him by the arm, and began to search his pockets. Almost at once she was able to bring forth a pair of very wet mittens. 'Well, I declare!' cried Aunt Martha. The two women went close to the lamp, and minutely examined the mittens, turning them over and over. Afterwards, when Horace looked up, his mother's sad-lined, homely face was turned towards him. He burst into tears.

His mother drew a chair near the stove. 'Just you sit there now, until I tell you to git off.' He sidled meekly into the chair. His mother and his aunt went briskly about the business of preparing supper. They did not display a knowledge of his existence; they carried an effect of oblivion so far that they even did not speak to each other. Presently they went into the dining- and living-room; Horace could hear the dishes rattling. His Aunt Martha brought a plate of food, placed it on a chair near him, and went away without a word.

Horace instantly decided that he would not touch a morsel of the food. He had often used this ruse in dealing with his mother. He did not know why it brought her to terms, but certainly it sometimes did.

The mother looked up when the aunt returned to the other room. 'Is he eatin' his supper?' she asked.

The maiden aunt, fortified in ignorance, gazed with pity and contempt upon this interest. 'Well, now, Emily, how do I know?' she queried. 'Was I goin' to stand over 'im? Of all the worryin' you do about that child! It's a shame the way you're bringin' up that child.'

'Well, he ought to eat somethin'. It won't do fer him to go without eatin',' the mother retorted, weakly.

Aunt Martha, profoundly scorning the policy of concession which these words meant, uttered a long, contemptuous sigh.

❧ 3 ❧

Alone in the kitchen, Horace stared with sombre eyes at the plate of food. For a long time he betrayed no sign of yielding. His mood was adamantine. He was resolved not to sell his vengeance for bread, cold ham, and a pickle, and yet it must be known that the sight of them affected him powerfully. The pickle in particular was notable for its seductive charm. He surveyed it darkly.

But at last, unable to longer endure his state, his attitude in the presence of the pickle, he put out an inquisitive finger and touched it, and it was cool and green and plump. Then a full conception of the cruel woe of his situation swept upon him suddenly, and his eyes filled with tears, which began to move down his cheeks. He sniffled. His heart was black with hatred. He painted in his mind scenes of deadly retribution. His mother would be taught that he was not one to endure persecution meekly, without raising an arm in his defence. And so his dreams were of a slaughter of feelings, and near the end of them his mother was pictured as coming, bowed with pain, to his feet. Weeping, she implored his charity. Would he forgive her? No; his once tender heart had been turned to stone by her injustice. He could not forgive her. She must pay the inexorable penalty.

The first item in this horrible plan was the refusal of the food. This he knew by experience would work havoc in his mother's heart. And so he grimly waited.

But suddenly it occurred to him that the first part of his revenge was in danger of failing. The thought struck him that his mother might not capitulate in the usual way. According to his recollection, the time was more than due when she should come in, worried, sadly affectionate, and ask him if he was ill. It had then been his custom to hint in a resigned voice that he was the victim of secret disease, but that he preferred to suffer in silence and alone. If she was obdurate in her anxiety, he always asked her in a gloomy, low voice to go away and leave him to suffer in silence and alone in the darkness without food. He had known this manœuvring to result even in pie.

But what was the meaning of the long pause and the stillness? Had his old and valued ruse betrayed him? As the truth sank into his mind, he supremely loathed life, the world, his mother. Her heart was beating back the besiegers; he was a defeated child.

He wept for a time before deciding upon the final stroke. He would run away. In a remote corner of the world he would become some sort of bloody-handed person driven to a life of crime by the barbarity of his mother. She should never know his fate. He would torture her for years with doubts and doubts, and drive her implacably to a repentant grave. Nor would his Aunt Martha escape. Some day, a century hence, when his mother was dead, he would write to his Aunt Martha, and point out her part in the blighting of his life. For one blow against him now he would, in time, deal back a thousand – aye, ten thousand.

He arose and took his coat and cap. As he moved stealthily towards the door he cast a glance backward at the pickle. He was tempted to take it, but he knew that if he left the plate inviolate his mother would feel even worse.

A blue snow was falling. People, bowed forward, were moving briskly along the walks. The electric lamps hummed amid showers of flakes. As Horace emerged from the kitchen, a shrill squall drove the flakes around the corner of the house. He cowered away from it, and its violence illumined his mind vaguely in new directions. He deliberated upon a choice of remote corners of the globe. He found that he had no plans which were definite enough in a geographical way, but without much loss of time he decided upon California. He moved briskly as far as his mother's front gate on the road to California. He was off at last. His success was a trifle dreadful; his throat choked.

But at the gate he paused. He did not know if his journey to California would be shorter if he went down Niagara Avenue or off through Hogan Street. As the storm was very cold and the point was very important, he decided to withdraw for reflection to the woodshed. He entered the dark shanty, and took seat upon the old chopping-block upon which he was supposed to perform for a few minutes every afternoon when he returned from school. The wind screamed and shouted at the loose boards, and there was a rift of snow on the floor to leeward of a crack.

Here the idea of starting for California on such a night departed from his mind, leaving him ruminating miserably upon his martyrdom. He saw nothing for it but to sleep all night in the woodshed and start for California in the morning bright and early. Thinking of his bed, he kicked over the floor and found that the innumerable chips were all frozen tightly, bedded in ice.

Later he viewed with joy some signs of excitement in the house. The flare of a lamp moved rapidly from window to window. Then the kitchen door slammed loudly and a shawled figure sped towards the gate. At last he was making them feel his power. The shivering child's face was lit with saturnine glee as in the darkness of the woodshed he gloated over the evidences of consternation in his home. The shawled figure had been his Aunt Martha dashing with the alarm to the neighbours.

The cold of the woodshed was tormenting him. He endured only because of the terror he was causing. But then it occurred to him that if they instituted a search for him, they would probably examine the woodshed. He knew that it would not be manful to be caught so soon. He was not positive now that he was going to remain away forever, but at any rate he was bound to inflict some more damage before allowing himself to be captured. If he merely succeeded in making his mother angry, she would thrash him on sight. He must prolong the time in order to be safe. If he held out properly, he was sure of a welcome of love, even though he should drip with crimes.

Evidently the storm had increased, for when he went out it swung him violently with its rough and merciless strength. Panting, stung, half blinded with the driving flakes, he was now a waif, exiled, friendless, and poor. With a bursting heart, he thought of his home and his mother. To his forlorn vision they were as far away as heaven.

🐟 4 🐟

Horace was undergoing changes of feeling so rapidly that he was merely moved hither and then thither like a kite. He was now aghast at the merciless ferocity of his mother. It was she who had thrust him into this wild storm, and she was perfectly indifferent to his fate, perfectly indifferent. The forlorn wanderer could no longer weep. The strong sobs caught at his throat, making his breath come in short, quick snuffles. All in him was conquered save the enigmatical childish ideal of form, manner. This principle still held out, and it was the only thing between him and submission. When he surrendered, he must surrender in a way that deferred to the undefined code. He longed simply to go to the kitchen and stumble in, but his unfathomable sense of fitness forbade him.

Presently he found himself at the head of Niagara Avenue, staring through the snow into the blazing windows of Stickney's butcher-shop. Stickney was the family butcher, not so much because of a superiority to other Whilomville butchers as because he lived next door and had been an intimate friend of the father of Horace. Rows of glowing pigs hung head downward back of the tables, which bore huge pieces of red beef. Clumps of attenuated turkeys were suspended here and there. Stickney, hale and smiling, was bantering with a woman in a cloak, who, with a monster basket on her arm, was dickering for eight cents' worth of something. Horace watched them through a crusted pane. When the woman came out and passed him, he went towards the door. He touched the latch with his finger, but withdrew again suddenly to the sidewalk. Inside Stickney was whistling cheerily and assorting his knives.

Finally Horace went desperately forward, opened the door, and entered the shop. His head hung low. Stickney stopped whistling.

'Hello, young man,' he cried, 'what brings you here?'

Horace halted, but said nothing. He swung one foot to and fro over the sawdust floor.

Stickney had placed his two fat hands palms downward and wide apart on the table, in the attitude of a butcher facing a customer, but now he straightened.

'Here,' he said, 'what's wrong? What's wrong, kid?'

'Nothin',' answered Horace, huskily. He laboured for a moment with something in his throat, and afterwards added, 'O'ny – I've – I've run away, and – '

'Run away!' shouted Stickney. 'Run away from what? Who?'

'From – home,' answered Horace. 'I don't like it there any more. I – ' He had arranged an oration to win the sympathy of the butcher; he had prepared a table setting forth the merits of his case in the most logical fashion, but it was as if the wind had been knocked out of his mind. 'I've run away. I – '

Stickney reached an enormous hand over the array of beef, and firmly grappled the emigrant. Then he swung himself to Horace's side. His face was stretched with laughter, and he playfully shook his prisoner. 'Come – come – come. What dashed nonsense is this? Run away, hey? Run away?' Whereupon the child's long-tried spirit found vent in howls.

'Come, come,' said Stickney, busily. 'Never mind now, never mind. You just come along with me. It'll be all right. I'll fix it. Never you mind.'

Five minutes later the butcher, with a great ulster over his apron, was leading the boy homeward.

At the very threshold, Horace raised his last flag of pride. 'No – no,' he sobbed. 'I don't want to. I don't want to go in there.' He braced his foot against the step and made a very respectable resistance.

'Now, Horace,' cried the butcher. He thrust open the door with a bang. 'Hello there!' Across the dark kitchen the door to the living-room opened and Aunt Martha appeared. 'You've found him!' she screamed.

'We've come to make a call,' roared the butcher. At the entrance to the living-room a silence fell upon them all. Upon a couch Horace saw his mother lying limp, pale as death, her eyes gleaming with pain. There was an electric pause before she swung a waxen hand towards Horace. 'My child,' she murmured, tremulously. Whereupon the sinister person addressed, with a prolonged wail of grief and joy, ran to her with speed. 'Mam-ma! Mam-ma! Oh, mam-ma!' She was not able to speak in a known tongue as she folded him in her weak arms.

Aunt Martha turned defiantly upon the butcher because her face betrayed her. She was crying. She made a gesture half military, half feminine. 'Won't you have a glass of our root-beer, Mr Stickney? We make it ourselves.'

Twelve O'Clock

Where were you at twelve o'clock, noon, on 9 June 1875?

Question on intelligent cross-examination

🕿 I 🕿

'Excuse *me*,' said Ben Roddle with graphic gestures to a group of citizens in Nantucket's store. 'Excuse *me*! When them fellers in leather pants an' six-shooters ride in, I go home an' set in th' cellar. That's what I do. When you see me pirooting through the streets at th' same time an' occasion as them punchers, you kin put me down fer bein' crazy. Excuse *me*!'

'Why, Ben,' drawled old Nantucket, 'you ain't never really seen 'em turned loose. Why, I kin remember – in th' old days – when –'

'Oh! damn yer old days!' retorted Roddle. Fixing Nantucket with the eye of scorn and contempt, he said, 'I suppose you'll be sayin' in a minute that in th' old days you used to kill Injuns, won't you?'

There was some laughter, and Roddle was left free to expand his ideas on the periodic visits of cowboys to the town. 'Mason Rickets, he had ten big punkins a-sittin' in front of his store, an' them fellers from the Upsidedown-P ranch shot 'em – shot em all – an' Rickets lyin' on his belly in th' store a-callin' fer 'em to quit it. An' what did they do! Why they *laughed* at 'im – just *laughed* at 'im! That don't do a town no good. Now, how would an eastern capiterlist' – (it was the town's humour to be always gassing of phantom investors who were likely to come any moment and pay a thousand prices for everything) – 'how would an eastern capiterlist like that? Why, you couldn't see 'im fer th' dust on his trail. Then he'd tell all his friends that "there town may be all right, but ther's too much loose-handed shootin' fer my money". An' he'd be right, too. Them rich fellers they don't make no bad breaks with their money. They watch it all th' time b'cause they know blame well there ain't hardly room fer their feet fer th' pikers an' tin-horns an' thimble-riggers what are layin' fer 'em. I tell you, one puncher racin' his cow-pony hell-bent-fer-election down Main Street an' yellin' an' shootin' an' nothin' at all done about it, would scare away a whole herd of capiterlists. An' it ain't right. It oughter be stopped.'

A pessimistic voice asked: 'How you goin' to stop it, Ben?'

'Organise,' replied Roddle pompously. 'Organise. That's the only way to make these fellers lay down. I – '

From the street sounded a quick scudding of pony hoofs, and a party of cowboys swept past the door. One man, however, was seen to draw rein and dismount. He came clanking into the store. 'Mornin', gentlemen,' he said civilly.

'Mornin',' they answered in subdued voices.

He stepped to the counter and said, 'Give me a paper of fine cut, please.' The group of citizens contemplated him in silence. He certainly did not look threatening. He appeared to be a young man of twenty-five years, with a tan from wind and such, with a remarkably clear eye from perhaps a period of enforced temperance, a quiet young man who wanted to buy some tobacco. A six-shooter swung low on his hip, but at the moment it looked more decorative than warlike; it seemed merely a part of his old gala dress – his sombrero with its band of rattlesnake skin, his great flaming neckerchief, his belt of embroidered Mexican leather, his high-heeled boots, his huge spurs. And, above all, his hair had been watered and brushed until it lay as close to his head as the fur lays to a wet cat. Paying for his tobacco, he withdrew.

Ben Roddle resumed his harangue. 'Well, there you are! Looks like a calm man now, but in less'n half an hour he'll be as drunk as three bucks an' a squaw, an' then . . . excuse *me*!'

🐚 2 🐚

On this day the men of two outfits had come into town, but Ben Roddle's ominous words were not justified at once. The punchers spent most of the morning in an attack on whiskey which was too earnest to be noisy.

At five minutes of eleven, a tall, lank, brick-coloured cowboy strode

over to Placer's Hotel. Placer's Hotel was a notable place. It was the
best hotel within two hundred miles. Its office was filled with armchairs
and brown papier-mâché receptacles. At one end of the room was a
wooden counter painted a bright pink, and on this morning a man was
behind the counter writing in a ledger. He was the proprietor of the
hotel, but his customary humour was so sullen that all strangers
immediately wondered why in life he had chosen to play the part of
mine host. Near his left hand, double doors opened into the dining-
room, which in warm weather was always kept darkened in order to
discourage the flies, which was not compassed at all.

Placer, writing in his ledger, did not look up when the tall cowboy
entered.

'Mornin', mister,' said the latter. 'I've come to see if you kin
grub-stake th' hull crowd of us fer dinner t'day.'

Placer did not then raise his eyes, but with a certain churlishness, as if
it annoyed him that his hotel was patronised, he asked: 'How many?'

'Oh, about thirty,' replied the cowboy. 'An' we want th' best dinner
you kin raise an' scrape. Everything th' best. We don't care what it
costs s'long as we git a good square meal. We'll pay a dollar a head: by
God, we will! We won't kick on nothin' in the bill if you do it up fine.
If you ain't got it in the house, russle th' hull town fer it. That's our
gait. So you just tear loose, an' we'll – '

At this moment the machinery of a cuckoo-clock on the wall began
to whirr, little doors flew open, and a wooden bird appeared and cried,
'Cuckoo!' And this was repeated until eleven o'clock had been announced, while the cowboy, stupefied, glass-eyed, stood with his red
throat gulping. At the end he wheeled upon Placer and demanded
'What in hell is that?'

Placer revealed by his manner that he had been asked this question
too many times. 'It's a clock,' he answered shortly.

'I know it's a clock,' gasped the cowboy; 'but what *kind* of a clock?'

'A cuckoo-clock. Can't you see?'

The cowboy, recovering his self-possession by a violent effort,
suddenly went shouting into the street. 'Boys! Say, boys! Com' 'ere a
minute!'

His comrades, comfortably inhabiting a nearby saloon, heard his
stentorian calls, but they merely said one to another: 'What's th' matter
with Jake? – he's off his nut again.'

But Jake burst in upon them with violence. 'Boys,' he yelled, 'come
over to th' hotel! They got a clock with a bird inside it, an' when it's
eleven o'clock or anything like that, th' bird comes out and says, *"toot-*

toot, *toot*-toot!" that way, as many times as whatever time of day it is. It's immense! Come on over!'

The roars of laughter which greeted his proclamation were of two qualities; some men laughing because they knew all about cuckoo-clocks, and other men laughing because they had concluded that the eccentric Jake had been victimised by some wise child of civilisation.

Old Man Crumford, a venerable ruffian who probably had been born in a corral, was particularly offensive with his loud guffaws of contempt. 'Bird a-comin' out of a clock an' a-tellin' ye th' time! Haw – haw – haw!' He swallowed his whisky. 'A bird! a-tellin' ye th' time! Haw-haw! Jake, you ben up agin some new drink. You ben drinkin' lonely an' got up agin some snake-medicine licker. A bird a-tellin' ye th' time! Haw-haw!'

The shrill voice of one of the younger cowboys piped from the background. 'Brace up, Jake. Don't let 'em laugh at ye. Bring 'em that salt cod-fish of yourn what kin pick out th' ace.'

'Oh, he's only kiddin' us. Don't pay no 'tention to 'im. He thinks he's smart.'

A cowboy whose mother had a cuckoo-clock in her house in Philadelphia spoke with solemnity. 'Jake's a liar. There's no such clock in the world. What? a bird inside a clock to tell the time? Change your drink, Jake.'

Jake was furious, but his fury took a very icy form. He bent a withering glance upon the last speaker. 'I don't mean a *live* bird,' he said, with terrible dignity. 'It's a wooden bird, an' – '

'A wooden bird!' shouted Old Man Crumford. 'Wooden bird a-tellin' ye th' time! Haw-haw!'

But Jake still paid his frigid attention to the Philadelphian. 'An' if yer sober enough to walk, it ain't such a blame long ways from here to th' hotel, an' I'll bet my pile agin yours if you only got two bits.'

'I don't want your money, Jake,' said the Philadelphian. 'Somebody's been stringin' you – that's all. I wouldn't take your money.' He cleverly appeared to pity the other's innocence.

'You couldn't *git* my money,' cried Jake, in sudden hot anger. 'You couldn't git it. Now – since yer so fresh – let's see how much you got.' He clattered some large gold pieces noisily upon the bar.

The Philadelphian shrugged his shoulders and walked away. Jake was triumphant. 'Any more bluffers 'round here?' he demanded. 'Any more? Any more bluffers? Where's all these here hot sports? Let 'em step up. Here's my money – come an' git it.'

But they had ended by being afraid. To some of them his tale was absurd, but still one must be circumspect when a man throws forty-five dollars in gold upon the bar and bids the world come and win it. The general feeling was expressed by Old Man Crumford, when with deference he asked: 'Well, this here bird, Jake – what kinder lookin' bird is it?'

'It's a little brown thing,' said Jake, briefly. Apparently he almost disdained to answer.

'Well – how does it work?' asked the old man, meekly.

'Why in blazes don't you go an' look at it?' yelled Jake. 'Want me to paint it in iles fer you? Go an' look!'

❧ 3 ❧

Placer was writing in his ledger. He heard a great trample of feet and clink of spurs on the porch, and there entered quietly the band of cowboys, some of them swaying a trifle, and these last being the most painfully decorous of all. Jake was in advance. He waved his hand toward the clock. 'There she is,' he said laconically. The cowboys drew up and stared. There was some giggling, but a serious voice said half-audibly, 'I don't see no bird.'

Jake politely addressed the landlord. 'Mister, I've fetched these here friends of mine in here to see yer clock – '

Placer looked up suddenly. 'Well, they can see it, can't they?' he asked in sarcasm. Jake, abashed, retreated to his fellows.

There was a period of silence. From time to time the men shifted their feet. Finally, Old Man Crumford leaned toward Jake, and in a penetrating whisper demanded, 'Where's th' bird?' Some frolicsome spirits on the outskirts began to call 'Bird! Bird!' as men at a political meeting call for a particular speaker.

Jake removed his big hat and nervously mopped his brow.

The young cowboy with the shrill voice again spoke from the skirts of the crowd. 'Jake, is ther' sure 'nough a bird in that thing?'

'Yes. Didn't I tell you once?'

'Then,' said the shrill-voiced man, in a tone of conviction, 'it ain't a clock at all. It's a bird-cage.'

'I tell you it's a clock,' cried the maddened Jake, but his retort could hardly be heard above the howls of glee and derision which greeted the words of him of the shrill voice.

Old Man Crumford was again rampant. 'Wooden bird a-tellin' ye th' time! Haw-haw!'

Amid the confusion Jake went again to Placer. He spoke almost in supplication. 'Say, mister, what time does this here thing go off agin?'

Placer lifted his head, looked at the clock, and said, 'Noon.'

There was a stir near the door, and Big Watson of the Square-X outfit, and at this time very drunk indeed, came shouldering his way through the crowd and cursing everybody. The men gave him much room, for he was notorious as a quarrelsome person when drunk. He paused in front of Jake, and spoke as through a wet blanket. 'What's all this – monkeyin' about?'

Jake was already wild at being made a butt for everybody, and he did not give backward. 'None a' your dam business, Watson.'

'Huh?' growled Watson, with the surprise of a challenged bull.

'I said,' repeated Jake, distinctly, 'it's none a' your dam business.'

Watson whipped his revolver half out of its holster. 'I'll make it m' business, then, you – '

But Jake had backed a step away, and was holding his left-hand palm outward toward Watson, while in his right he held his six-shooter, its muzzle pointing at the floor. He was shouting in a frenzy, 'No – don't you try it, Watson! Don't you dare try it, or, by Gawd, I'll kill you, sure – *sure*!'

He was aware of a torment of cries about him from fearful men; from men who protested, from men who cried out because they cried out. But he kept his eyes on Watson, and those two glared murder at each other, neither seeming to breathe, fixed like two statues.

A loud new voice suddenly rang out: 'Hol' on a minute!' All spectators who had not stampeded turned quickly, and saw Placer standing behind his bright pink counter, with an aimed revolver in each hand.

'Cheese it!' he said. 'I won't have no fightin' here. If you want to fight, git out in the street.'

Big Watson laughed, and, speeding up his six-shooter like a flash of blue light, he shot Placer through the throat – shot the man as he stood behind his absurd pink counter with his two aimed revolvers in his incompetent hands. With a yell of rage and despair, Jake smote Watson on the pate with his heavy weapon, and knocked him sprawling and bloody. Somewhere a woman shrieked like windy, midnight death. Placer fell behind the counter, and down upon him came his ledger and his inkstand, so that one could not have told blood from ink.

The cowboys did not seem to hear, see, nor feel, until they saw numbers of citizens with Winchesters running wildly upon them. Old Man Crumford threw high a passionate hand. 'Don't shoot! We'll not fight ye for 'im.'

Nevertheless two or three shots rang, and a cowboy who had been about to gallop off suddenly slumped over on his pony's neck, where he held for a moment like an old sack, and then slid to the ground, while his pony, with flapping rein, fled to the prairie.

'In God's name, don't shoot!' trumpeted Old Man Crumford. 'We'll not fight ye fer 'im!'

'It's murder,' bawled Ben Roddle.

In the chaotic street it seemed for a moment as if everybody would kill everybody. 'Where's the man what done it?' These hot cries seemed to declare a war which would result in an absolute annihilation of one side. But the cowboys were singing out against it. They would fight for nothing – yes – they often fought for nothing – but they would not fight for this dark something.

At last, when a flimsy truce had been made between the inflamed men, all parties went to the hotel. Placer, in some dying whim, had made his way out from behind the pink counter, and, leaving a horrible trail, had travelled to the centre of the room, where he had pitched headlong over the body of Big Watson.

The men lifted the corpse and laid it at the side.

'Who done it?' asked a white, stern man.

A cowboy pointed at Big Watson. 'That's him,' he said huskily.

There was a curious grim silence, and then suddenly, in the death-chamber, there sounded the loud whirring of the clock's works, little doors flew open, a tiny wooden bird appeared and cried 'Cuckoo' – twelve times.

Moonlight on the Snow

The town of Warpost had an evil name for three hundred miles in every direction. It radiated like the shine from some stupendous light. The citizens of the place had been for years grotesquely proud of their fame as a collection of hard-shooting gentlemen, who invariably 'got' the men who came up against them. When a citizen went abroad in the land, he said, 'I'm f'm Warpost.' And it was as if he had said, 'I am the devil himself.'

But ultimately it became known to Warpost that the serene-browed angel of peace was in the vicinity. The angel was full of projects for taking comparatively useless bits of prairie, and sawing them up into town lots, and making chaste and beautiful maps of his handiwork, which shook the souls of people who had never been in the West. He commonly travelled here and there in a light waggon, from the tailboard of which he made orations, which soared into the empyrean regions of true hydrogen gas. Towns far and near listened to his voice, and followed him singing, until in all that territory you could not throw a stone at a jack-rabbit without hitting the site of a projected mammoth hotel, estimated cost, fifteen thousand dollars. The stern and lonely buttes were given titles like grim veterans awarded tawdry patents of nobility: Cedar Mountain, Red Cliffs, Look-out Peak. And from the East came both the sane and the insane with hope, with courage, with horded savings, with cold decks, with Bibles, with knives in boots, with humility and fear, with bland impudence. Most came with their own money; some came with money gained during a moment of inattention on the part of somebody in the East. And high in the air was the serene-browed angel of peace, with his endless gabble and his pretty maps. It was curious to walk out of an evening to the edge of a vast silent sea of prairie, and to reflect that the angel had parcelled this infinity into building lots.

But no change had come to Warpost. Warpost sat with her reputation for bloodshed pressed proudly to her bosom, and saw her mean neighbours leap into being as cities. She saw drunken old reprobates selling acres of red-hot dust, and becoming wealthy men of affairs, who congratulated themselves on their shrewdness in holding land which, before the boom, they would have sold for enough to buy a treat all round in the Straight Flush Saloon – only, nobody would have given it.

Warpost saw dollars rolling into the coffers of a lot of contemptible men who couldn't shoot straight. She was amazed and indignant. She saw her standard of excellence, her creed, her reason for being great, all tumbling about her ears, and after the preliminary gasps she sat down to think it out.

The first man to voice a conclusion was Bob Hether, the popular barkeeper in Stevenson's Crystal Palace.

'It's this here gun-fighter business,' he said, leaning on his bar, and, with the gentle, serious eyes of a child, surveying a group of prominent citizens who had come in to drink at the expense of Tom Larpent, a gambler. They solemnly nodded assent. They stood in silence, holding their glasses and thinking.

Larpent was chief factor in the life of the town. His gambling-house was the biggest institution in Warpost. Moreover, he had been educated somewhere, and his slow speech had a certain mordant quality which was apt to puzzle Warpost, and men heeded him for the reason that they were not always certain as to what he was saying.

'Yes, Bob,' he drawled, 'I think you are right. The value of human life has to be established before there can be theatres, waterworks, street-cars, women, and babies.'

The other men were rather aghast at this cryptic speech, but some-body managed to snigger appreciatively, and the tension was eased.

Smith Hanham, who whirled roulette for Larpent, then gave his opinion.

'Well, when all this here coin is floatin' round, it 'pears to me we orter git our hooks on some of it. Them little tin-horns over at Crowdger's Corner are up to their necks in it, an' we ain't yit seen a centavo – not a centavetto. That ain't right. It's all well enough to sit round takin' money away from innercent cowpunchers s'long's ther's nothin' better; but when these here speculators come 'long flashin' rolls as big as water-buckets, it's up to us to whirl in an' git some of it.'

This became the view of the town, and, since the main stipulation was virtue, Warpost resolved to be virtuous. A great meeting was held, at which it was decreed that no man should kill another man, under penalty of being at once hanged by the populace. All the influential citizens were present, and asserted their determination to deal out a swift punishment which would take no note of an acquaintance or friendship with the guilty man. Bob Hether made a loud, long speech, in which he declared that he, for one, would help hang his 'own brother', if his 'own brother' transgressed this law which now, for the good of the community, must be for ever held sacred. Everybody was enthusiastic, save a few Mexicans, who did not quite understand; but as they were more than likely to be the victims of any affray in which they engaged, their silence was not considered ominous.

At half-past ten on the next morning Larpent shot and killed a man who had accused him of cheating at a game. Larpent had then taken a chair by the window.

✦ 2 ✦

Larpent grew tired of sitting in the chair by the window. He went to his bedroom, which opened off the gambling hall. On the table was a bottle of rye whisky, of a brand which he specially and secretly imported from the east. He took a long drink; he changed his coat, after laving his hands and brushing his hair. He sat down to read, his hand falling familiarly upon an old copy of Scott's *Fair Maid of Perth*.

In time, he heard the slow trample of many men coming up the stairs. The sound certainly did not indicate haste; in fact, it declared all kinds of hesitation. The crowd poured into the gambling hall; there was low talk; a silence; more low talk. Ultimately somebody rapped diffidently on the door of the bedroom.

'Come in,' said Larpent. The door swung back and disclosed Warpost, with a delegation of its best men in the front, and at the rear men who stood on their toes and craned their necks. There was no noise. Larpent looked up casually into the eyes of Bob Hether. 'So you've come up to the scratch all right, eh, Bobbie?' he asked kindly. 'I was wondering if you would weaken on the blood-curdling speech you made yesterday.'

Hether first turned deadly pale, and then flushed beet-red. His six-shooter was in his hand, and it appeared for a moment as if his weak fingers would drop it to the floor.

'Oh, never mind,' said Larpent in the same tone of kindly patronage. 'The community must and shall hold this law for ever sacred, and your own brother lives in Connecticut, doesn't he?' He laid down his book and arose. He unbuckled his revolver belt and tossed it on the bed. A look of impatience had come suddenly upon his face. 'Well, you don't want me to be master of ceremonies at my own hanging, do you? Why don't somebody say something or do something? You stand around like a lot of bottles. Where's your tree, for instance? You know there isn't a tree between here and the river. Damned little jack-rabbit town hasn't even got a tree for its hanging. Hello, Coats, you live in Crowdger's Corner, don't you? Well, you keep out of this thing, then. The Corner has had its boom, and this is a speculation in real-estate which is the business solely of the citizens of Warpost.'

The behaviour of the crowd became extraordinary. Men began to back away; eye did not meet eye; they were victims of an inexplicable influence, it was as if they had heard sinister laughter from a gloom.

'I know,' said Larpent considerately, 'that this isn't as if you were going to hang a comparative stranger. In a sense, this is an intimate affair. I know full well you could go out and jerk a comparative stranger into kingdom-come and make a sort of festal occasion of it. But when it comes to performing the same office for an old friend, even the ferocious Bobbie Hether stands around on one leg like a damned white-livered coward. In short, my milk-fed patriots, you seem fat-headed enough to believe that I am going to hang myself if you wait long enough; but unfortunately I am going to allow you to conduct your own real-estate speculations. It seems to me there should be enough men here who understand the value of corner lots in a safe and godly town, and hence should be anxious to hurry this business.'

The icy tones had ceased, and the crowd breathed a great sigh, as if it had been freed of a physical pain. But still no one seemed to know where to reach for the scruff of this weird situation. Finally there was some jostling on the outskirts of the crowd, and some men were seen to be pushing old Billie Simpson forward amid some protests. Simpson was on state occasions the voice of the town. Somewhere in his past he had been a Baptist preacher. He had fallen far, very far, and the only remnant of his former dignity was a fatal facility of speech when half drunk. Warpost used him on those state occasions when it became bitten with a desire to 'do the thing up in style'. So the citizens pushed the blear-eyed old ruffian forward until he stood hemming and hawing in front of Larpent. It was evident at once that he was brutally sober, and hence wholly unfitted for whatever task had been planned for him. A dozen times he croaked like a frog, meanwhile wiping the back of his hand rapidly across his mouth. At last he managed to stammer –

'Mister Larpent – '

In some indescribable manner, Larpent made his attitude of respectable attention to be grossly contemptuous and insulting.

'Yes, Mister Simpson?'

'Er – now – Mister Larpent,' began the old man hoarsely, 'we wanted to know – ' Then obviously feeling that there was a detail which he had forgotten, he turned to the crowd and whispered, 'Where is it?' Many men precipitately cleared themselves out of the way, and down this lane Larpent had an unobstructed view of the body of the man he had slain. Old Simpson again began to croak like a frog.

'Mister Larpent.'

'Yes, Mister Simpson.'

'Do you – er – do you – admit – '

'Oh, certainly,' said the gambler, good-humouredly. 'There can be no doubt of it, Mister Simpson, although, with your well-known ability to fog things, you may, later possibly prove that you did it yourself. I shot him because he was too officious. Not quite enough men are shot on that account, Mister Simpson. As one fitted by nature to be consummately officious, I hope you will agree with me, Mister Simpson.'

Men were plucking old Simpson by the sleeve, and giving him directions. One could hear him say, 'What? Yes. All right. What? All right.' In the end he turned hurriedly upon Larpent and blurted out –

'Well, I guess we're goin' to hang you.'

Larpent bowed. 'I had a suspicion that you would,' he said, in a pleasant voice. 'There has been an air of determination about the entire proceeding, Mister Simpson.'

There was an awkward moment.

'Well – well – well, come ahead – '

Larpent courteously relieved a general embarrassment.

'Why, of course. We must be moving. Clergy first, Mister Simpson. I'll take my old friend, Bobbie Hether, on my right hand, and we'll march soberly to the business, thus lending a certain dignity to this outing of real-estate speculators.'

'Tom,' quavered Bob Hether, 'for Gawd sake, keep your mouth shut.'

'He invokes the deity,' remarked Larpent, placidly. 'But no; my last few minutes I am resolved to devote to inquiries as to the welfare of my friends. Now, you, for instance, my dear Bobbie, present today the lamentable appearance of a rattlesnake that has been four times killed and then left in the sun to rot. It is the effect of friendship upon a highly delicate system. You suffer? It is cruel. Never mind; you will feel better presently.'

❧ 3 ❧

Warpost had always risen superior to her lack of a tree by making use
of a fixed wooden crane, which appeared over a second-storey window
on the front of Pigrim's general store. This crane had a long tackle
always ready for hoisting merchandise to the store's loft. Larpent,
coming in the midst of a slow moving throng, cocked a bright bird-like
eye at this crane.

'Mm – yes,' he said.

Men began to work frantically. They called each to each in voices
strenuous but low. They were in a panic to have the thing finished.
Larpent's cold ironical survey drove them mad, and it entered the
minds of some that it would be felicitous to hang him before he could
talk more. But he occupied the time in pleasant discourse.

'I see that Smith Hanham is not here. Perhaps some undue tenderness of sentiment keeps him away. Such feelings are entirely unneces-
sary. Don't you think so, Bobbie? Note the feverish industry with
which the renegade parson works at the rope. You will never be hung,
Simpson. You will be shot for fooling too near a petticoat which
doesn't belong to you – the same old habit which got you flung out of
the church, you red-eyed old satyr. Ah, the Cross Trail coach ap-
proaches. What a situation.'

The crowd turned uneasily to follow his glance, and saw, truly
enough, the dusty rickety old vehicle coming at the gallop of four lean
horses. Ike Boston was driving the coach, and far away he had seen and
defined the throng in front of Pigrim's store. First calling out excited
information to his passengers, who were all inside, he began to lash his
horses and yell. As a result, he rattled wildly up to the scene just as they
were arranging the rope around Larpent's neck.

'Whoa,' said he to his horses.

The inhabitants of Warpost peered at the windows of the coach, and
saw therein six pale, horror-stricken faces. The men at the rope stood
hesitating. Larpent smiled blandly. There was a silence. At last a
broken voice cried from the coach –

'Driver! driver! What is it? What is it?' Ike Boston spat between the
wheel horses and mumbled that he s'posed anybody could see, less'n

they were blind. The door of the coach opened, and out stepped a beautiful young lady. She was followed by two little girls, hand clasped in hand, and a white-haired old gentleman, with a venerable and peaceful face. And the rough West stood in naked immorality before the eyes of the gentle East. The leather-faced men of Warpost had never imagined such perfection of feminine charm, such radiance, and as the illumined eyes of the girl wandered doubtfully, fearfully, toward the man with the rope around his neck, a certain majority of practised ruffians tried to look as if they were having nothing to do with the proceedings.

'Oh,' she said, in a low voice, 'what are you going to do?'

At first none made reply, but ultimately a hero managed to break the harrowing stillness by stammering out, 'Nothin'!' And then, as if aghast at his own prominence, he shied behind the shoulders of a big neighbour.

'Oh, I know,' she said. 'But it's wicked. Don't you see how wicked it is? Papa, do say something to them.'

The clear, deliberate tones of Tom Larpent suddenly made everyone stiffen. During the early part of the interruption he had seated himself upon the steps of Pigrim's store, in which position he had maintained a slightly bored air. He now was standing with the rope around his neck and bowing. He looked handsome and distinguished and – a devil, a devil as cold as moonlight upon the ice.

'You are quite right, miss. They are going to hang me; but I can give you my word that the affair is perfectly regular. I killed a man this morning, and you see these people here who look like a fine collection of premier scoundrels are really engaged in forcing a real-estate boom. In short, they are speculators, land barons, and not the children of infamy, which you no doubt took them for at first.'

'O-oh!' she said, and shuddered.

Her father now spoke haughtily. 'What has this man done? Why do you hang him without a trial, even if you have fair proofs?'

The crowd had been afraid to speak to the young lady, but a dozen voices answered her father.

'Why, he admits it.' 'Didn't ye hear?' 'There ain't no doubt about it.' 'No.' 'He *ses* he did.'

The old man looked at the smiling gambler. 'Do you admit that you committed murder?'

Larpent answered slowly. 'For the first question in a temporary acquaintance that is a fairly strong beginning. Do you wish me to speak as man to man, or to one who has some kind of official authority to meddle in a thing that is none of his affair?'

'I – ah – I,' stuttered the other. 'Ah – man to man.'

'Then,' said Larpent, 'I have to inform you that this morning, at about 10.30, a man was shot and killed in my gambling house. He was engaged in the exciting business of trying to grab some money, out of which he claimed I had swindled him. The details are not interesting.'

The old gentleman waved his arm in a gesture of terror and despair, and tottered toward the coach; the young lady fainted; the two little girls wailed. Larpent sat on the steps with the rope around his neck.

❦ 4 ❦

The chief function of Warpost was to prey upon the bands of cowboys who, when they were paid, rode gaily into town to look for sin. To this end there were in Warpost many thugs and thieves. There was treachery and obscenity and merciless greed in every direction. Even Mexico was levied upon to furnish a kind of ruffian which appears infrequently in the northern races. Warpost was not good; it was not tender; it was not chivalrous, but –

But –

There was a quality to the situation in front of Pigrim's store which made Warpost wish to stampede. There were the two children, their angelic faces turned toward the sky, weeping in the last anguish of fear; there was the beautiful form of the young lady prostrate in the dust of the road, with her trembling father bending over her; on the steps sat Larpent, waiting, with a derisive smile, while from time to time he turned his head in the rope to make a forked-tongued remark as to the character and bearing of some acquaintance. All the simplicity of a mere lynching was gone from this thing. Through some bewildering inner power of its own, it was carried out of the hands of its inaugurators, and was marching along like a great drama, and they were only spectators. To them it was ungovernable; they could do no more than stand on one foot and wonder.

Some were heartily ill of everything, and wished to run away. Some were so interested in the new aspect that they had forgotten why they had originally come to the front of Pigrim's store. These were the poets. A large practical class wished to establish at once the identity of the newcomers. Who were they? Where did they come from? Where were they going to? It was truthfully argued that they were the parson for the new church at Crowdger's Corner, with his family.

And a fourth class – a dark-browed, muttering class – wished to go at once to the root of all disturbance by killing Ike Boston for trundling up in his old omnibus, and dumping out upon their ordinary lynching party such a load of tears and inexperience and sentimental argument. In low tones they addressed vitriolic reproaches.

'But how'd I know?' he protested, almost with tears – 'how'd I know the'd be all this here kick-up?'

But Larpent suddenly created a great stir. He stood up, and his face was inspired with new, strong resolution.

'Look here, boys,' he said decisively, 'you hang me tomorrow – or, anyhow, later on today. We can't keep frightening the young lady and these two poor babies out of their wits. Ease off on the rope, Simpson, you blackguard. Frightening women and children is your game, but I'm not going to stand it. Ike Boston, take your passengers on to Crowdger's Corner, and tell the young lady that, owing to her influence, the boys changed their minds about making me swing. Somebody lift the rope where it's caught under my ear, will you? Boys, when you want me, you'll find me in the Crystal Palace.'

His tone was so authoritative that some obeyed him at once, involuntarily; but, as a matter of fact, his plan met with general approval. Warpost heaved a great sigh of relief. Why had nobody thought earlier of so easy a way out of all these here tears?

⁓ 5 ⁓

Larpent went to the Crystal Palace, where he took his comfort like a gentleman, conversing with his friends and drinking. At nightfall two men rode into town, flung their bridles over a convenient post, and clanked into the Crystal Palace. Warpost knew them in a glance. Talk ceased, and there was a watchful squaring aback.

The foremost was Jack Potter, a famous town marshal of Yellow Sky, but now the sheriff of the county. The other was Scratchy Wilson, once a no-less famous desperado. They were both two-handed men of terrific prowess and courage, but Warpost could hardly believe her eyes at view of this daring invasion. It was unprecedented.

Potter went straight to the bar, behind which frowned Bobbie Hether.

'You know a man by the name of Larpent?'

'Supposin' I do?' said Bobbie, sourly.

'Well, I want him. Is he in the saloon?'

'Maybe he is, an' maybe he isn't,' said Bobbie.

Potter went back among the glinting eyes of the citizens.

'Gentlemen, I want a man named Larpent. Is he here?'

Warpost was sullen, but Larpent answered lazily for himself.

'Why, you must mean me. My name is Larpent. What do you want?'

'I've got a warrant for your arrest.'

There was a movement all over the room as if a puff of wind had come. The swing of a hand would have brought on a murderous *mêlée*. But after an instant the rigidity was broken by Larpent's laughter.

'Why, you're sold, sheriff,' he cried. 'I've got a previous engagement. The boys are going to hang me tonight.'

If Potter was surprised, he betrayed nothing.

'The boys won't hang you tonight, Larpent,' he said calmly, 'because I'm goin' to take you into Yellow Sky.'

Larpent was looking at the warrant. 'Only grand larceny,' he observed. 'But still, you know, I've promised these people to appear at their performance.'

'You're goin' in with me,' said the impassive sheriff.

'You bet he is, sheriff,' cried an enthusiastic voice; and it belonged to Bobbie Hether. The barkeeper moved down inside his rail, and, inspired like a prophet, he began a harangue to the citizens of Warpost. 'Now, look here, boys, that's just what we want, ain't it? Here we were goin' to hang Tom Larpent jest for the reputation of the town, like. 'Long comes Sheriff Potter, the reg-ulerly con-sti-tuted officer of the law, an' he says, "No; the man's mine." Now, we want to make the reputation of the town as a law-abidin' place; so what do we say to Sheriff Potter? We says, "A-a-ll right, sheriff; you're reg'lar; we ain't; he's your man." But supposin' we go to fighten over it; then what becomes of the reputation of the town which we was goin' to swing Tom Larpent for?'

The immediate opposition to these views came from a source which a stranger might have difficulty in imagining. Men's foreheads grew thick with lines of obstinacy and disapproval. They were perfectly willing to hang Larpent yesterday, today, or tomorrow as a detail in a set of circumstances at Warpost, but when some outsiders from the alien town of Yellow Sky came into the sacred precincts of Warpost, and proclaimed their intention of extracting a citizen for cause, any citizen for any cause, the stomach of Warpost was fed with a clan's blood, and her children gathered under one invisible banner, prepared to fight as few people in few ages were enabled to fight for their points of view. There was a guttural murmuring.

'No; hold on,' screamed Bobbie, flinging up his hands. 'He'll come clear all right. Tom,' he appealed wildly to Larpent, 'you never committed no g'damn low-down grand larceny?'

'No,' said Larpent, coldly.

'But how was it? Can't you tell us how it was?'

Larpent answered with plain reluctance. He waved his hand to indicate that it was all of little consequence.

'Well, he was a tenderfoot, and he played poker with me, and he couldn't play quite good enough. But he thought he could; he could play extremely well, he thought. So he lost his money. I thought he'd squeal.'

'Boys,' begged Bobbie, 'let the sheriff take him.'

Some answered at once, 'Yes.' Others continued to mutter. The sheriff had held his hand because, like all quiet and honest men, he did not wish to perturb any progress toward a peaceful solution, but now he decided to take the scene by the nose and make it obey him.

'Gentlemen,' he said formally, 'this man is comin' with me. Larpent, get up and come along.'

This might have been the beginning, but it was practically the end. The two opinions in the minds of Warpost fought in the air and, like a snow squall, discouraged all action. Amid general confusion Jack Potter and Scratchy Wilson moved to the door with their prisoner. The last thing seen by the men in the Crystal Palace was the bronze countenance of Jack Potter as he backed from the place.

A man, filled with belated thought, suddenly cried out –

'Well, they'll hang him for this here shootin' game anyhow.'

Bobbie Hether looked disdain upon the speaker.

'Will they? An' where 'll they get their witnesses? From here, do y' think? No; not a single one. All he's up against is a case of grand larceny, and – even supposin' he done it – what in hell does grand larceny amount to?'

Manacled

◆◈◆◈

In the First Act there had been a farm scene, wherein real horses had drunk real water out of real buckets, afterward dragging a real waggon off stage L. The audience was consumed with admiration of this play, and the great Theatre Nouveau rang to its roof with the crowd's plaudits.

The Second Act was now well advanced. The hero, cruelly victimised by his enemies, stood in prison garb, panting with rage, while two brutal warders fastened real handcuffs on his wrists and real anklets on his ankles. And the hovering villain sneered.

' 'Tis well, Aubrey Pettingill,' said the prisoner. 'You have so far succeeded; but, mark you, there will come a time – '

The villain retorted with a cutting allusion to the young lady whom the hero loved.

'Curse you,' cried the hero, and he made as if to spring upon this demon; but, as the pitying audience saw, he could only take steps four inches long.

Drowning the mocking laughter of the villain came cries from both the audience and the people back of the wings. 'Fire! Fire! Fire!' Throughout the great house resounded the roaring crashes of a throng of human beings moving in terror, and even above this noise could be heard the screams of women more shrill than whistles. The building hummed and shook; it was like a glade which holds some bellowing cataract of the mountains. Most of the people who were killed on the stairs still clutched their play-bills in their hands as if they had resolved to save them at all costs.

The Theatre Nouveau fronted upon a street which was not of the first importance, especially at night, when it only aroused when the people came to the theatre, and aroused again when they came out to go home. On the night of the fire, at the time of the scene between the enchained hero and his tormentor, the thoroughfare echoed with only the scraping shovels of some street-cleaners, who were loading carts with blackened snow and mud. The gleam of lights made the shadowed pavement deeply blue, save where lay some yellow plum-like reflection.

Suddenly a policeman came running frantically along the street. He charged upon the fire-box on a corner. Its red light touched with flame each of his brass buttons and the municipal shield. He pressed a lever. He had been standing in the entrance of the theatre chatting to the lonely man in the box-office. To send an alarm was a matter of seconds.

Out of the theatre poured the first hundreds of fortunate ones, and some were not altogether fortunate. Women, their bonnets flying, cried out tender names; men, white as death, scratched and bleeding, looked wildly from face to face. There were displays of horrible blind brutality by the strong. Weaker men clutched and clawed like cats. From the theatre itself came the howl of a gale.

The policeman's fingers had flashed into instant life and action the most perfect counter-attack to the fire. He listened for some seconds, and presently he heard the thunder of a charging engine. She swept around a corner, her three shining enthrilled horses leaping. Her consort, the hose-cart, roared behind her. There were the loud clicks of the steel-shod hoofs, hoarse shouts, men running, the flash of lights, while the crevice-like streets resounded with the charges of other engines.

At the first cry of fire, the two brutal warders had dropped the arms of the hero and run off the stage with the villain. The hero cried after them angrily –

'Where are you going? Here, Pete – Tom – you've left me chained up, damn you!'

The body of the theatre now resembled a mad surf amid rocks, but the hero did not look at it. He was filled with fury at the stupidity of the two brutal warders, in forgetting that they were leaving him manacled. Calling loudly, he hobbled off stage L, taking steps four inches long.

Behind the scenes he heard the hum of flames. Smoke, filled with sparks sweeping on spiral courses, rolled thickly upon him. Suddenly his face turned chalk-colour beneath his skin of manly bronze for the stage. His voice shrieked –

'Pete – Tom – damn you – come back – you've left me chained up.'

He had played in this theatre for seven years, and he could find his way without light through the intricate passages which mazed out behind the stage. He knew that it was a long way to the street door.

The heat was intense. From time to time masses of flaming wood sung down from above him. He began to jump. Each jump advanced him about three feet, but the effort soon became heart-breaking. Once he fell, and it took time to get upon his feet again.

There were stairs to descend. From the top of this flight he tried to fall feet first. He precipitated himself in a way that would have broken his hip under common conditions. But every step seemed covered with glue, and on almost every one he stuck for a moment. He could not even succeed in falling downstairs. Ultimately he reached the bottom, windless from the struggle.

There were stairs to climb. At the foot of the flight he lay for an instant with his mouth close to the floor trying to breathe. Then he tried to scale this frightful precipice up the face of which many an actress had gone at a canter.

Each succeeding step arose eight inches from its fellow. The hero dropped to a seat on the third step, and pulled his feet to the second step. From this position he lifted himself to a seat on the fourth step. He had not gone far in this manner before his frenzy caused him to lose his balance, and he rolled to the foot of the flight. After all, he could fall downstairs.

He lay there whispering. 'They all got out but I. All but I.' Beautiful flames flashed above him, some were crimson, some were orange, and here and there were tongues of purple, blue, green.

A curiously calm thought came into his head. 'What a fool I was not to foresee this! I shall have Rogers furnish manacles of papier-mâché tomorrow.'

The thunder of the fire-lions made the theatre have a palsy.

Suddenly the hero beat his handcuffs against the wall, cursing them in a loud wail. Blood started from under his finger-nails. Soon he began to bite the hot steel, and blood fell from his blistered mouth. He raved like a wolf.

Peace came to him again. There were charming effects amid the flames . . . He felt very cool, delightfully cool . . . 'They've left me chained up.'

An Illusion in Red and White

❧   ☙

Nights on the Cuban blockade were long, at times exciting, often dull. The men on the small leaping despatch boats became as intimate as if they had all been buried in the same coffin. Correspondents, who in New York had passed as fairly good fellows, sometimes turned out to be perfect rogues of vanity and selfishness, but still more often the conceited chumps of Park Row became the kindly and thoughtful men of the Cuban blockade. Also each correspondent told all he knew, and sometimes more. For this gentle tale I am indebted to one of the brightening stars of New York journalism.

'Now, this is how I imagine it happened. I don't say it happened this way, but this is how I imagine it happened. And it always struck me as being a very interesting story. I hadn't been on the paper very long, but just about long enough to get a good show, when the city editor suddenly gave me this sparkling murder assignment.

'It seems that up in one of the back counties of New York State a farmer had taken a dislike to his wife; and so he went into the kitchen with an axe, and in the presence of their four little children he just casually rapped his wife on the nape of the neck with the head of this axe. It was early in the morning, but he told the children they had better go to bed. Then he took his wife's body out in the woods and buried it.

'This farmer's name was Jones. The widower's eldest child was named Freddy. A week after the murder, one of the long-distance neighbours was rattling past the house in his buckboard when he saw Freddy playing in the road. He pulled up, and asked the boy about the welfare of the Jones family.

' "Oh, we're all right," said Freddy, "only ma – she ain't – she's dead."

' "Why, when did she die?" cried the startled farmer. "What did she die of?"

' "Oh," answered Freddy, "last week a man with red hair and big white teeth and real white hands came into the kitchen, and killed ma with an axe."

'The farmer was indignant with the boy for telling him this strange childish nonsense, and drove off much disgruntled. But he recited the incident at a tavern that evening, and when people began to miss the familiar figure of Mrs Jones at the Methodist Church on Sunday mornings, they ended by having an investigation. The calm Jones was arrested for murder, and his wife's body was lifted from its grave in the woods, and buried by her own family.

'The chief interest now centred upon the children. All four declared that they were in the kitchen at the time of the crime, and that the murderer had red hair. The hair of the virtuous Jones was grey. They said that the murderer's teeth were large and white. Jones only had about eight teeth, and these were small and brown. They said the murderer's hands were white. Jones's hands were the colour of black walnuts. They lifted their dazed, innocent faces, and crying, simply because the mysterious excitement and their new quarters frightened them, they repeated their heroic legend without important deviation, and without the parroty sameness which would excite suspicion.

'Women came to the jail and wept over them, and made little frocks for the girls, and little breeches for the boys, and idiotic detectives questioned them at length. Always they upheld the theory of the murderer with red hair, big white teeth, and white hands. Jones sat in his cell, his chin sullenly on his first vest button. He knew nothing about any murder, he said. He thought his wife had gone on a visit to some relatives. He had had a quarrel with her, and she had said that she was going to leave him for a time, so that he might have proper opportunities for cooling down. Had he seen the blood on the floor? Yes, he had seen the blood on the floor. But he had been cleaning and skinning a rabbit at that spot on the day of his wife's disappearance. He had thought nothing of it. What had his children said when he returned from the fields? They had told him that their mother had been killed by an axe in the hands of a man with red hair, big white teeth, and white hands. To questions as to why he had not informed the police of the county, he answered that he had not thought it a matter of sufficient importance. He had cordially hated his wife, anyhow, and he was glad to be rid of her. He decided afterward that she had run off; and he had never credited the fantastic tale of the children.

'Of course, there was very little doubt in the minds of the majority that Jones was guilty, but there was a fairly strong following who insisted that Jones was a coarse and brutal man, and perhaps weak in his head – yes – but not a murderer. They pointed to the children and declared that children could never lie, and these kids, when asked, said that the murder had been committed by a man with red hair, large white teeth, and white hands. I myself had a number of interviews with the children, and I was amazed at the convincing power of their little story. Shining in the depths of the limpid up-turned eyes, one could fairly see tiny mirrored images of men with red hair, big white teeth, and white hands.

'Now, I'll tell you how it happened – how I imagine it was done. Sometime after burying his wife in the woods Jones strolled back into the house. Seeing nobody, he called out in the familiar fashion, "Mother!" Then the kids came out whimpering. "Where is your mother?" said Jones. The children looked at him blankly. "Why, pa," said Freddy, "you came in here, and hit ma with the axe; and then you sent us to bed." "Me?" cried Jones "I haven't been near the house since breakfast time."

'The children did not know how to reply. Their meagre little sense informed them that their father had been the man with the axe, but he denied it, and to their minds everything was a mere great puzzle with no meaning whatever, save that it was mysteriously sad and made them cry.

' "What kind of a looking man was it?" said Jones.

'Freddy hesitated. "Now – he looked a good deal like you, pa."

' "Like me?" said Jones. "Why, I thought you said he had red hair?"

' "No, I didn't," replied Freddy. "I thought he had grey hair, like yours."

' "Well," said Jones, "I saw a man with kind of red hair going along the road up yonder, and I thought maybe that might have been him."

'Little Lucy, the second child, here piped up with intense conviction. "His hair was a little teeny bit red. I saw it."

' "No," said Jones. "The man I saw had very red hair. And what did his teeth look like? Were they big and white?"

' "Yes," answered Lucy, "they were."

'Even Freddy seemed to incline to think it.

' "His teeth may have been big and white."

'Jones said little more at that time. Later he intimated to the children that their mother had gone off on a visit, and although they were full of wonder, and sometimes wept because of the oppression of an incomprehensible feeling in the air, they said nothing. Jones did his chores. Everything was smooth.

'The morning after the day of the murder, Jones and his children had a breakfast of hominy and milk.

' "Well, this man with red hair and big white teeth, Lucy," said Jones. "Did you notice anything else about him?"

'Lucy straightened in her chair, and showed the childish desire to come out with brilliant information which would gain her father's approval.

' "He had white hands – hands all white – "

' "How about you, Freddy?"

' "I didn't look at them much, but I think they were white," answered the boy.

' "And what did little Martha notice?" cried the tender parent. "Did she see the big bad man?"

'Martha, aged four, replied solemnly, "His hair was all yed, and his hand was white – all white."

' "That's the man I saw up the road," said Jones to Freddy.

' "Yes, sir, it seems like it must have been him," said the boy, his brain now completely muddled.

'Again Jones allowed the subject of his wife's murder to lapse. The children did not know that it was a murder, of course. Adults were always performing in a way to make children's heads swim. For instance, what could be more incomprehensible than that a man with two horses, dragging a queer thing, should walk all day, making the grass turn down and the earth turn up? And why did they cut the long grass and put it in a barn? And what was a cow for? Did the water in the well like to be there? All these actions and things were grand, because they were associated with the high estate of grown-up people, but they were deeply mysterious. If then, a man with red hair, big white teeth, and white hands should hit their mother on the nape of the neck with an axe, it was merely a phenomenon of grown-up life. Little Henry, the baby, when he had a want, howled and pounded the table with his spoon. That was all of life to him. He was not concerned with the fact that his mother had been murdered.

'One day Jones said to his children suddenly, "Look here; I wonder if you could have made a mistake. Are you absolutely sure that the man you saw had red hair, big white teeth, and white hands?"

'The children were indignant with their father. "Why, of course, pa, we ain't made no mistake. We saw him as plain as day."

'Later young Freddy's mind began to work like ketchup. His nights were haunted with terrible memories of the man with the red hair, big white teeth, and white hands, and the prolonged absence of his mother made him wonder and wonder. Presently he quite gratuitously developed the theory that his mother was dead. He knew about death. He had once seen a dead dog; also dead chickens, rabbits, and mice. One day he asked his father, "Pa, is ma ever coming back?"

'Jones said: "Well, no; I don't think she is." This answer confirmed the boy in his theory. He knew that dead people did not come back.

'The attitude of Jones toward this descriptive legend of the man with the axe was very peculiar. He came to be in opposition to it. He protested against the convictions of the children, but he could not move them. It was the one thing in their lives of which they were stonily and absolutely positive.

'Now that really ends the story. But I will continue for your amusement. The jury hung Jones as high as they could, and they were quite right: because Jones confessed before he died. Freddy is now a highly respected driver of a grocery waggon in Ogdensburg. When I was up there a good many years afterwards people told me that when he ever spoke of the tragedy at all he was certain to denounce the alleged confession as a lie. He considered his father a victim to the stupidity of juries, and some day he hopes to meet the man with the red hair, big white teeth, and white hands, whose image still remains so distinct in his memory that he could pick him out in a crowd of ten thousand.'

Wordsworth American Library

IRVING BACHELLER
Eben Holden

AMBROSE BIERCE
Can Such Things Be?

KATE CHOPIN
The Awakening

JAMES FENIMORE COOPER
The Deerslayer

STEPHEN CRANE
The Red Badge of Courage
Maggie: A Girl of the Streets

RICHARD HENRY DANA JR
Two Years Before the Mast

FREDERICK DOUGLASS
The Life and Times of
Frederick Douglas

THEODORE DREISER
Sister Carrie

BENJAMIN FRANKLIN
Autobiography of
Benjamin Franklin

ZANE GREY
Riders of the Purple Sage

EDWARD E. HALE
The Man Without a Country

NATHANIEL HAWTHORNE
The House of the Seven Gables
The Scarlet Letter

HENRY JAMES
Washington Square
The Awkward Age

JACK LONDON
The Iron Heel
Call of the Wild/White Fang

HERMAN MELVILLE
Moby Dick

HARRIET BEECHER STOWE
Uncle Tom's Cabin

MARK TWAIN
The Man That
Corrupted Hadleyburg
The Tragedy of Pudd'nhead
Wilson

HENRY DAVID THOREAU
Walden

EDITH WHARTON
Ethan Frome
The House of Mirth

OWEN WISTER
The Virginian

WORDSWORTH DISTRIBUTION

Great Britain and Ireland
Wordsworth Editions Limited
Cumberland House, Crib Street
Ware, Hertfordshire SG12 9ET
Telephone 01920 465 167
Fax 01920 462 267

USA, Canada and Mexico
Universal Sales & Marketing Inc
230 Fifth Avenue, Suite 1212
New York, NY 10001, USA
Telephone 212-481-3500
Fax 212-481-3534

South Africa
Struik Book
Distributors (Pty) Ltd
Graph Avenue,
Montague Gardens
7441 P O Box 193 Maitland 7405
South Africa
Telephone 021-551-5900
Fax 021-551-1124

Italy
Magis Books SRL
Via Raffaello 31c
Zona ind Mancasale
42100 Reggio Emilia, Italy
Telephone 0522-920999
Fax 0522-920666

Germany, Austria and Switzerland
Swan Buch-Marketing GmbH
Goldscheuerstrabe 16
D-7640 Kehl am Rhein, Germany

Portugal
International Publishing
Services Limited
Rua da Cruz da Carreira, 4B
1100 Lisboa
Telephone 01-570051
Fax 01-352-2066

Spain
Ribera Libros S L
Poligono Martiartu, Calle 1, no 6
48480 Arrigorriaga, Vizcaya
Telephone
34-4-671-3607 (Almacen)
34-4-441-8787 (Libreria)
Fax
34-4-671-3608 (Almacen)
34-4-4418029 (Libreria)

India
Om Book Services
1690 First Floor, Nai Sarak
Delhi 110006
Telephone 327 9823– 326-5303
Fax 327-8091